Sparkle
Life

Sparkle Life

Kara Lindstrom

— a novel —

Other Press · New York

Copyright © 2006 Kara Lindstrom

Production Editor: Robert D. Hack
Text design: Natalya Balvova
This book was set in Janson Text by Alpha Graphics of Pittsfield, NH.
ISBN-13: 978-1-59051-232-6

10 9 8 7 6 5 4 3 2 1

Library of Congress Cataloging-in-Publication Data

Lindstrom, Kara.
    Sparkle life / by Kara Lindstrom.
       p. cm.
    ISBN 1-59051-232-4 (hardcover : alk. paper) 1. Women motion picture producers and directors–Fiction. 2. Armenian Americans–Fiction. 3. Women immigrants–Fiction. 4. New York (N.Y.)–Fiction. I. Title.
    PS3612.I537S67 2006
    813'.6–dc22

                                              2005022026

Part One

1

*Y*ou're sweating because you're about to be caught, Liv told herself. You know the jig is almost up and you're going to be *found out.*

Liv knew that in less than two months at the first screening of her documentary, the world would see ninety-nine running minutes of *flaw.* Everyone would finally know the truth: Liv Johansson wasn't talented, pretty, and smart; she was a mess. She could smell her sweat, now. She really shouldn't have worn polyester, today.

"Can you turn up the air?" Liv asked her driver.

She aimed the air conditioner blower at her face, closed her eyes and breathed in, out, in, out. Stop over-amping, she told herself. Worst-case scenario: they hate the movie, and the party after the screening will be a drag. Liv pictured herself depressed for two months and then waking up one sunny morning, ready to do something else. The jig isn't up, she thought. What is a *jig,* anyway?

Relax. Focus on where you are now: being driven to your editing suite in a fully loaded Range Rover, coming from a nine-room co-op on the Upper West Side. That doesn't suck. Focus on the Range Rover's ad campaign: *Climb in and ignore the world.* Do that, Liv commanded herself.

She closed her eyes and breathed in, out, in, out. She nestled into a mantra: *I'm lucky.* My mother was a waste product, but Daddy saved me. Breathe in. I live rent-free in Manhattan. Breathe out. I'm lucky. Breathe in. Out: *ig.* In: *nore.* Out: *the.* In: *world.* She exhaled a long sigh. I'm lucky, and that means I'm rich and smart and pretty enough, to be able to *ig-nore-the-world.*

It was working. Liv felt herself relaxing. *What's my problem? I've never been caught before. Why should it happen now? People who get caught play loose with their luck. I respect my luck,* Liv thought, mouthing these words, as if someone higher up was actually listening to this deposition.

She felt her underarms drying in the cool air. *I'm lucky and I'm grateful for the luck,* she reaffirmed to the higher-up person/spirit-thingy. *The film is okay—good, even. I'm lucky; I always manage to come through. I don't make failures. I'm not flawed. Bad shit happens around me, but not to me.* She mouthed the words, *Don't worry. You're lucky.*

Liv cut herself off. She wasn't showing her respect. *Don't worry; you're lucky* was plain old gloating, and failures gloated. Stop it, she told herself. The universe bites gloaters in the ass.

Liv had been to college—grad school, even. She knew her myths. She knew about hubris. Liv was a 37-year-old New Yorker and an Armenian immigrant which meant that she had an inborn understanding of the evil eye. To ward it off, you should say the bad, because saying the good was gloating, which was flirting with disaster. To undo the damage done by her gloating, she mouthed to the higher-up, *My film sucks.*

Her car passed an electronics store with a banner for a sale starting on Saturday. It was Thursday, and Liv idly counted backward, ticking off the days since her last period: twenty-four. *Wait a second,* she thought, *this stressing is just hormonal. I'm getting my period. I am lucky.*

She exhaled and felt her panic recede. But, just in case, Liv reached out and tapped the Range Rover's genuine burl-wood dashboard. Whether her film sucked or not; whether she was premenstrual or not; whether the jig was up on her luck or not: knocking on wood, even glued-on trim, was always a good idea.

When Liv got to the editing suite, Dahlia, her editor, ran a sequence where a 27-year-old Palestinian looked down into the High-8 Video Handycam he held between his thighs and said, "I wish I was seeing this with you, mama. God willing, we will be together soon." It was what Liv dubbed *another shameless sentimental moment* in her documentary about a group of Israeli Jews and Arab Muslims on a bus tour of California.

Liv said, "You took out the part where he says, 'We'll make a home together.'"

"There was a flare," Dahlia said.

Liv stared at the paused image. Naim: cropped dark hair, dark eyes, 5' 10". Her height. When she started production, she had called him the "time bomb." What else is a young, reserved Palestinian who videotapes his vacation for the mother he hasn't seen since he was 18 when they both finally got out of Lebanon, she to domestic work in Bahrain, he to an apprenticeship in Amman?

Eight days into the tour, when the group was at a Central Valley water park, Liv changed her mind. He wasn't a suicide bomber waiting to happen. Not even close.

Liv's best sequence at the water park was of a 50-year-old Jordanian grandmother going down a giant water slide in the housedress she insisted on wearing over her bathing suit. The water, flowing at one thousand-plus gallons per minute—a half hour of water-slide action equaling the total water consumption of a Gaza Strip refuge camp—had the dress, *cum* chador, clinging suggestively to everything it was intended to cover. Her arms flew up. She threw back her head, her gold-filled teeth exposed in the bright sun. She was the sole caregiver for her seven grandchildren. *Feel it!* was what the billboard at the water park's ticket window commanded in script decorated with waves, suns, and rainbows.

Although unexpressed, the group of thirty-two Jews and Muslims acted as if they had signed a contract agreeing to be "nice" on this all-expenses-paid vacation. They wanted to see everything and participate fully. They were all up for being moved by things other than each other: water park slides; trained whales at Sea World; roller coasters at Magic Mountain; battles at a virtual-reality arcade; a new studio release on the largest screen at Universal City Walk. In two weeks, they'd return home, rested; *then* they could start shouting at each other again.

The vacationers proved to be everything Liv had hoped for when planning the film—two populations who, when stuck together on a bus, could be more than "warring."

What Liv hadn't expected was how exhausting they were. Their tears expressed anguish, their laughter, joy. The earnest emotion was suffocating. It might have been pure cinema, but by the time she reached the water park, all Liv wanted was to watch television and drink a martini alone.

The group was staying at the Red Roof Motel, but Liv slipped away and checked into the Sacramento Hyatt Regency where she drank at the lobby bar. A guy played pop songs on a keyboard and a couple danced to "I Will Survive." The anonymity was a relief.

She was on her second martini when Naim walked into the restaurant and, from the maitre d' stand, started filming the bar. His mouth was moving, narrating for his mother, Liv guessed.

A waiter told him that he couldn't shoot in the bar, and Liv heard Naim say that he'd buy a drink at a table. The waiter told him that the tables were reserved for dinner. Naim told the waiter that it was eleven o'clock. Who was eating dinner? He spotted Liv.

"It's just policy. You can't film here without permission," the waiter said.

Liv went to try to help, and she saw that Naim's camera was still recording, even with the lens pointing at the turquoise carpet. Would he send the audio track to his mother? she wondered.

"Excuse me, but he's a friend of mine, and he's here on vacation with a tour group. They were at the water park this afternoon where they had a fantastic time," Liv said. "The hotel's so nice that he wants to show it to his mother." She knew it was obvious that she was drunk.

"It's bothering some of the customers," the waiter said.

The music stopped. There were two tables finishing dinner. Three men at the bar. Liv wondered which one had picked up Naim's accent. Which customer had he bothered?

"He really can't shoot here," the waiter said.

Such an unfortunate verb, Liv thought.

"The guy's a prick. Let's go," Liv said to Naim.

"You can't say that," the waiter said.

"Sure, I can," Liv said, heading toward the exit, hoping that Naim was behind her.

Naim shot the lighted pool below her room on the sixth floor.

"I don't think you're going to get much," she said.

"This is more sensitive than you think," he said.

Liv looked through the viewfinder to see pinpricks of light reflected off the water ruffled by the night breeze. "You think your mother will find this interesting?"

"She likes water," he said.

He zoomed in and shot through the windows of the restaurant, focusing on the waiter serving the last table a piece of cream pie with two forks. Liv handed Naim a beer from the minibar.

"I came here because I wanted to see a four-star hotel," he said. "I walked. It's three miles."

At last count, Liv had slept with 126 men. When she talked about sex, which was hardly ever, she claimed that sleeping with a man right away was "dating condensed." The anonymity was respectful, not cold, and the sex usually felt great like an airport hotel bar—all needs taken care of with the swipe of a credit card. She had done it so many times that she was confident in her ability to read a man's signals. She knew that an apparently innocent sentence like "I forgot to buy coffee today" could be her cue to say, "Stay with me. I have coffee." But Naim's "I walked. It's three miles," stumped her. Was this a pretext? Should she invite him to stay? It made her nervous and aggravated that he wasn't easy to read. Liv needed to know as quickly as possible: is this going to happen or not?

She saw that he still hadn't opened the beer, and she felt like an idiot. He doesn't drink; he's Muslim, she thought.

"They have *Braveheart*," he said, pointing to the pay-per-view movie advertisement on the television.

He opened his Corona.

After *Braveheart*, Naim lay down with his clothes still on and then crawled under the covers because the air conditioning was so high. Liv followed his cue and crawled into the bed wearing a T-shirt and gym shorts. They would undress each other later under the blankets. This is what he wants, she thought.

He curled up, his back to her, and fell immediately asleep. She pulled up the acrylic bedspread for warmth.

It was dark when she woke, finding his hand on her shoulder. She wanted him to put his hand between her legs, and she wriggled closer to him.

His eyes opened. "Don't tell anyone about this," he said, his voice clear and awake.

"Okay," she said. Did he mean about sleeping with her or did he mean about the waiter kicking him out of the bar?

"Promise?" he asked.

"Promise."

She started to pull off her T-shirt, but he held her hands to stop her. Oh, he means *act as if this night never happened*, she thought.

"I promise I won't tell anyone that you slept fully dressed in my bed," Liv said.

He turned away from her. "You don't have to laugh at me."

"I'm not laughing."

He was quiet, and she waited. Maybe if she were quiet long enough, he'd relax, like a scared animal adapting to a stranger's presence.

"I don't believe in God," he said quietly.

She kept still. *This* must be the opening. Maybe he was the kind of man who needed to confess before having sex, like a married man who had to spit out everything about his wife before cheating on her.

"You thought I did," he said.

"Yes," she admitted.

"It is why we are interesting to you people," he said.

It was unpleasant to hear Naim refer to her as "you people."

"You say our love of God makes us crazy. Sometimes you say our love of God makes us strong. It depends on where the camera points," he said.

"Yes, it does," Liv said. They were definitely not going to have sex, she realized.

"When I know there is no God, I feel very free," Naim whispered.

"He's such a presence. You really got lucky that he speaks English to his mom," Dahlia said, turning off the machine. "Think of what you saved on subtitling with Mr. Photogenic Arab speaking decent English into his camera."

Liv's style was bohemian and sophisticated. A lot of black clothes. A studied casualness. Her affect was of a woman not easily tripped up. But this—Dahlia's simple question about Naim's English—this tripped her up. Jesus, Liv thought. He had an agenda. He wanted to be the star of the movie, so he spoke English. I wanted to sleep with him, and it made me dumb and blind, she thought.

"His mother spent fifteen years in London," Liv said. She was punting, and she immediately asked herself if there was any way she could be caught in this lie. No, she decided. The chances were slim to none that anyone would guess that Naim only spoke English to ensure his presence in her movie. I'm lucky, always have been, always will be. Remember that, Liv told herself.

2

*J*oy Brundage sussed out the people at Beth Meisner's brunch, looking for her entrée. She was there to gain notoriety, admiration, new power relationships, and a better social standing. Joy was a line producer, which meant she was the one the film studios paid a lot of money to get the job done. She hired the crew, and she watched the numbers. She followed directions. She wasn't the kind of movie producer who found the story, developed it, and then raised the money to make the film. That was the kind of producer Beth Meisner was. That was a *creative* producer, and that's what Joy wanted to be, because that was the next thing on the career ladder, and because Joy was convinced that she was creative.

Joy wandered into the kitchen where several women stood around the center island, picking at what was left of the fruit salad. Joy knew none of them, but if they were at Beth Meisner's, she should. Know them.

One of the women was talking about how *frustrated* she had gotten with an unresponsive man at a party last night. "What's wrong with them?" she asked. The other women standing at the kitchen island commiserated. Who said that men were oversexed? The women in the kitchen knew the truth; it's women who want it all the time.

A story, Joy thought. They'll like to hear a story.

She straightened the bottom edge of her sweater, liking how her hip bones stuck out, her stomach flat between them. She ran her hand through her hair, quickly arranging the ends to show off her neck. Good neck, she thought.

"I don't usually tell this story, but it is frustration to the max," Joy said.

The women turned toward her.

"I was on the 405. That's the freeway that goes to LAX," Joy said for these New Yorkers who didn't know one L.A. freeway from another, knowing that it added to her allure that she did. "I was on the second repeat of 'All Things Considered,' and I was stopped dead. There was a gardener's truck behind me, and a guy in a BMW on my right. There was a Jeep ahead, and I couldn't see the driver."

She could feel the women relax into the narrative, which, by her tone, held the promise of being too intimate, perhaps even inappropriate.

"What was I going to do? You can't exactly do script notes on a freeway, no matter how stuck you are," Joy said, happy to have gotten in a reference to her career, to the scripts that were always at hand. "And I was in a cell phone dead zone."

Joy described slipping her hand between her legs and shimming her fingers under the silk panties, adding that it was one of ten she had recently bought because it's important to treat yourself right by buying the best.

The women nodded, and Joy knew they understood her.

"And then I let my fingers slip into place," she said, pausing to make sure her audience all knew where "place" was.

She told her audience that she tried to keep her face "normal" as she pulsed her fingers. She didn't tell the women that she fantasized about Mr. BMW and then thought about how her breasts looked in the new bras she bought as part of the commitment she had made in therapy to take pride in and "own" her body, which meant, concretely, never again hiding her tits in discount-store lingerie. Joy didn't talk about how she had always been intimidated by the idea of moving from L.A. to New York and how the lingerie vow had given her the courage to swap one coast for another, the east being the more exciting of the two. "Exciting" was code for "New York has more available men than Los Angeles."

She got to the part in the story where she let her eyes close, and she was warm between her legs.

Joy watched the women, their lips resting on their champagne flutes, their breath fogging the glass. She had them right where she wanted them. Too bad Beth Meisner was in the living room.

She said that she moaned. "And then someone honked, and I had to fucking *shift*," she said.

One of the women laughed so hard that she snorted up champagne and sent it spraying over the cat bowl. "I hope you wiped off the gear shift," the woman said. Her name was Sara.

"With a Kleenex," Joy lied.

The women started wandering back to the living room to gather up coats, bags, children, and partners.

Joy watched Sara leave the party alone. Was she a producer, an executive, a sales agent? Joy liked Sara's haircut—short, boyish, and sexy. Joy would have to ask Beth about her, later.

At home Joy immediately pulled on her running clothes. She saw herself in a high-end athletic-shoe ad, her skin oiled so that the light could catch her muscles' ripples. It was an ad designed for people like me, she thought. Although not yet at her new career goal, the studios did pay her a lot. Enough to live downtown with views of both rivers, a garage for the Saab, a doorman always on duty, a weekly massage, a skin care regime, nice underwear, *The New Yorker*, *Granta*, and *Daily Variety* subscriptions, a private yoga teacher to stretch open the heart chakra. To most people Joy looked rich, but more important than the dollar amount, she was a good shopper, knowing which bits and pieces were worthy of acquisition.

I am a good shopper. I have a plan. Just do it, she thought, pulling on her shoes.

Outside, drizzle was followed by gusts of wind. Storm clouds passed quickly over the sun, and the turbulent air turned up the silver gray undersides of the season's last leaves. If the day were any indication, it would snow before Thanksgiving.

Joy's ipod had an album from junior high. She knew all the words and had once been able to play the songs on the piano. There was a guy up ahead. Longish red-blond hair. A baseball cap. Did she know him? She picked up her pace, stretching her legs to make them look more lean and athletic.

I feel the earth move, the music played.

Joy was closer now. Yep, she definitely knew him. A documentary filmmaker who had once come to her for advice about a film he was making about the Velvet Revolution. The documentary had been an accident—footage gotten only because he had just happened to be in Prague with a Handycam and his girlfriend, Ruth. All Joy could remember was shaky footage of people running.

I just lose control.

What's his name? Donald. Not Donald. That was his partner on the project. Peter. This guy was Peter.

"Joy?"

"Peter," Joy smiled. He was better looking than she remembered. What was he doing now? When had she seen his footage? When *was* the Velvet Revolution? 1992 or something? No, '89. Had she ever slept with him?

Down to my very soul.

From her early teenage years, Joy believed that any male she met could be president someday. If he wanted her, she could wind up being First Lady. You just never know; you have to be open to these possibilities. Joy had never questioned where the belief had come from. She also never questioned that the boy was to be Jewish—the first Jewish U.S. president.

All over, all over, all over, Carole King kept singing.

Joy imagined herself standing on a cold Pennsylvania Avenue, listening to Peter—who she believed was Jewish—swear to the American people, "I do."

Joy made the calculation: at approximately nine calories a minute, she had burned only 135 in a quarter-hour of running. It wasn't enough to leach the brioche French toast from brunch (she estimated 340 calories, happy she hadn't used syrup). She'd add fifteen minutes to tomorrow's workout. She couldn't just run past Peter; you have to be open to possibilities. You just never know.

She shifted her smile—less grin, more mystery—and took off her headphones.

"Do you live around here?" Peter asked.

Joy nodded. "You?"

"Brooklyn. I was at a friend's." He pointed up at a building on Battery Place.

Joy was disappointed. Brooklyn. Then she rallied. Lots of people lived in Brooklyn. People like Norman Mailer and Paul Auster. Even Nick Gorelich, the man she had been going out with nearly every Saturday night for the last two years, but who had not yet touched her, and whose apartment she had never seen. So what if her therapist, Linus Kezian, thought Nick represented nothing more than an obsessive search for validation.

"I sold the doc to European TV."

"That's great." Joy wondered which channel. Arte? Arte was supposed to be the "classy" channel.

"Yeah, it turned out okay. I've done two other projects for them, and I'm talking to people about a feature."

Joy knew that when Peter said, "I'm talking to people about a feature," he really meant (1) there's no deal in place, and so (2) there's room for a wanna-be ambitious creative producer—you, Joy Brundage—to muscle in. She reminded herself that people like Beth Meisner would consider a documentary aired on European TV as a stamp of approval. People like Beth Meisner knew that making a documentary was a great proving ground for a feature-film director. Joy saw it all very clearly: walking into an awards event as the producer of this handsome, established documentarian's first feature film.

"I sold it to Arte," Peter said. "Do you know them?"

Joy thought about their career trajectory: first there would be strictly independent movies, then, after two films together, she and Peter would go on to make bigger studio films. The kind that were nominated for Academy Awards because they were important.

"That's fantastic," she said, wondering if they should get a drink somewhere.

He looked like a director, she thought. A little spacey, like he was thinking about the next shot. Joy wondered whom Peter knew with an apartment over here. An owner or a renter? Was it a woman? He wasn't wearing a ring. What was his girlfriend's name during the Velvet–Revolution period? Ruth. "How's Ruth?" she asked.

"We broke up a while ago," he answered.

Joy stuck out her bottom lip and made her forehead wrinkle. It was a face for a child with a scraped knee. Joy wanted Peter to know that she would kiss his boo-boo to heal the pain. She congratulated herself again for being courageous enough to move to New York.

In L.A. you're stuck in your cars, and everything goes on behind closed doors in people's houses or offices. In New York, you can actually meet an amazing documentary filmmaker for Arte in the street. There's life on the street in New York, she imagined telling a journalist doing a profile on her.

Joy knew she would continue waiting for things to change between her and Nick Gorelich, but, in the meantime, it was important to be open to other possibilities. You just never know. She asked Peter up to her place for a glass of wine.

"Oh my God, both rivers," Peter said, standing at the wraparound windows, where everyone stood the first time they walked into Joy's apartment.

"All I have is red," Joy said, opening a Bordeaux she knew would be good because it was the same one Nick had brought to dinner at an important studio executive's loft.

Nick Gorelich grew up in Madison, Wisconsin, the son of classics professors. While he didn't have the perfect husband-profile, Joy knew Nick was most likely the one for her. He was good in public. He really *knew* things. He could hold his own. He had gone to private schools. He tested well. He interviewed well. He remembered everything. To Joy, he had never appeared to be someone from a fly-over state. Nick knew that the small painting in the important studio executive's loft was a Twombly.

"That's all I like," Peter said, more of a beer drinker.

"I smell," Joy said before taking a quick shower after which she put on a pair of pants (no underwear), and a sweater with a bra that would show off her nipples when she stepped from the warm shower into the living room.

Peter pushed a strand of hair away from her face, and she kissed him. He backed her against the wall. She reached for him, and he took her hands to pin them over her head. He slipped his other hand down her pants, her skin still wet from the shower.

Humid, she thought.

There was some fumbling about condoms, but she had one in the nightstand.

"Handy," he said, parroting a line from his script.

Peter's script was a romantic comedy: boy likes girl while girl doesn't like boy; then boy doesn't like girl while girl likes boy; then girl snags boy, and boy likes it.

"Don't move yet," he whispered.

Joy followed directions.

3

$\mathscr{S}$ara Koehl walked home to Brooklyn from Beth Meisner's downtown loft, wondering what she always wondered whenever she saw Beth: When would she be dropped from the invitation list? When would Beth Meisner realize that being at Hampshire College together sixteen years ago wasn't the social glue that lasted forever? Beth was a *producer* with films at Cannes and Venice. Sara was a *copy editor* at a medical trade journal. Beth flew first class. Sara flew coach on her rare business trips, greedily saving frequent-flyer miles. She didn't have a car. She had never even been in a Saab convertible like the one she saw the producer who had told the masturbation story picking up from the parking garage across from Beth's building. What was her name? Jill. Jill? Joy.

Sara noticed details—commas and column width at work, the clothes and gestures of Beth's guests. She made patterns out of the details, and she made up explanations—ecological, sociological, cultural, historical—for the patterns. Now, for example, the string of white SUVs clogging the Brooklyn Bridge was an indication that car owners had more time to wash their vehicles. The preponderance of a certain athletic shoe worn by the pedestrians and runners on the bridge was proof that people *did* watch a certain sit-com where its main character wore the same shoe. The oncoming gusting wind blowing soot in the runners' eyes was all the evidence needed to prove global climate change.

Sara had been making up the explanations for so long that she understood that they "explained" nothing. Instead, they were her stories. And making stories had become the point—full stop—even if her therapist, Linus Kezian, thought they kept her disengaged from the world, dangerous for someone like Sara.

A long time ago, right after college, Sara had thought about working in the film business—maybe a screenwriter, maybe a director, whatever. But that was before she came to understand, with the help of her therapist, that the film business wasn't a good fit, because you had to always be "on." You couldn't look depressed—which was exactly how Sara knew she looked, even on her current dose of Paxil.

The light wavered as clouds passed in and then out of the sun. Had she and Beth *ever* been friends at Hampshire College?

She remembered tripping and making snow angels while playing with a black Labrador retriever who she alternately saw as a messenger from the "spirit side" and an incarnation of America—big, bordering on fat, and a little stupid. "Is this dog Lazarus or Archie?" she asked her boyfriend, Thumper, who was kneeling with his face on the ice to better study grass caught at peak green during a flash freeze the night before.

He had been her boyfriend since the second week of freshman year. The first week she called him "White Rabbit" because his eyebrows were so blond that they were invisible. He became "Thumper" after their first night together.

"Archie who?" Thumper asked.

"Archie, from the comics," she said. "You know, Betty, Veronica, Archie, Jughead."

"It's all mosaic tile," Thumper said, staring at the frozen grass, dumbfounded that he was only just now noticing the extravagant Moorish tile terrace in front of the college library. Thumper had taken three hits of blotter acid, Sara, one.

The Labrador jumped on Sara to lick her face. Archie, she thought. He's definitely Archie. The lamps lining the walk between the student center and the library switched on, and Sara watched her breath crystallize into a blue halo around the dog's thick head. No, he's Lazarus. Definitely Lazarus, she decided.

Beth Meisner crunched across the snow toward the library with a backpack full of books. "It's Simone de Beauvoir," Sara said to the dog. Beth smiled, and Sara waved the dog's paw at her.

Did this moment mean they were friends for life?

Thumper never understood Sara's connection to all things Beth. Why, when she came out of eight hours of hallucinating or living on black beauties to read her comp-lit syllabus in a weekend, were Sara's first thoughts always about Beth? Why was the article about Julio Cortázar and the French New Wave that Beth was rumored to be publishing her sophomore year, so *amazing*? Why was an article more important than his new connection for 500 hits of acid?

"I'm making our life qualitatively better," Thumper said, talking about his LSD connection. "In the scheme of things, her article's only a tick on her résumé." *The scheme of things* was something Thumper often claimed to see.

What Thumper missed was that Sara and Beth were connected. They came from the same background—progressive, secular, and urban. Both had gone to private schools where the message was clear: you have unlimited capacities; your life will be fabulous. Beth got the message, but Sara had doubts. Even at 7, while being exposed to Mozart during a New York Philharmonic young people's concert or during a workshop with human rights lawyers to sensitize her third-grade class to issues of race, Sara knew something was up. Sara saw patterns, and *special* was not an adequate descriptor—certainly not of her.

After college, when no job interviewer cared about unlimited capacities and fabulousness, Sara finally found the adequate words to describe the world's pattern: there was *regular*, and there was *better*. She was regular. Beth was better. And then Reagan, Thatcher, deregulation, junk bonds, neo-cons, globalization, and her own serotonin levels joined together to confirm her position. She wasn't an alcoholic, but she lived as if she were—alert to the things she could change, accepting of those she couldn't. And she knew she would never measure up to the likes of Beth Meisner.

From her kitchen, Sara watched the wind stir up leaves, a Starbucks cup, and the river, which she could just glimpse through two buildings. She watched a couple on the street duck to avoid a blowing plastic garbage can lid. When they straightened, the man lifted the woman's hand to sip from her to-go cup, brushing his lips across her hand. The phone rang, and Sara picked up and then dropped the receiver. It was only the voicemail reminder she had set to start getting dressed for dinner.

Verizon Communications' reminder call service made her feel not exactly as if she had friends, but sort of. Three calls a day: the morning wakeup, the reminder that Charlie Rose was about to begin, and the "floater," like the one tonight that told her to get ready for dinner with her mother, her brother, and his new girlfriend. At twenty-five cents per call, Sara paid $273.75 a year for the illusion of phone pals. This was nothing compared to the months after being released from her mother's care when she had randomly programmed the reminder call option to ring her throughout the day, $2.50 days being the norm. That was a $973.00 year.

She had never told her therapist about this for the obvious reason that people who believed that computer-generated calls came from their friends were crazy. They were the kind of people who staged talk shows in their living rooms, taking the role of both David Letterman and the celebrity guest. She wasn't like that. She was sure about that.

Sara stood behind a potted cypress at the unoccupied maitre d' stand to watch her brother, Peter, and her mother at a back table. It was the first time seeing her mother since their "spa getaway" in Cabo San Lucas. Yoga in the morning, hikes, hot stone massages, peels, and wraps. Fifteen hundred calories a day.

From day one, Jan, the yoga instructor, made her mother his favorite, pushing her into deeper forward bends, massaging her neck during cool down. His head was shaved; his eyes bulged. When he leaned over Sara during supta padangushtasana to roll her thighs in, she imagined projectile vomiting into his face.

Sara skipped yoga classes after the second day to read on the beach.

"You hurt Jan's feelings," her mother said, appearing after class, standing on Sara's towel. Sara shaded her eyes to look up at her mother in a skinny T-shirt and Adidas workout pants. Her breasts were small. Her arms muscled. Backlit by the sun, she could have been 20 years old.

"I'm sure he didn't notice. You're his pet," Sara said.

"You sound like a child," her mother said.

"How would you know what I sound like? You're so involved with reinventing yourself that you can't see that I'm struggling with my own personal transformation here," Sara said. A child was exactly what she sounded like.

"What's there to see? You're a 38-year-old playing Sleeping Beauty, waiting for someone to wake you up," her mother said.

Sara had been in therapy long enough to know that it was wrong—therapeutically speaking—to long for a TV drama world where a mom's hug and a kiss always make the ouchy go away. She knew that the right thing was to value the richness and complexity that real life offered.

"What's a fucking middle-aged woman doing on vacation with her mother, anyway?" In the last few years her mother had begun talking like a Quentin Tarantino movie.

"Well, why's a fucking mother more concerned about some Nazi yoga instructor than her own daughter?" Sara asked.

"He's Dutch," her mother said, sprinting across the scalding sand back to the hotel.

"Fuck you," Sara said when her mother was too far away to hear.

Her mother laughed and touched Peter's hand. Like a flirt, Sara thought. No, not like a flirt, she corrected herself. Like a lonely person. Like a maiden aunt. Like an *elderly* woman. My mother's getting *old*.

"May I help you?" the maitre d' asked.

"I'm with them," Sara said, pointing to her brother and mother.

"Oh, the Nancy party," the maitre d' said, waving Sara on back. Her mother had recently stopped using her last name.

"I've been talking to people at the studios, and today I ran into an old friend who has become a pretty successful independent producer," Peter was saying to their mother as Sara sat down.

"Beware of men in independent-producer clothing," she said, taking the chair next to her mother, across from Peter.

"A woman in independent-producer clothing," Peter said.

"I know I'm not in the business, but it all sounds exciting," Nancy said.

"Exciting isn't the word. It's a lot of wheel spinning and meetings. But it's a game, and if I want to make feature films, I have to play it," Peter said. "I have to act *as if* I'm a director. The idea is that sooner or later someone will believe me."

Sara wondered if her brother was as good at seducing other people as he was their mother. Had he started calling her Nancy?

"I don't want to brag or anything, but I'm pretty good at making people want to be around me," Peter said, standing up, his arms open to a tall woman hurrying across the restaurant. "Liv Johansson," Peter said, presenting her to his mother and sister.

"Sorry I'm late," Liv said.

Sara took in her brother's new girlfriend. Closer to her age than to Peter's 34. Uncombed, long, dark hair. Her green eyes were tired, and the black jeans had definitely been taken from the floor by the side of the bed.

Liv kissed Peter and brushed his hair away from his face. Then she turned, reached her hand across the table and said, "You're Nancy."

"Yes, I am," Nancy said.

Her voice was high and singsong, and Sara watched her mother's neck redden and bloom into an eczema patch. It was her mother's anxiety meter, and Sara wondered if the rash would bloom in the panic before death. Would her mother be declared dead with a red splotch on her neck, the embalmer stuck trying to cover it? Would they have to bury her mother with a scarf around her neck? No open casket, Sara decided. Maybe cremation.

"Hi, I'm Sara," Sara said, taking Liv's hand.

Liv sat next to Peter. "I'm trying to get this thing done for the mix, and I just lost track of time," she said.

Peter scooted his chair closer to Liv. "Liv's finishing this amazing documentary about a group of Arabs and Israelis who go on a bus tour of California. There are these Palestinians from the occupied territories . . ."

"Well, there were visa problems, so it's mainly Jordanians and some Lebanese," Liv interrupted. "It's part of this 'peace project' that's been going on for years. Arabs and Israelis on vacation together in some neutral spot—not that the States is all that neutral, mind you."

"It's wild," Peter said. "They're all crammed on this tour bus, and they're visiting wineries in Napa, which is kind of weird because the Arabs don't drink . . ."

"Some do," Liv said.

"Still, you get the irony," Peter said. "Then they go to the Hearst Castle, and no one can believe what they're seeing. The best is when they're all at Disneyland. Like do you laugh or cry? I mean, is Disneyland going to end up being the great equalizer?"

"Since when do you use the word *equalizer*? Sara asked.

Peter looked startled. "Since always," he said.

She had blurted this out too quickly. Too aggressive and weird, Sara thought. So what if her dyslexic brother had just used a rare four-syllable word? No reason to *broadcast* it.

"Why?" Peter asked.

"I don't know," Sara said. "Sorry." She looked at Liv, hoping for more conversation from this girl who seemed like she was socially adept.

"The real equalizer was when we went to this huge mall in Orange County," Liv said. "When I'd ask them about property or water rights, they were like snarling dogs. But when we went to Best Buys, it was like a block party. I think it's hard to think about lighting your neighbor on fire when you're checking out new hard drives," Liv said.

Sara wondered what happened to Peter's last girlfriend. Ruth. Ruth Rosner.

"What's pathetic is that the world's in big fat trouble, and no one's screaming 'Fire!' I mean, why isn't anyone coming up with anything better than shopping?" Liv said.

She's nervous, Sara thought, noticing that Liv's wine glass was already empty.

Nancy held her blouse closed at the collar, feigning a chill to cover her rash.

With his right hand Peter sliced off a piece of vegetable mousse. Peter was a leftie, and Sara wondered where her brother's left hand was. On Liv, she realized, trying to get a glimpse of their laps.

A burst of laughter came from a long table lined with women, one chair piled with presents. Sara watched her mother, Liv, and Peter look over at the table where a woman with Pilates arms wearing a tight electric-blue dress was waving for the waiter.

"I know why no one's coming up with real solutions," Sara said.

Sara could see that everyone at the table had forgotten what they had been talking about.

"You wanted to know why no one was coming up with anything better than shopping," she reminded Liv. "Well, it's because other solutions are hard. They force people to take stands or make sacrifices," Sara said. "And that's a drag. All anyone really wants is to be *liked*, right?" Sara wasn't exactly sure what she was talking about.

Nancy said, "I don't know. I think people take stands. They have opinions."

"I was at a brunch this morning with all these movie types," Sara said, ignoring her mother. "Everyone stood around smiling and nodding, and that was it. How can anything change if all people do is nod at each other?"

The waiter came with a list of specials. Nancy ordered oysters and champagne for the table. When the waiter left, they were quiet. What had Sara been saying?

"We're all like sloppy, enthusiastic puppies. Americans." Sara said. "That's what Americans are like."

Liv smiled, distracted. She hasn't heard a thing I just said, Sara realized.

Peter's left hand appeared to reach for his water.

"We're like extras in an 'I heart America' ad," Sara said. "No one wants their mellow to be harshed." *Don't harsh my mellow*, was what Thumper used to say, Sara remembered. "We want to shop, watch TV, and have people smile at us. America, the land of life, liberty, and an unharshed mellow," she said.

"There's nothing wrong with being nice," Nancy said.

"Whose brunch was it?" Peter asked.

"Beth Meisner's," Sara said, realizing that Beth Meisner was someone her brother probably wanted to know.

The waiter put a tray of oysters on the table and began working the champagne cork.

"The bad thing about 'nice' is that it doesn't go anywhere. You only know who you are by rubbing up against something," Sara said, understanding this for the first time.

"Nicely put," Liv said, looking straight at Sara.

I've impressed her, Sara thought, hoping that Peter and her mother had noticed. How pathetic, Sara thought, imagining herself as a puppy rolling over for approval.

"There's a bit of La Pasionaria in you, isn't there?" Liv said.

Sara pictured a grainy photo of a foreign-looking woman in a black dress. Was she picturing La Pasionaria or Edith Piaf?" she wondered.

"Spanish Civil War?" Nancy asked.

"Yes," Liv said. "She was this charismatic leader in a black dress who stood at the barricades saying something like 'the fascists shall not pass.'"

"¡No Pasaràn!" Sara whispered, her high-school Spanish coming back.

The Veuve Cliquot gave way in a professional "pop." The lights dimmed, and waiters came out with a birthday cake. The lady with Pilates arms at the long table with the presents piled on a chair made her friends happy by appearing surprised as they sang "Happy Birthday."

4

$\mathscr{A}$fter dinner Sara walked to Bob Nascent's building where she stood across the street, counted up eight floors and then drew her finger across the building to the corner apartment. To Planet Bob. A light was on.

Bob was gangly with longish dirty blond hair and pale skin. He was 27, the same age as Thumper when he disappeared. Sara had noticed him the first day he started working at the medical association journal. She collected gossip about him, saw the patterns and made assumptions. So far this is what she knew about Bob Nascent: he had gone straight from the University of Illinois to a start-up in San Jose, and then to another one in San Francisco, and then five years ago to another one in New York. After this one choked in six months, he came to work at the medical association's on-line journal. He had furnished his apartment in an afternoon at Conran's, had never had a steady girlfriend, was called Jez in "Gate Keeper," the on-line text-based fantasy game he had played since he was 14, had his groceries delivered from the deli downstairs, and had most likely never worked less than sixty hours a week since leaving college. He had supposedly never had anyone up to his apartment, even his parents visiting from Chicago. Sara was confident that two nights ago—Friday—she had gotten closer than anyone else had ever been.

Friday had started with Bob hanging over Sara's cubicle, pointing his grande mocha to the four strangers in the conference room, asking, "Should we know about that?" When he saw an improvised spitball session in a conference room, he knew to be ready to jump in.

Sara checked her planner and scrolled through current e-mail chatter. "I don't think so. There's no mention of it anywhere," she said. She wanted to keep Bob at her cubicle for as long as possible, so she added, "Hey, I checked out that Web site."

Bob smiled. "Pretty sick, right?"

"Sick" for Bob was a fusion of cool, strange, scary, and weird. "Sick" was "funny." The site was devoted to home bomb construction, mainly nails and fertilizers, and Sara had studied the site, noting proportions, such as the quantity of liquid fertilizer to the length of the fuse. She imagined throwing a Molotov cocktail into the conference room. "Not so sick," Sara said.

They watched Cyndy Jacoby rise up from her cubicle, looking disoriented. She removed her phone headset and walked to the Human Resources Department offices. Mike Noritz, who had recently sent out an e-mail saying, "The value of work is the camradry!" appeared in his office door and pulled Cyndy Jacoby in. Sara had replied to Noritz's e-mail, correcting the spelling of camaraderie. Noritz had never responded.

"Show's over," Bob said, and he left Sara to go to his cubicle.

Mike Noritz and Cyndy Jacoby emerged from his office and walked together to the conference room where one of the strangers handed Cyndy what looked to be a cappuccino.

Sara called Bob's extension, "They're handing out cappuccinos," she said.

"What?" Bob asked.

"The show isn't over. Numnuts walked Cyndy with two Y's to the conference room. They gave her a cappuccino."

"They're firing," Bob said. He had seen this before.

He came back to Sara's cubicle where he used the green padded walls as a duck blind to survey the alley between Noritz's office and the conference room. "Sheridan, ten o'clock," he said when Tom

Sheridan walked from his cubicle to Noritz's office and then to the conference room. Bob set his watch. Three minutes and six seconds later, Tom Sheridan emerged from the conference room with a coffee, and Bob leaned out of Sara's cubicle to wave him over.

"They told me that they're joining with another association and they don't need as many people. Those guys are counselors." Tom sipped the coffee, the steam fogging a half moon on his smeared glasses. "They've got someone in the kitchen with an espresso machine. I counted thirty cups, so they're probably axing thirty of us, right?"

Sara had taken this job because her shrink, Linus Kezian, thought that her old job, working from home as a freelance copy editor for a dental journal, was too "isolating." Linus felt that Sara needed "the community of the water cooler."

The medical association had no water cooler. What it had was a refrigerator where people put the bag lunches they ate at their desks.

"We'll be at Marino's later if you want to come by," Bob said to Tom.

Sara's breath caught. *This* is what Linus had been hoping for. Sara and Bob: Team Bob Nascent. *We'll* be at Marino's.

"But you guys might not get the axe," Tom said.

"We'll still be there," Sara said.

Sara and Bob were not fired on Friday, but from seven to midnight they were at Marino's with those who were. Bob played video games and insisted that the bartender play a Chemical Brothers CD three times in a row. Sara drank tequila because Bob ordered a bottle and made a big show of laying cut limes and saltshakers on the tables pushed together at the back of the room. She danced with someone from graphics while watching Bob figure out a complicated magic trick involving a folded dollar bill.

Sara's future rolled out as smooth as a new freeway; she and Bob would share a cab, and he would tell her not to bother going on to Brooklyn. She would spend the night at his place where they would have easy sex. The two of them would hang out Saturday in a comfortable hung-over haze, reliving the gossip of the night before. Saturday night, they would rent a video and eat take-out. On Sunday Bob would go with her to Beth Meisner's brunch and then maybe even to dinner with her mother, Peter, and Liv.

But what happened was this: she and Bob shared a cab. He held her hand, and before he got out of the cab at his apartment, he kissed her. Sara's mouth was stiff, and she knew it was as stale as his.

"I'm finishing up a graphic interface tomorrow," he said, paying the driver for his leg of the trip.

Sara rode home to Brooklyn wondering what Bob meant by "I'm finishing up a graphic interface tomorrow." Was he trying to say that he was going into the office and he wanted her to be there with him? Or did he mean that he'd be at home working all day Saturday, and that she should call him? Tears welled up. She hated herself for not knowing what Bob Nascent meant.

Sara decided to ring Bob's bell and go on up. They'd have a beer and then maybe watch TV. She would salvage what this weekend could have been. She stepped off the curb to cross the street. The light went off in his apartment. Sara stepped back up onto the curb.

A metal roll-up door rattled down over a grocery store, and a little girl scurried under, shouting, "Daddy, wait." Bob Nascent opened his window and sat on the windowsill, talking on the phone. He was laughing, and Sara saw his breath in the cold air. She saw the tableau, and the tableau contained the truth: Bob Nascent was up there. She was down here. She would never make it up to his apartment. How could she?

Bob Nascent stepped back into his apartment and closed the window. There was a siren somewhere close. A cab turned onto the street, and Sara raised her arm to flag it.

The cab smelled of patchouli, and the driver was talking on his cell phone, his other ear closed off by puffy scar tissue.

"I'm going to Grace Court in Brooklyn," Sara said.

He put the car in gear, and Sara lay back on the seat. The streetlights flashed by. She thought about the bomb Web site, picturing a mushroom cloud over Bob Nascent's building.

"Race?" the driver shouted at her.

"Grace," Sara said loudly.

I work in a cubicle, Sara thought. No one has seen me naked for a long time. I'm 38 years old, and there isn't much time.

"What?" the driver said, turning to her.

"Grace. I'm going to Grace Court," Sara said in something close to a whisper.

5

$\mathcal{L}$iv lay staring at the bedside clock, her film running in her head. Was it too much that Naim took up almost twenty percent of her movie? Was she an idiot to devote this much screen time to a man who used his camera to talk to his mother? If she were a real artist, she would have the guts to cancel the mix tomorrow and recut the whole film. I'm overcranking, she thought. Naim got twenty minutes, but the Israeli mother of five who had lost her oldest son in a bus bombing got seventeen minutes.

Breathe, she told herself. It's okay. It's not a *total* piece of shit. The film made sense. Her editor liked it. Naim was photogenic and sad. His twenty minutes were going to give her an edge for an Oscar nomination. She thought about the award ceremony and how she'd take Naim.

Peter came out of the bathroom. "So, what did you think of them?" he asked.

"Your family?"

Peter nodded. Of course his family.

"They're eager."

"Eager. My sister is not eager."

"She is, too," Liv said, remembering Sara's passion—something about how Americans were like Labrador retrievers.

"So what's wrong with eager?" Peter asked.

"Nothing," Liv said. There was nothing to be gained by telling him that eagerness was usually just nervous energy.

"Do you want to do it?" Peter asked, climbing into bed and wrapping his arms around her from behind.

"No."

"My hand cramped up at the table," Peter said.

"The waiter saw what we were doing," Liv said.

"Oh yeah? What did he do?"

"Glanced. I'm sure he's seen boyfriends trying to give their girl-friends orgasms under the tablecloth before."

The clock flashed to 12:33. Five and a half hours until she could get into the editing room early to watch the Naim stuff again. Maybe she *had* given him too much screen time.

"Well, did you come?" Peter asked.

"Yeah," Liv said.

"Marry me," Peter whispered.

She heard her father in the kitchen, and she pictured him squint-ing into the Sub Zero refrigerator light to pull out the yogurt tub. She and Peter had probably woken him when they came in.

"Did you hear me?"

"Yes," Liv said.

Liv knew that her father was thinking about her. He would have already said his nightly prayer, which always included his younger brother, Linus; and his factory, Sparkle Life Fashions. Now, at the refrigerator, he would be taking the opportunity to reassure God that Liv would soon have a husband.

"And?" Peter asked.

The kitchen was quiet, and Liv knew her father was flooding the bowl of yogurt with honey.

"Yes," Liv answered.

6

At 5 a.m. Liv was at the kitchen table making her day's to-do list:

PU dry cleaning
Call lab re: additional print costs
Accounts
Confirm restaurant
Peter: future
Call Nick Gorelich

"Say your prayers," John said, kissing her on the head.

"Why would I bother writing that down when you're always reminding me?" she asked, covering the part about Peter and the future.

John was dressed for running, a Discman and rosary in his fanny pack. He went to Mass after his morning run.

"Did you have fun last night?"

"Fun. I met his family."

"Come on. Not fun like 'whoopee,' but fun like were they nice?" He dumped two bananas, orange juice, and protein powder into the blender.

"Nice enough. His mother wasn't how I imagined her," Liv said, thinking of the one photo she had of her own mother, Inga, in her SAS flight attendant uniform, an A-line skirt, and white blouse. Even though her father had never ducked telling Liv about Inga—ditzy, pill-addicted, unpredictable, dangerous, dead in 1980, promiscuous, uncouth, selfish—this photo represented the sentimental version of "mother" that Liv maintained. Although Liv knew that she had come out of a four-night stand, Liv never considered the word "accident" when considering her conception.

"Blender on," John said, pushing number 8 on the machine, churning the viscous, beige super-drink against the sides of the blender pitcher.

In Armenia, John had worked in a textile co-op in Spitak. In the late 60s, the co-op decided to specialize in wedding ware, and John was chosen to go to Paris to learn more about Western tastes and manufacturing techniques at the *Salon du Mariage*. It was almost two days of travel: Yerevan to Moscow and then Moscow to Paris. It was an Aeroflot scheduling foul-up in Moscow that put John on an SAS flight.

Inga, the stewardess on John's flight, was going to be in Paris on hiatus and said "Call me" to John as he deplaned. "I'm at the Hôtel de Suède," she said as he walked down the plane's stairs to the tarmac. The tossed-off two words, "Call me," excited John in a way he had never felt before. On the tarmac, he looked back to the plane's door, the sun flaring in his eyes as he tried to make out the SAS stewardess who could be so sexy with two tossed-off words.

At baggage claim, John saw a man in a brown suit watching him, and John was flattered that he was important enough to warrant a minder from the Soviet State. *Defecting*, John thought, trying the word out in his head, having no intention of doing so.

Consumed by the erotic casualness of "Call me," and puffed up by the self-importance he got from the minder, John called Inga as soon as he reached his hotel room.

For the four days of the wedding convention, John dutifully visited every stand, collecting samples of dresses, fabrics, and trims. He attended seminars on the latest trends in wedding parties. He had a meeting with a company who made a detachable wedding-dress train. Every day when the exhibitors were shutting down their stands and Mr. Brown Suit Soviet Minder was eating a crepe at the convention café, John went straight back to his hotel on Rue de Turenne. John was Mr. Brown Suit's easiest job, for John stayed in his hotel room—bound to his SAS stewardess—all night, every night. In room 5, he wrapped Inga in samples and then peeled them off. She blindfolded him with pink satin and dragged marabou across his stomach. It was the first time he had ever heard the word "fuck." She was the first woman who seemed to want it.

After the convention, back in Spitak, the co-op began producing copies of the samples John had brought back, and every Armenian bride was assured that she looked liked a European. Although a new factory chief was elected every six months, the vision and energy that John brought back from France made him the real boss.

A year and a half later, while John was in Yerevan on a business trip and Linus was home studying for his medical exams, a letter arrived from Sweden. Linus tried calling John to get permission to open the letter, but the phone at the Yerevan factory was always busy. Linus paced with the letter, knowing the name on the return address from the few stories John had shared. John's stories about Inga had been spare, but Linus retained the essential details: her eye color, the way she walked unapologetically naked in the hotel room. Linus slit open the envelope.

Dear John Kezian,

I had a baby, and you are her father. But I find that I cannot keep her. I want someone to adopt her, and maybe it's you!

Perhaps you could. She is healthy and good. Please contact me immediately.

> *Sincerely,*
>
> *Inga Johansson*

The letter was written in block letters. No signature, just Inga's name in the same block letters.

Linus kept trying to reach John at the Yerevan factory. Only once did someone pick up, but that person dropped the receiver on the desk, leaving Linus with the disembodied sounds of someone eating. Finally, Linus went to the police station where he paid a policeman to use his overseas line to call Sweden.

When Inga answered, Linus said, "I am John."

"Thank God," Inga said, launching into the story of the pregnancy—how it had been so easy, how she had really felt good, but how, once the baby was here, it was too hard. She wasn't up to it. "It's not me, you know? I'm not like a mother," she said, giggling.

How could he have had sex with this idiot? Linus thought.

"I wanted to give her away to farmers. Farmers need children, but Gunner, he's my friend, said I should ask you first. Do you want baby? It's a girl."

"Yes, I want," Linus said quickly. "I come soon." He was suddenly aware of how thick his accent was. Did he sound anything like John? How could Inga possibly believe he was John? he wondered. Maybe she's slept with so many men that the only memory she has of John is an address on a scrap of paper, he thought. Again, he decided that Inga was an idiot.

Linus paid more money to the policeman to get an exit visa for his brother, and less than a week later, Linus was hurrying John to the airport. John never questioned Linus's decision to open the letter, his masquerade with Inga on the phone, or Linus's conviction that the baby girl had to be saved from the spaced-out stewardess.

"You're here. Thank, God," Inga said, opening her door, quickly swallowing two of the white pills that she usually took for those layovers when she didn't want to sleep right away.

John found himself stuck on the English word for "hello," so he nodded.

A TV was blaring a commercial where a woman scrubbed a floor, her mop sending off animated sparkles.

"Look, look," Inga said, grabbing John's coat sleeve so he would look at the television.

"*Jag bara älskar mitt golv!*" the actress in the commercial squealed, proudly surveying her shiny floor.

"Her name's Liv. The actress. Isn't she beautiful? I named the baby after her. Liv, like the actress." The actress winked at the camera, and the commercial ended.

"Where is baby?" John asked.

"Here, here," Inga said, leading John down the hall to a back room. "This is Liv," she said, opening the door.

A crib was pushed between the washing machine and an Exercycle. A sodium-vapor streetlight lit the room orange and threw shadows of the crib's slats up the wall. John leaned close to the child. Dark hair. Like him, a slight fold to her eyelids. The baby stared back at her father: she, the aquarium fish, he, the ichthyologist.

"She is quiet," John said.

"I don't want her. I made a mistake. We made a mistake." She showed him the birth certificate. "You can take her with you. No problem. You're her father. See? Yes, yes, her name is Johansson, but you are the father. John Kezian. It's spelled okay, right? I can go with you to the airport to make sure there are no hitches. I'm the mother, and you have my permission to take her." Gunner's white pills were kicking in.

John struggled with the word "hitches." What were "hitches?"

"You live in a place that's set up for babies. There are always women around who would love to take care of a baby like her. It won't cost you much. How much can a baby cost? Girls are easier than boys. They don't go out as much. Not like boys who are always out at bars and nightclubs. When a girl goes out, the boy pays. So it's less money, too."

She picked at the skin under her fingernail.

John picked a blanket with dancing cows off the floor and covered his daughter. It was a long trip to Spitak, and he wondered about formula. Would Inga have diapers to give him? Had he ever changed a diaper?

"Maybe when she's older, she'll want to meet me. We could arrange it, but it should be up to her, don't you think?"

Inga rubbed her eyes and then started closing and opening the drapes, the fabric whooshing as she pulled the curtain pulls like utters. Right, left, right, left.

"You have family in Tirana. You're equipped for a baby."

Tirana, John thought. She said, "Tirana," and for the first time, he understood that he had tricked himself into believing that Inga was smart just because she spoke English better than he and had let him have sex with her in a way that made him feel special. The stupid cow doesn't know that Tirana is in Albania, John thought, tucking the blanket around Liv's feet.

"I really think we're doing the right thing. She won't even remember me."

John slapped her. Inga was still, and John watched the right cheek redden. He was surprised that his hand hurt.

"Fuck you," Inga said, leaving the room.

Liv started to cry, and John picked her up. "*Khosk em dalees, sa verchin angam eh vor gdesnes inds ayspesie vad ararkh gadarelutz,*" he murmured, apologizing for scaring the baby, pressing her to his wool coat, assuring her that he didn't hit people. This was the first and last time, and he meant it. "*Khosk em dalees.*"

And Liv, at 6 months, went from hearing her mother's Swedish to her father's Armenian.

John drank his protein drink from the blender pitcher.

"I think the sister, Sara, is depressed. If I had to guess, I'd say she's on medication. It's like there's a roll of cotton around her, you know?" Liv said.

"But they liked you."

"Yeah. Dad, look, it's not a sure thing that I'm going to marry him."

"But you said you wanted to."

"I said that I thought he might be my husband. I was a mess when I met him. You know that. Don't go all super-Catholic on me," Liv said, remembering last night's "yes."

John wiped the protein drink scum from his lips. "Do you remember Armenia, Liv?" he asked.

Liv knew he was talking not about Armenia, but about how they had left Armenia, the event that cemented the family into an unbreakable troika—John, Linus, Liv. Every family has their event. Some have the Mayflower or slave ships or hot treks across the Sonora desert or Ellis Island, or container ships. Some have terrifying wagon-train journeys over mountains where they get stuck in the Donner Pass and have to resort to cannibalism to survive. For Liv's family the event was a bumpy truck ride out of the Soviet state.

"Of course I do. It's The Event. It's our Donner Party except we ate pork sausage instead of each other," she said.

Liv saw her father clamp his top lip over his teeth as he rinsed the blender pitcher. Shit, he's mad, Liv realized. *The Event. The Donner Party.* Wrong word choices. She had made their story—*their* story—into anecdote. She had given it a punch line, and he wasn't in that kind of mood. Shit.

"Let me do that, Dad" she said, taking the pitcher from him. "The blades need to be cleaned." She got out a scouring pad to clean all the blender's hard-to-reach parts.

7

As he did before all his couch patients, Linus Kezian moved one of the Vassily chairs behind and slightly to the left of the couch, annoyed that after twenty years he was still giving in and granting early morning sessions to those patients who insisted that their schedules were *too* impossible for anything during the normal working day. Seven fifteen a.m. for Joy Brundage. He hoped she had a lot to say. He wasn't in the mood for much more than listening. The light beside the door flashed. Joy was waiting.

Joy started the session with, "So, I went to this brunch on Sunday at Beth Meisner's. I think I told you about her. She's a pretty big producer."

Then Joy told Linus the story she had told at the brunch—the one about masturbating in her car on the 405 freeway.

Linus tried to imagine the 405, remembering news footage of the police chasing O. J. Simpson. Was that the 405? What's wrong with me that I've never been to L.A.? Linus wondered. It was only because of some twisted reverse snobbery—L.A. having the largest Armenian population outside Yerevan—that he had never made the trip to California. It's time I get out there, he thought. A week on the beach. A hotel in Santa Monica. No, he thought. I'll stay in Hollywood. *The Hollywood Hills. The Strip*, he thought.

Joy told Linus that the women had seemed to like the story and her.

Linus had to work at remembering what Joy had been saying. Something about putting her hands down her pants. She had told this story at a party, he reminded himself. Yesterday, a brunch, Linus remembered.

"But why this story?" he asked.

She was quiet, and he knew she was offended. He knew she thought it was a funny story. A *risqué* story. He knew that she thought such stories were social currency. It's what people did at parties. Why the hell was Linus questioning her about *this*?

"It's funny, and everyone does it," Joy said.

"Do you mean everyone masturbates in traffic jams or that everyone tells a story like this to strangers?" Linus asked.

She was quiet again. She's going to cry in ten, he predicted to himself. One, two, three, four. He noticed that some sand from his desktop Zen garden had spilled onto a teak side table, and he lost count. He licked his finger to pick up the grains and then brushed them onto the garden floor. Still no tears from Joy. He would have been at seventeen or so by now.

"Beth Meisner's signing a huge producing contract, and it's important that we get to know each other," Joy said. "My job's all about people, and I should know everyone Beth Meisner knows. The story was an icebreaker."

Linus thought about renting an apartment in Los Angeles. A short-term furnished rental. Something with a hot tub. He'd do the whole clichéd thing. He'd rent a fancy car and watch fabulous people. *Be* fabulous. Eat at The Ivy.

"I don't see what's wrong with the story," she said. "I feel so bad when you ask why I do something so *normal* like tell that story. It makes me start thinking that there's something really wrong with me, and how I'm alone and needy. It's too obvious how needy I am. I mean I know I'm needy, but people shouldn't know it. People don't want to be around needy people. But it's hard because I *am* needy. When I leave these parties, what do I have waiting for me? An empty apartment. God, some of the women at the party have a husband *and* a baby."

Now she was crying.

Linus thought about actors who could cry on a dime just by remembering their dog's death forty years ago. If it *looks* like emotion, then it must *be* emotion: that's what Joy believes, Linus thought. The tears were a flash card for emotion.

"Why are you crying about something you've never had?" he asked.

She answered him with something about how love is part of the human genome. At $250 a session, Linus almost admired Joy's proud resistance to the therapeutic process. She was going to try to get her way for as long as it took. This therapy was part of the agenda: accelerate the career, find a man and have a baby before age forty. Linus knew that he was right there alongside all her other personal service providers. He assumed he was listed somewhere near her masseuse. Above or below, he didn't know.

"Do you think you could be crying about something else?" he asked.

"Why don't you tell me?" she spit out.

"I'm not sure you can feel an absence if you've never had the thing before," he said.

"I know what I feel," she said.

Linus kept himself quiet. He knew she was broaching a new subject.

"I ran into this guy on Sunday, and we had sex," she said. "I felt good about having sex with him because there was an authentic connection, you know?"

Linus knew Joy wanted him to be impressed. He had made an offhand remark a month ago about how, even if she was unhappy, she was at least getting what most people craved—sex. He made Joy very happy with that remark, because it made her sound successful. He knew that ever since, she had used every opportunity to show him how proactive she was.

"I was *with* him. It wasn't a bullshit fantasy. I was really with Peter," she said.

Linus heard Joy say "Peter" as he dragged the small rake across the Zen garden's sand. "Peter" was the name of his niece's boyfriend—the one John wanted Liv to marry, mainly because he was so tired of the string of men she had been bringing home for nearly twenty years now. He loosened his grip on the rake, and the lines became more artful and even. There were only five minutes left, so he was off the hook. Not enough time to probe Joy's need to please any man who came along, or to question her assertion that fantasy was not part of the afternoon with Peter. She might as well be wearing an "All Offers Considered. As Is." banner, he thought.

Joy sat up as Linus began a new set of lines in the sand.

Busted, he thought, surprised by how he calmly finished the line in the sand before putting down the rake.

8

"$\mathcal{B}$ob Nascent is awesome, and I'm not. It's that simple," Sara said as she entered Linus's office. "I got an e-mail from him this morning. You know what he did this weekend? He went to see Noritz, from Human Resources. What did I do? I had dinner with my mother and then stared at Bob's building."

She threw her coat on the couch and sat in one of the Vassily chairs to face Linus. Sara was not a couch patient. Never had been. Linus needed to see her face.

"You're feeling inferior only because you're comfortable with that feeling," he said.

"Wrong. I don't *feel* inferior; I *am* inferior. Bob Nascent actually confronted Numnuts to see justice done, and I did zero."

"So use it as a catalyst to act," Linus said.

Just fucking do something! Linus thought. He imagined shaking Sara until she cried and how nice it would be to dry her tears.

He had a recurring dream about meeting Sara at the Angelika movie theater. When he said hello, she didn't recognize him. When he started to undress her, she didn't notice. When he entered her on the theater's lobby floor, moaning, "I'm Linus, your therapist," she was watching the usher collect tickets.

Linus had realized a long time ago that he was incapable of entering Sara's world. What was disappointing to Linus was that his dream world had nothing more to add to this fact. Even after being his patient for fifteen years, Sara still made Linus feel stuck, like he was in a Hansel and Gretel hunt with the breadcrumbs gone and the path cut off at every turn by a fast-growing privet. Sometimes he tried jumping through the privet to grab Sara. Other times he let her scurry away to give her the sense, however false, of progressing in her therapy. Both tactics were shots in the dark. Sara was unknowable, and the truth was that Linus didn't have a clue what to do other than to adjust her dosage.

What he could give her was consistency, and that translated into maintaining eye contact during their sessions. So, even when she was looking away, Linus made sure his eyes were there when she finally did turn back. He told himself that this contact—however small—was important to her therapy. He knew that this was a rationalization of his ineptitude.

"To do what? What should I do?" Sara asked.

Linus glanced at the clock. Thirty more minutes.

"Try to find open windows," Linus said. "You have to grab onto those moments when you can be direct. With Bob or anyone. Sara, I think you wanted to sleep with this kid, but you never made that clear."

Sara was quiet.

"Were you ever really with him? Bob."

Linus knew Sara was in her late thirties, but she carried herself like a teenager, horribly embarrassed by her body and the disappointing stupid illogic of the world. Her mouth was half smirk, half grimace. He had just asked her *the* question of her therapy. Was she really ever present? This was of course her issue.

Linus watched Sara staring over his head at the new Paul Klee print that went along with the room's new furniture, paint job, and rug. He had spent $30,000 on the room's makeover. One room. My empire, Linus thought.

"I need to make the visible *visible*," she said, still staring at the Klee print. "That's what you're saying I should do, right?"

That's clever, Linus thought. Hadn't Klee said he wanted to

make the *invisible* visible? When I close up the practice, I'll give her the print, he decided, suddenly seeing, very clearly, the office closed for good. He'd put the mid-century modern furniture on e-Bay. The couch, he'd keep.

"Yes, try to see what's actually there," Linus said to Sara.

After therapy, Sara headed straight for Bob's cubicle. "What do you mean 'his explanation was lame'?" she asked, blocking the cubicle's entrance.

Several windows of a branching program were open on his screen. "Lame," Bob said. He couldn't really explain it.

"I really want to know how Noritz explained the firing. Can't you remember anything else?" She was seizing an opportunity. She thought about how she'd describe this to Linus: there she was, standing firm in Bob Nascent's cubicle, demanding more than one-word answers. She was using this moment as a catalyst for change. She saw herself as fierce and passionate, because, well, because she was. Liv had gotten it right. La Pasionaria.

"He said he's sending an e-mail to everyone that's going to explain everything," Bob said. His computer beeped. "Shit," he said, leaning into the screen. He typed quickly, and a new window appeared. He looked up at her, and Sara thought he was trying to remember her name.

"Sara," she said.

"Yeah, yeah, I know. Sometime it takes me a while to enter this window."

Sara understood that he was talking about real life. "You want to get lunch?" It just came out. That was spontaneous, she thought.

Bob didn't respond, and she wondered if he had heard her. She gave him more time.

"I think they're ordering from Ozzies or something. It usually gets here around 1:00." Bob Nascent had never gone out to lunch. "How long would it take?" he asked.

"An hour. Tops," Sara said.

They went to Moustache where Bob excitedly ordered two loomis to drink right away. He told Sara that he had worked with a Jordanian programmer in San Francisco who turned him on to loomi, the sweet citrus drink infused with dried fruit.

The waiter put down hummus, falafel, tabouli, and stuffed grape leaves. Bob said, "Oh, man," just before he scooped up his first bit of hummus.

"So tell me about Numnuts's explanation for the massacre."

"It was lame. He said he had to fire people who weren't necessary," Bob said.

The rush of getting this far—asking Bob out, sitting in a restaurant together, talking—was gone, and Sara was embarrassed. I chase Bob; then I pay Linus to chase me, she thought. There they were—the three of them, Linus, Bob, and Sara—projected onto a cyclorama, forever chasing each other, no one ever gaining. Chasing, not talking. Drowning, not waving.

"What was the apartment like? Numnuts's apartment," she asked.

"He has a big couch."

The reflection off the copper table made his skin glow too pink. He looked corn-fed and confused, like he had been raised on literal bible interpretations and now was comfortable only with the certainty of binary code. One. Zero.

"I don't know. I can't really explain it." Bob said, watching the CNN news ribbon on the TV over the counter.

I can't really explain it. Her fork was heavy. The air was too thick. The light shuddered like a fluorescent tube with bad ballast.

"What did you do the rest of the weekend?" she asked, trying again. Maybe he just needed some encouragement.

"Mainly Gate Keeper."

Gate Keeper was an on-line text-based fantasy game where the participants became characters like wizards, monsters, and warriors who had to fight their way through increasingly complex scenarios. A character stayed in the game only by acquiring enough arms to keep him adequately defended. After thirteen years, Bob had garnered telekinesis and levitation skills, swords of all sizes, knives and arrows, and a hefty bag of magic potions, including one that could freeze an adversary in place. Bob was very good in this window.

What Sara remembered about the site was the dialogue she witnessed between two players. Player one: *Wave wand.* Player two: *Open door. Escape.*

"I slayed a wiz, but I didn't know that he could re-an," Bob said.

Sara guessed that "wiz" was wizard.

"Re-an?" she asked.

"He could move again," Bob said.

"Reanimate?" Sara guessed.

"Yeah, that's it," Bob said, getting up from the table. "I'm going to order some more stuff to go." And he headed to the deli case.

When Sara was 17, she read *The Sound and the Fury*, writing in her journal, *If someone could convince me that God created Faulkner, then God might exist. Then again, if Faulkner described God, he would definitely exist.* Linus was wrong; there was no opportunity to be had here with Bob Nascent. Bob couldn't come up with the words. He would never want to have a conversation. It would never be possible to train him as her partner. This window was not a possibility.

She got up from the table. *Push restaurant door. Escape to the sidewalk outside.*

Bob was adding dessert pastries to his order as Sara ran down the subway stairs. She was going home at 1:45 on a Monday afternoon. Lunch with Bob Nascent had lasted thirty-three minutes.

9

Peter called Joy to ask where to send his script: home or the production office of the movie she had recently brought in on budget for Paramount. Her assistant answered.

"We're working at Joy's place today. I could send a messenger to pick it up," the assistant said.

Coffee and a chat with Joy would be a good tack. Put everything on an even keel before Joy read the script, and they became director and producer, Peter thought.

"I'll bring it by," Peter said.

Peter laid the script on the coffee table. The assistant was out making photocopies and getting lunch.

"At the very least, I think it's a good read," Peter said. He felt the soft sell was always best.

Joy wore a thin wool-silk blend sweater. "What's the budget?" she asked.

Peter licked his finger and stuck it in the air as if testing the wind. "A guess? Four million, maybe six."

"My assistant won't be here before 2:30."

"Joy, look. Yesterday was pretty weird," Peter said.

Joy maintained her smile and then raised her chin.

Peter knew "weird" was the wrong word. "It happened so fast," he said.

He knew he should tell Joy about Liv, but he also knew that that would blow everything. Didn't everyone say to follow the gut? Well, the gut was saying to wait until Joy's viability as a real producer checked out. If she didn't check out, he would move on, and the confession scene about having a girlfriend could be avoided all together. Peter watched her open the script, and for the first time he considered that she might not like it.

"Oh, they meet in a laundromat. That's good," she said.

Peter kneeled in front of her and slid his hands up her legs. He took hold of the silk panties.

"Lift up your sweater," he said.

"Not here," she said.

Her face was covered by the sweater caught on her arms.

"Yes, here," he said, pulling her off the chair, keeping the sweater over her head. "Stay there," he said, unbuttoning his fly.

Joy's arms stuck up stiffly like a presidential candidate accepting a nomination.

Peter hoped that being on the floor like this with Joy would seal their deal. He buried his face in her neck, coming almost immediately. Peter thought he heard Joy moan.

"Sorry that was so fast," Peter said.

"It's okay. I have work," Joy said.

Peter rolled off Joy, and she got up to pull down her sweater and pull up her pants. Peter heard a helicopter and the apartment's heater blower. He sat up and saw his script on the coffee table, still opened to page one.

"I'll know more when I read it, but maybe the script could be something for Beth Meisner. She has a new deal, you know," Joy said.

"That would be great," Peter said, playing it calm, but already thinking about calling Donald, his partner on the last two documentaries, with the fantastic news. This was *it*. *It* was going to happen, Peter thought.

Of course, Donald would warn him about trusting Joy Brundage. He'd say she was a wanna-be. He'd say that Joy had no creative point of view, and that if Peter were honest with himself, he'd know that he'd rather be kicking her than fucking her. Donald always got to the heart of the matter. But Peter knew that even Donald couldn't deny the gravitas of someone like Beth Meisner. She had a deal. She could make things happen.

The phone rang.

"I should take this," Joy said, glancing at Caller ID. It was Nick Gorelich.

Peter left the apartment as Joy answered the phone.

"I got an invitation to a screening of a documentary about Palestinians, or something," Nick said to Joy. "Friday the eighteenth."

"Who's the filmmaker?" Joy asked.

"Liv Johansson. She got into some trouble in Nagorno Karabagh. Her dad called the senator's office and made a big contribution. The senator got an oil company to fly her out. I lost track of her, but I guess she's making documentaries, now."

Joy knew how her evening with Nick would unroll. There would be dinner after the screening. Then a kiss. And then. Nothing. He still wouldn't want to have sex with her. He still wouldn't want to marry her. In her next therapy session, Linus would tap his pen and ask her what the obsession with Nick was *really* about. Linus's inference that she was a loser would be, as usual, so transparent.

"I have a meeting right before, so I have to meet you at the theater," he said.

Joy highlighted the evening on her PDA calendar and canceled her other plans for that night. "I'll be there," Joy said. Of course she would be. You just never know.

10

$\mathcal{L}$iv and Dahlia celebrated finishing the mix with the champagne that John had sent to the editing room.

"It is a fucking great doc, even if the world hates Arabs," Liv said, toasting her editor. "And Jews," she added after her first sip.

The guy from the mailroom dropped off the day's last delivery— a large envelope to Liv from Naim. She felt a cassette inside the envelope.

Liv took a super-8 video camera from the postproduction facility equipment room and got her jacket to go.

"What? You're leaving our celebration after two sips?" Dahlia said.

"Yeah. I'm trashed," Liv said. "Take the rest of the champagne home, if you want."

Liv told the cab driver she was in a hurry.

"It's not a good day, miss," the driver said. "All day has been one of those weird days, you know? All week, really."

The cab was stopped dead in traffic on Park. Liv considered loading the video camera and watching the cassette in the cab, but she decided the tape deserved more attention. She should watch it someplace dark and calm. Not here. Too exposed.

"I'll get out, here," Liv said.

Liv walked to Grand Central Station and then into the dim Campbell Apartment bar where she ordered a martini and loaded the tape. Then, as if leaning into a microscope, she pressed into the eyepiece, put on headphones, and toggled the switch to "play."

Naim appeared distorted as he leaned into the lens to check the controls. "Hello, Liv," he said, sitting back, his features released from the fish-eye distortion.

He stared at her. The time code ran. Fifteen seconds.

Then he started talking, telling her about his job at a car-parts distributor, about how he had just sold new shocks to the manufacturer that made the bus that took them around California.

"It's a Swedish company, and they make the bus I take to work, too. They want to get out of the Middle East. Too many explosions," he said, smiling for the first time since the tape began.

He told her about his neighbor who listened to the BBC World Service very loudly at dawn.

"He apologizes, and says he's going deaf, but I think he's lying. He wants me up for first prayer."

Naim sat forward and rested his face in his hands. The time code ran: 22 seconds without a word.

"Liv, I go to my job every day so people will think that I am responsible and normal. I read religious books at lunch so people will think that I am a believer. You believed this about me, didn't you? I fooled you, too, right? You thought I was a suicide bomber."

Liv expected a smile here. No smile. She wondered why Naim had chosen to make the tape in a kitchen—his kitchen, she supposed. Was she supposed to be gleaning significance from its yellow walls, the two-burner cooktop and espresso pot, the tiny refrigerator, and the open shelves where she could make out canned soups? She wondered if there was beer in the refrigerator. He had lost weight since she had last seen him. His hair was longer. She liked it.

"What I am doing alone? I talk into this camera to my mother, and now I talk to you. People who want to be alone should have a reason, like they are great thinkers or maybe artists like Van Gogh or Gauguin, the one who went to the island."

Liv thought the neighbor's BBC was helping Naim's English. She paused the tape and looked away from the eyepiece, blind for a moment in the bar's dimness. She blinked and then saw two men with scotches near the middle of the bar, a woman wearing a black patent leather raincoat drinking a Manhattan at the far end. There were three men in low club chairs drinking champagne. When had men waiting to take commuter trains home started drinking champagne? Liv wondered. They were red-faced and puffy, and their ties held their necks too tightly. One of them started laughing so hard that he coughed and gasped and then laughed even harder. His friends laughed, threatening the Heimlich maneuver as they slapped him on the back. Liv wondered what they dreamed of, men giddy from Veuve Clicot who pounded each other on the back. Escaping to the South Pacific? Their mothers?

She released pause.

"I'm waiting. I feel like I'm in a bus station, waiting. There is a story about a girl who sleeps and doesn't wake up until a prince kisses her. Do you know that story? Sometimes I feel like that girl. I'm not waiting for a prince, but I'm waiting. I'm preparing."

His face distorted again as he leaned in to turn off the camera. Color bars and then video noise. She leaned away from the eyepiece. The champagne men were gone. A small dark woman with a fake flower in her chignon cleared their bottle and glasses, making way for six women, loudly exclaiming how ready they were for cocktails.

As soon as she left the bar, Liv felt the street's nerves. There was a doorman whistling frantically for a cab, a bicycle messenger belting out "Back in the USSR," a toddler swinging at his mother with closed fists. Am I projecting my own edginess? Liv asked herself. Is that why I see only the jumpy people? Are there calm moments out here that I'm blind to? No, she decided. I'm not projecting. I'm just *looking*. This isn't about *me*; it's simply about camera position. One angle gives you the "dynamic" Manhattan; another angle gives you the death of Western civilization. She mumbled Christopher Isherwood's Berlin assertion, "I am a camera."

But that's not it, either, Liv thought. He wasn't just a camera. He was as edgy with prewar jitters as the next Berliner. I'm connected to these people, Liv thought, weaving through the crowd coming up from the subway. Who am I, out here on the street? Liv asked herself. I am the woman walking the fastest on this sidewalk. I'm the one carrying a video camera bag, weaving in and out of the less determined masses.

A pigeon swooped on a discarded hamburger bun. A man leaned against a building to adjust his socks. Liv stepped off the curb.

A green-felt beret blew off a woman's head, flew straight up and then hovered over a street lamp before disappearing behind a Gap billboard. A parking garage's neon chasing arrows started blinking. Liv weaved through the cars blocking the intersection. The street sign was folded back on itself, and the street's one hundred and seventy beats per minute downshifted to a waltz. Liv felt clean and calm. Why the change? She couldn't say. Maybe this was the feeling her father told her about. "When you *know* God is close by," he said. "You feel the ecstasy." Naim's videotape was a sign. He was coming to New York. Not to visit, but to stay. Liv smelled the air—the street's breath. Snow.

Empty Chinese takeout cartons were on the kitchen table and Peter was watching a reality show when Liv got home.

"I went by the editing room, but Dahlia said you left. That was four hours ago," Peter said. "I called your cell."

"I turned it off," Liv said. "I'm sorry. I was crashing from the mix, and I had to walk. I forgot we were supposed to meet down there."

"It's going to get crazy with the screening and everything. It's okay to forget your boyfriend sometimes, but you can't forget producers and stuff. And they're going to start calling; I promise."

Liv kissed him. When it came to almost everything, Peter was pretty decent, she thought.

"Your dad went to a church meeting. Do you want to go to bed?" he asked.

Liv shook her head. She didn't want to fuck him. She was very tired of fucking him.

"Why do you want to be with a heavy, spaced-out Armenian who still lives with her father?" she asked.

"You're not heavy."

"*Spiritually* speaking."

"You're *serious*, and you're only half Armenian."

"But you're so pleasant. You're agreeable." He was a pool toy—airy and fun, she thought. Naim wasn't airy. He wasn't fun.

"And you're not?"

Liv shook her head. She only acted agreeable when she wanted something. Didn't Peter know that about her yet?

"I think you're very agreeable," he murmured in her ear. "Do you remember what I asked you?"

Liv nodded.

"Do you remember what you said?"

She straddled him on the kitchen chair, smoothed his hair, and took off her T-shirt. "I changed my mind. I want to fuck," she said.

"I want to marry you."

"Right now?"

She pulled him off the chair to the floor, yanking down his pants part way to keep his legs bound up. She had his prick in her hand and held herself away from him.

"Come on," he said. "Talk to me."

"Later," she said.

She felt his pulse in her hand. His eyes closed, and he moaned.

After that they went to her room where Peter got hard again.

"Are you taking Viagra or something?" Liv asked.

"No," Peter said. "I think you should put Beth Meisner on the screening list."

"Do you know her?"

"She's reading my script, and she's supposed to be signing a deal with Media Capital."

"Maybe they'll want you and your script, but I make documentaries. It's not their mandate," Liv said.

"Docs are hot, remember? That suicide bomber type—he's a real character. The way he talks to his mom into his video camera—it's total Hollywood movie stuff."

He pulled the covers tighter around them.

"Invite my sister," he said.

Liv imaged Sara standing alone at the wine bar after the screening.

"We need to talk about marriage," he said.

"Go to sleep," Liv said, stroking his face like he was in a fever dream.

"You really don't want to fuck?" he asked.

"No," she whispered.

"Okay, but let's talk about a wedding, soon," he said.

"Yes," she said, watching his face relax. He was almost asleep, and she counted: one, two, three, four. His breath was heavier. His mouth hung slightly open. His cheek was smashed into the pillow, puffy like a toddler's. Peter was asleep.

They had met over ten years ago in Paris when she was in the trench that had split her life into before and after. It was the summer her head sprouted its first gray, and the lines between her eyebrows began deepening into furrows.

Liv leaned close to look for cracks and gullies in Peter's skin, for hair in the wrong places. But there was nothing. He was a smooth, inflatable pool toy. The ten years that had happened to her face hadn't yet happened to his.

The *New York Times* had sent Liv to Azerbaijan because she spoke Armenian and enough Russian, and, unlike their foreign policy expert journalists, she didn't complain about staying in an Azerbaijani village without electricity that was rumored to be the Russians' and Armenians' next battleground.

She found a place to stay with a village family headed by a 65-year-old woman named Marina. Marina took Liv's housing allowance, folding the U.S. currency into a pocket sewn on the inside of the smock she wore every day over one of her three dresses. For the money, Liv got a room, meals, and an introduction to the villagers who had not yet fled the region. Liv was there to provide human-interest stories of life during wartime, and so she insisted to everyone she met that she must be treated as a normal member of the community. The villagers smiled and nodded. "Of course." But of course the American with good teeth would never be a normal member of the community.

There had been looting in the area, and so the village began a twenty-four-hour watch on the local granary. Liv insisted on taking part and was conscripted into the watch team. She was given a stick and put in the command of a 16-year-old boy who was disgusted to learn on their first night together that Liv could not recite the list of atrocities committed so far by the Armenians in this most recent war.

Marina's dog accompanied Liv on her nightly watch. His barking—nonstop during the day—stopped at nightfall when he sat, quiet and alert. Vigilant. Bred to guard. Liv's teenage commander taught her how to clean his gun and roll a cigarette with one hand. He filled in her sorry sense of history by making her memorize the sites of eleven recent atrocities. The towns of Khojaly, Shusha, Lachin, Kelbaja, Agdere, Angdan, Fizuili, Djebrail, Kuatly, Zangelam, Goradiz. Liv never learned her commander's name.

On what was to be their last night together, they heard a noise coming from the far side of the granary. The dog was up on his feet. Liv's commander pointed at the ground, and the dog sat back down. The commander would go alone to investigate: no Liv, no dog. He needed to be alone to act. What if there was real violence? No place for a woman in that. He was her leader, and what he said went. Thirty minutes later, he was back, smelling of shit, his face streaked with dirt and tears.

"Shut up," he screamed at Liv. She hadn't said a word.

The next evening, Marina called her family to the house and announced they were going to a nearby town because it would be safer in a city. What Marina said went in her family. "We're stupid deer sitting in this village," Marina said, meaning they were vulnerable. If Marina said it, the family knew it must be true.

"No," Liv said, the word startling the room.

The background material that Liv had read on the trip from New York said that a ceasefire was in the works. She recited to the family the *New York Times* and *Foreign Policy Review*'s analyses: the Russians needed stability in the area because they wanted access to the Azerbaijan oil reserves and the Caspian. The Russians couldn't let BP or Exxon get to all that oil before they did.

"This is a new kind of conflict," Liv said. "Okay, it's true that the Russians have always been on the Armenian side when it came to Karabagh, but it's different now," Liv said. She explained that the Soviet Union was now broke, and that they wouldn't—they *couldn't*—let the conflict continue. "So," Liv said to the family, "We really should just sit tight. It'll be over soon."

Marina patted Liv's arm. She said that she didn't mean to insult Liv's heritage, but it was an unfortunate fact that the Armenians were animals who had caused the death of at least one person in every Karabagh family. She talked as if Liv was a slow child struggling to understand a fundamental Azerbaijani concept: when Russians, Armenians, or Americans wanted anything, they just took it.

The family turned their attention to packing, and Liv saw herself for the caricature she was: the Western fool. Oil? Pipelines? The family knew that nothing as fucked up as this war could be about pipelines. All the geopolitics that these people needed to know was that the Armenian Catholics were racist and arrogant; that the Russians, getting trounced in Afghanistan, needed to feel like a superpower by beating the shit out of the Azerbaijanis; and that the Americans would never support anyone who seemed so like the Iranians just across the border.

Liv fell into line with the family. She was here to report on life during wartime, so she stuffed her things into her knapsack to make the exodus. Dog hair covered her jeans; mud was caked on the hem. She went to collect the dog. He wasn't at the back door where he usually lay. He wasn't at the empty goat pen. There hadn't been a goat or cow alive in the region for weeks. She whistled. No dog.

Marina ladled meat and potatoes onto the bulgur at dinner.

"We'll need protein. It's a long walk," Marina said.

It was the dog on her plate. Liv folded her hands, and then for the first time in her life, she unfolded them to cross herself. No one

said anything as she refolded her hands, bowed her head and murmured the Lord's Prayer. She had never said it before, but she knew
every word.

They reached the foothills after midnight. Artur, Marina's 4-year-
old grandson, started crying, and Marina swatted him to shut up. He
stopped walking to whimper as the family passed by. No one said,
"Come on, hurry up," but that's what Artur was expected to do.

Liv picked him up and murmured into his ear, "Hold on tight."

His legs gripped around her waist; his arms clamped her neck.

They passed through high summer pastures populated with quiet
cows. Artur pushed his face into her neck. Liv needed him to turn
his head. Her back was stiffening in this position, and they had hours
to go.

"Look at the cows," she whispered to Artur. "As soon as we pass
by, they're going to stand up on their hind legs just like people."

Liv was imagining Gary Larson cartoons with cows that only
pretended to be cows because that's what people wanted them to
be. What silly people didn't know was that cows were worldly ru-
minates who lounged and made cocktail-hour chatter about the silly
people who acted, well, just like cows.

Artur turned to look at the cows, and Liv's back was released.
She told him that cows were the smartest animal on earth and that
they were laughing at her and Artur as they passed, because people
were so dim. Artur giggled, and Liv put her hand over his mouth.

"Shh," she whispered. "Cows don't like to be laughed at. They're
very sensitive."

Four men with guns stepped out from behind trees at dawn. The
family stood still. Liv peed in her pants. Her arms shook—every
single muscle shook as she shoved Artur's face into her neck.

Marina's dress was wet as she held out the roll of Liv's American dollars. Liv could smell her from ten feet away. One of the men snatched the money. Liv felt Artur shaking now. His legs tightened around her waist. His pants were wet. She felt his vomit on her neck.

How could she run with Artur? She kept looking back at the cows. Don't look at the cows, think of a plan. Save yourself. Save Artur. The men have guns. Stop looking at the cows. Liv was her own commander, now.

The men crowded around the man with the money. He counted while the others watched. Liv took off, racing for the cows, Artur bouncing over her shoulders. You're moving too slowly, she screamed to herself. Move! Fucking move! she screamed in her head.

There was a pop. Marina fell; her kerchief stayed on her head.

Those are guns. They shot Marina. Move. Don't look at the cows. Don't look back. Move, keep moving.

The men were shouting at her. Holding Artur was slowing them both down. The men were going to catch them both this way. There were more pops.

She forced Artur onto his feet. "Run," she said, shoving him toward the cows. She whirled around and held up her blue American passport, screaming, "American. Don't you fucking dare."

The men understood. They lowered their guns. They hadn't figured on an American. Liv could see that the man with the money was calculating, figuring; an American hostage could be a good thing.

"I can get you more money," she said to the men. "Dollars." There was so much water in her eyes. Her shirt was drenched. The sweat kept pouring, and her snot ran thick. Her eyes were fogged. There were people on the ground. Not people anymore, but dead bodies. A cowherd whistled from across the field. Something went "pop," like the last firecracker on Puerto Rican Independence Day. There was a man Liv hadn't seen before now. He stood in the woods next to a jeep. He lowered his hunting rifle.

Liv couldn't see Artur. The cowherd was gone. Liv took off running toward the cows, "you fucking cocksuckers. You scum. You motherfucking assholes," she screamed in English as she ran toward where she had last seen Artur. She expected to hear another "pop," imagining what a bullet in her back would feel like. She kept running. There was no shot.

Instead, she heard the jeep drive away. The men with guns were gone. Liv stopped running. There were cow paddies all around her. Artur wasn't there. Liv was alone with the five dead bodies. She threw up a thin viscous stream—what remained of the vigilant dog. Liv thought she wanted to die.

No one came that day and the bodies bloated in the sun. There was a smell. Birds circled. Liv thought about wolves. The next night, a dog ran into the pasture. He raced for Marina's dead family, and a young boy yelled at him from a coppice of ash trees. The dog left the bodies and went to work, dodging the cows into formation. Liv followed, hurrying to catch up with the boy.

No, the boy hadn't seen Artur. No, he hadn't heard the shooting. He took Liv to his family, and she promised them money if they told her where Artur was. They swore to Liv that they hadn't heard or seen anything. They knew nothing about a 4-year-old boy in a red T-shirt. Liv could see that money wasn't talking; what they wanted was Liv out of the house. A message was gotten to her father.

John called the *New York Times* who said they could get her out in two days. It wasn't fast enough, and John called his senator. He promised money for the senator's campaign in return for a plane to get Liv out of Azerbaijan in the next twenty-four hours. It was a lot of money, and the senator ordered his aide, Nick Gorelich, to find a BP plane, ASAP.

Nick arranged for a plane out of the region and then a regularly scheduled commercial flight from Odessa to Paris where he made sure that a driver with a cardboard sign—*Johansson*—was waiting in Arrivals.

And then Liv was in the lobby of the Hotel Lutetia, her teeth chattering, her ankle bouncing, wanting to believe that she was slouched and curled in the overstuffed chair because she felt guilty that she was alive and they weren't. She wanted to believe she was suffering from survivor guilt.

But guilt wasn't it at all.

She jerked her body to fold her leg under her. Since the cow pasture incident, Liv found that if she jerked or twitched her body, she could sometimes keep the image away. But this time, she had jerked her leg too late, for there it was again: a dead dog, cows, and dead people. There was something in her abdomen. Maybe she could find a doctor in Paris to fix her. Her thighs tightened. Her hands were hot and then numb. An operation. Maybe she needed something cut out. God damn it. When was the goddamn sun going to set? she thought, closing her eyes to the sun flaring off a mirror on the far wall.

She bent over and put her ears to her knees. They were ringing. Her ears. The cows wore bells, and they rang, too. Was there someplace she hadn't looked in that pasture? Had Artur been bleeding to death while Liv failed to find him? Had the silent cows witnessed the 4-year-old dying in the field while she stumbled through, not seeing anything?

It shouldn't be this way after seeing people you know shot dead in a field, but being alive was all that mattered. What Liv felt in the

Hotel Lutetia lobby was relief. Khojaly, Shusha, Lachin, Kelbaja, Agdere, Angdan, Fizuili, Djebrail, Kuatly, Zangelam, Goradiz—Liv recited the atrocities to herself.

"Can I get you anything?" a waiter asked.

"I need a parka," she said. It was July.

"Liv?"

Someone was blocking the light.

"It's Ruth."

Liv finally saw her: Ruth Rosner, from grad school.

"Can I borrow a sweater?" Liv asked.

Ruth worked for U.N. Famine Relief. She had been in Sudan with a stopover in Paris to break up with her boyfriend before going to a conference in Geneva.

"I don't think you know Peter," Ruth said. "He's wonderful, but I'm leaving him."

How could Ruth be talking about breaking up with a boyfriend in a world where people were shot after eating their pets? Liv thought.

"It's all me. I can't stand someone else to be there with an opinion about me." Ruth was crying. "I know it's fucked up, but if I think someone else doesn't see things the way I see them, I get weak and I can't function. I have to be able to function. You know what I mean?"

Liv nodded because she wanted Ruth to shut up.

"This is what I found," the waiter said, holding a puffy red parka out to her. Fifteen hundred francs. Liv put it on. She was still cold.

Two days later, she met Peter at breakfast.

"You're Liv, right?" He was unshaven, and Liv smelled liquor. He sat down, and they drank coffee with the cognac he had in a plastic Volvic bottle.

Ruth left for Geneva, paying for five more days of the room for Peter. Liv's father had put her room on his Amex. She didn't yet know how many days she'd need to form a moat between Azerbaijan and Manhattan.

For three afternoons, she and Peter drank in the Lutetia lounge. One night they went to see an Atom Egoyan movie. Liv smoked opium in the toilet. Peter drank vodka from the Volvic bottle. Afterward, they went for artichoke hearts and mussels, and Peter got in a fight with the waiter, which Liv never even tried to stop.

On Peter's last day, he appeared in the breakfast room, shaved and wearing freshly pressed pants and a button-down shirt. A costume change made him into a serious documentary filmmaker that executives at Arte were excited to meet, and Liv finally saw Peter: a man who could be whatever the audience wanted him to be, a man who surfed and didn't sink.

She went to Le Bon Marché and bought new clothes for the flight to New York. She threw all her old clothes, except for the red parka, into a garbage can on Rue de Sevres. In the ladies' room at Charles de Gaulle, she smoked the rest of her opium.

Peter had never asked Liv one question about Azerbaijan. They never slept together in Paris. That came years later.

Liv slipped out of bed. She needed to shower. Her stomach growled, and she went to the kitchen to see if there was anything left in the takeout cartons. Broccoli and mushrooms. She checked her voicemail:

"Hello. I come on Wednesday." It was Naim.

She played the message again. Had a boy ever made her feel like this? Was she finally 14 and in love?

She looked at the kitchen clock. 12:10. Today was already Tuesday.

11

$\mathscr{F}$or the third night in a row, Linus started, fully awake at three a.m. In his 60 years, he could remember scattered bouts of insomnia, but waking up with a start at three a.m.? Never. He was a mental health professional, and this was psychic upheaval.

He had woken up out of a dream that was something about wanting to be liked in the way that Joy always wanted people to like her. Linus wondered if he was compensating for his failure to help Joy create a stronger identity by enfeebling his own. Watch Linus the therapist go down the toilet, he thought.

Since practically their first session, Linus had kept himself from telling Joy that she had sex with men who cared nothing about her in order to bolster her weak ego. Such bald judgments were not part of his treatment style, and besides, he knew she would only react by defensively snapping, "I get on well in this world. I'm not hurting anyone," the inference being, "Who are *you* to say this?"

Who was he, indeed? Linus wondered. When you get down to it, shouldn't the rest of his patients be striving to be like the high-functioning Joy? Like Sara, for example. Who would deny that Sara's life would improve if only she were more like Joy? Linus wondered why he was continuing to be a pretentious jerk, implying through his therapeutic style that his patients' reliance on the external could change—that each could find an inner compass, more stable and secure than anything on the outside? The world needed them all—Linus and his patients—to maintain their attachments. The world needs us to keep consuming, Linus thought. Why do I kid patients by implying that there's something "better" or "more authentic" than the nonstop images we receive from the advertising machine?

Linus couldn't answer his own question; nor would he ever be able to tell Joy what he thought was the truth: "Joy, your pathological need for approval is the essential component of evil." Instead, Linus had been taking the namby-pamby route of simply keeping her on the rails. The realization had been creeping up on him, but in the wake of the sleep disturbances, he finally saw his job for what it had become: keep the patients from running amok. For the patients who worked in the shitty offices with bad air, synthetic carpeting, and fluorescent lighting, he prescribed medication. For the richer analysands, the ones with better offices, he acted like a priest, there to absolve them.

I'm a collaborator taking their money. I'm no wiser than the worst off of them. Linus knew that his ego, just like his patients', needed to clamp onto externals to create a story where he was always the hero. His psychic closet was full of attachments: meticulously filed record collections, reading lists, pop-culture references, fantasy sex partners, gilded nostalgia for perfect orgasms, the impassioned glance of a stranger from a passing subway, and, of course, the rows of media stars onto which he/everyone could project anything at all.

Making reality might as well be catalogue shopping, he thought. And my reality is as secure as a blow-up sex doll. Real until punctured by a tack. "I am Joy Brundage," Linus said out loud.

He finally got out of bed, pulled on a worn pair of khaki pants and a torn sweatshirt, and took out his manuscript—a complicated, rambling screenplay about art heists. It had started as a script based on his patients, but it was really his story—his and his brother's—about getting out of Armenia.

Joy had started as Brigitte, a half-Greek, half-French Europol babe, tracking down art thieves. But nothing Linus could do on the page got Joy to let go of her fantasy that any American man could become president, and she, a version of Jackie Kennedy. He gave up on Joy as sexy Europol babe and morphed her into "Rachel," the Orthodox Jewish wife of the art thief's New York auction-house contact. Rachel breathed as a character. She took off and acted. Sara, who had started as a glue-sniffing teenager in a Greek port town, got the part of Brigitte, Europol babe who longed for Robert, the handsome art thief. Robert was, of course, Linus.

Linus started in on a scene where Rachel was lighting the Shabbat candles. She was beautiful in the light. She belonged there, tiny and insubstantial, engulfed in the millennia of Jewish culture called up by the simple gesture of lighting a candle. It was time to cut away to a scene between the Europol babe and Robert in a dingy warehouse, but Linus pivoted the computer screen away from him. He wasn't up to a confrontation scene right now.

He ran his hands over the three rocks on his desk: one from Armenia, one from Crete, and one from the construction site of the Ellis Island museum. He rubbed his finger over Armenia, and he imagined Joy with a bowed head before the Wailing Wall. He imagined her feeling guilty and responsible for everything she had done or said. She looked good like that.

Years of medical school, then training in his specialty, then the years spent conquering English. He was a psychiatrist. Wasn't he supposed to have insight? Why were his patients just meat puppets to him? What was wrong with him that he seemed to care so little?

He picked up the rock from Crete and heaved it at the door to the next room. He missed, squarely hitting a glass sconce instead. The room went dim. He aimed the New York stone at a second sconce, and the room went dark. He held Armenia to his third eye.

What his patients needed was to feel real, and the only time they felt real was when someone was watching them. His patients needed a judgmental creator hanging over their shoulder like a surveillance camera. They needed God, not a shrink.

Freud's Vienna must have been heady. He had a better patient pool than my billing list, Linus thought. Things had definitely devolved. His patients weren't up to the rigors of therapy; they didn't have what it took to do anything more than chase their tails.

His clock radio clicked on. Ninety minutes before his 7:00 session with Joy. Linus swept up glass shards and made plans. In therapy he hadn't managed to do a thing for Joy. But in his script, after he had given her character God, she had come alive with assuredness and grace. Joy had fallen too far from her Jewish God. Her problem was that she had gotten too secular. I'll make her rediscover her Jewishness, he thought, recognizing the insanity of this notion. But still, it worked for the character; why wouldn't it for the woman? She'll be my marker, he decided. Once she's got God looking over her; once I make her into a good Jewish woman, I can close up shop, he thought, certain this was a violation of some oath he had taken along the way toward New York certification.

The screenplay was already 200 pages, and he hadn't yet gotten to the heist.

12

$\mathcal{I}$n lower Manhattan, Joy finished reading Peter's script, *Bound Lover*. It wasn't the kind of story that won awards and garnered commentary, but it felt commercial. She could see the poster for the film, and wasn't this what everyone said predicted an eventual commercial success? She imagined a megaplex on a Saturday night. Date night: the girls wanting to see the new romantic comedy, *Bound Lover*. The boyfriends would grumble about this movie choice, but they knew that their acquiescence would assure sex later that night. Joy thought about actresses who could do the movie and she made a list: mainly TV actresses with symmetrical good looks. She wondered if they should shoot in Canada to keep production costs down; she decided that Canada was a bad idea, since New York was really a character in the movie. She'd call Beth Meisner in the morning and send over a copy of the script. She'd attach her name to the cover sheet as the "producer."

The clock radio turned on. Six a.m. Time to shower and dress for therapy.

13

$\mathcal{S}$ara was halfway through *Middlemarch*, and Eliot was closing a chapter with the moon rising above her characters, who were each poised before the crevasse that separated them from their futures.

Snow wisped across the streetlight outside Sara's bedroom window.

"It's snowing," Sara said to the empty apartment before picking up the phone to cancel today's Verizon Communications' 6:30 wakeup call.

14

"*I* saw that director this weekend, and I really think that we could make something good together. We're both hungry, and that's what counts," Joy said. "It gives us the energy we need, you know?"

"Is this what you want to be spending your time on?" Linus asked.

"What do you mean?"

"Do you want to spend your time making *this* movie with *this* man?"

"I want to be a real producer. I like him. He likes me. He has a project. Yes, this is what I want to be doing."

"Have you looked for projects that might be more fulfilling?" Linus had never before asked Joy about the specifics of her job.

"What do you mean, fulfilling?"

"I don't know. Something other than a romantic comedy."

"I like romantic comedies," Joy said.

Linus was quiet. What the hell was he doing playing career counselor? Stick to God, he thought.

"How did you know it's a romantic comedy?" Joy asked.

"I didn't. It was just the first thing that came to mind. I could have said action film."

Why did he say "romantic comedy?" he wondered. Had Joy described the director—Peter—in such a way that automatically pegged him as a lightweight?

"What's wrong with romantic comedies?" she asked.

"Why do you like them?" He was back on track. Weakening her faith in the movie business would be the first step in making her an observant Jew, too devoted to home and family to ever feel sorry for herself again.

"I don't know. They're light and no one gets hurt and the boy and girl wind up together."

Linus was quiet.

Joy started to cry.

Linus counted to ten, waiting for her question about why no one ever wanted to marry her. She said nothing, and he counted to ten again.

"I probably only want to do this project because he's kind of cute, and he needs a producer, and well, why the hell not," Joy said, her voice deeper than Linus had ever heard it before.

For the first time, Linus wished they were sitting face to face.

"Peter's just one of those guys that's floating around, you know? I mean, he makes his living by selling documentaries to European television, and he seems cool. I liked the sex we had, but I don't really *know* him. He doesn't talk about anything other than his career. I know he had a girlfriend a few years ago who was with the U.N. or something, but that's about all I know. I thought he was Jewish. His old girlfriend went to Brandeis, so Jewish, right? But he's not. His name's spelled K-o-*e*-h-l. Just regular German."

Linus put down his pen and ran the tip of his finger across the edge of his pad so that the paper cut the skin below the nail. *Peter Koehl.* This was Liv's Peter. He squeezed the skin and watch blood bead up. He imagined telling Joy the truth about Peter and watching her sob, maybe shout with rage. He imagined plotting with his brother to straighten out this SOB who was cheating on Liv. He imagined hauling Peter out into the street to kick him in the stomach.

"Does he have a girlfriend?" Linus asked.

"What?" Joy lifted herself up on her elbow and turned to Linus.

"Does Peter have a girlfriend?" Linus asked again.

Joy sat up. "I said he *had* a girlfriend a few years ago."

"Yes, but you also said that you don't know anything about him. You even thought he was Jewish."

"I don't need this," Joy said, reaching for her coat.

"What is it you don't need?"

"That tone. You're supposed to be my therapist, and you're acting like my fucking inquisitor."

For a second, there, Linus found Joy sexy.

"I'm sure this is all about transference, and I'm sure I'll realize that we've made a lot of headway, but right now I think you're an asshole."

He watched her pull on her coat, buttoning every button and then belting it, wrapping her scarf around her neck and face, pulling on her cap. She likes being watched, he thought.

Linus decided to sell his apartment when he packed up this office. He would buy something downtown, maybe TriBeCa. He wanted a view like the one Joy said she had. When she rediscovers her Judaism, she'll stop having sex with other people's boyfriends. Linus Kezian knew he was doing the world a service.

15

For the last month John Kezian had been transferring bolts of fabric from the stockroom of his Brooklyn factory to self-storage units in Queens. In a few weeks, a shipper was to move this fabric to John's new Sparkle Life Fashion factory in Spitak, Armenia. John Kezian was moving offshore, and until today, he had been the only one who knew about it.

He was surprised at how easy it was to ease stock out of the factory without anyone on the production floor seeming to notice. At one point he wondered if he might be able to walk away from the whole Brooklyn enterprise without saying anything at all. Maybe he could leave the ten thousand square feet and two hundred employees in the same way he had left Armenia some thirty years ago—without a trace. But this afternoon, his foreman reported a security problem: "A lot of fabric's missing from the stockroom," he said.

John came clean. "I've been moving it out. I'm closing the factory," he said, surprised how flat his voice sounded.

"You're going offshore?" the foreman asked.

And John nodded, ashamed for the first time by his decision.

The production floor knew within forty-five minutes, and by the time John left in his Range Rover loaded with more bolts of fabric for the storage units, the accountant was writing severance checks, one week's salary for every year worked, the most senior employee having fifteen years.

During his first years in America, John produced what he already knew—wedding dresses. But somewhere in the late 70s he discovered knits, changed the company name from Solemn Promise to Sparkle Life, and began producing stretchy halter tops, elastic waistband harem pants, swimsuits with plunging necklines and high legs, quinceaños and sweet-sixteen outfits, majorette and ballet-recital costumes.

In December 1988, when over twenty-five thousand people were killed in Spitak during a 7.0 earthquake, John returned to Catholicism and began diverting twenty percent of Sparkle Life's profits to the Armenian Catholic Church.

But even though his twenty percent tithe got heftier and heftier with Sparkle Life's continued success, John wanted to do more for his church and for Armenia. To send more money meant he needed more profit, which of course pointed toward "offshore production." He had first considered Mexico, but then he came up with Spitak. Build a factory in Armenia; support the locals and his homeland's struggling economy; make more profits and be able support his church with even higher donations. John knew he was screwing his Brooklyn workers, but he decided that Spitak and the Armenian Catholic Church were more worthy. He told himself that he couldn't save everyone, that every transaction had its loser. He was sorry for that, but he was a businessman. He hoped God would judge his actions as complex, but in the end, more good than bad.

The alleys between the rows of cinderblock storage units were empty. He backed the Ranger Rover up to unit 43, alley C-12. He rolled up the unit's gray metal door and started loading his bulky load of fifteen bolts of knits into the unit. The fabric was from what he still called his "disco" line, and the knits' metallic threads caught the overhead light.

When he closed the storage unit's door, he was breathing hard. He squatted against the wall to rest, his hands pressed together in prayer.

He liked it out here where his cell phone often found no cell, and he was always alone. God was closer out here. Close enough to hover over his right shoulder and notice how much his hair had thinned on top but how flexible his hips still were. It was something for a Western man to be able to squat like this at 65. He was proud that he could still load the storage units under his own steam.

He could hear the highway from here, the sound coming in waves, not at all disagreeable. John could see his breath, and his nose was running. The sky was the same flat gray as the metal rollup storage unit doors. It would snow out here tonight, probably rain in the city.

John wondered when he would tell Liv and Linus about the move. Linus would of course have some shrink thing to say about his behavior, like how John's need for total control kept him from sharing information with his family and his workers. Liv would probably shrug and say something about how ironic it was that the free-market system was leading him back to an old Soviet client state that happened to offer up dirt-cheap labor.

This would make him feel guilty, but only for a little while. One dollar and fifty cents to make a leotard in Spitak. Three dollars and sixty-two cents to make it in New York. The leotard was always twenty-five dollars at Target.

"Buy low. Sell high," John said out loud.

With the increased profits, he'd expand and build a second factory in Armenia, maybe in Yerevan. No, John thought, with increased profits, I'll build a church in Spitak. He imagined something new and sleek. He thought about how proud the country would be of the church and its benefactor. But don't think about that, John thought. That's just ego. The church should be about "giving back to Armenia." Building a church is about faith. He knew that he would never be able to make his brother and daughter understand that his decision to build a factory in Spitak was as much about God as about profits. But it didn't matter. Not really. He knew that even if they didn't understand, Sparkle Life Fashion's increased profits would serve them all well on earth and in heaven.

John's cell phone beeped on the highway. Three missed calls, all from Liv. The kid from her movie, Naim, was stuck in immigration at JFK. Could he go with her to the airport to help? It was important.

If she had a husband, she'd be calling him to help her out, John thought. If there were a husband around, I could be home sooner for wine, pasta with pesto, and a movie on cable. No, even better, John thought: If there were a husband, there wouldn't even *be* a strange man calling from JFK asking to get him out of immigration.

The cell phone rang. "What's going on, Liv?"

"The guy with the video camera in the movie. Remember him?" she asked.

"Naim," John said.

"Right. He came to New York, and they held him back at immigration."

John turned on the window defroster.

"What's that?"

"The defroster."

John had once asked his brother if, in his opinion as a psychiatrist, Liv's love life was her "fuck you" to John's Catholicism. Linus answered no, it was about sex, pure and simple, and even though Liv had been raised by an uptight father, she had managed to wind up liking it. Linus thought John was the one with the problem.

"Liv, don't you read the papers? If they want to put him in jail, they can. I don't know how much we can do. He's an *Arab*."

There was a traffic helicopter above him. He was stopped dead in the fast lane. John thought, Linus was wrong. Liv's men were *all* about affronting his faith.

"You can get him out, Daddy," Liv said.

The traffic knot gave way. He was moving. Twenty miles per hour, but it was movement. I'm her Daddy, John thought. Until he died: "Daddy." How could Inga have let that baby lie in the crib without her blanket? Keeping his lips closed, he formed the word in his mouth: "Daddy." He turned off the defroster and cracked his window.

"I'm closer than you are, so I'll go straight there," he said.

"I'll meet you."

"Traffic's awful. I'll call if you need to come."

"What are you doing out there?" Liv asked.

"I was at a storage place," John said, knowing she wouldn't be interested enough to ask for more details.

Naim was sitting in a plastic chair in a long fluorescent-lit hall. After the flights from Amman to Beirut, Beirut to Paris, and Paris to New York, his face was ashen with fine lines of cracked skin around his mouth and eyes. As soon as Naim saw John, he stood up and grabbed his hand.

"Liv told me what a wonderful father you are," he said.

John doubted that Liv had said this, but he was impressed that Naim thought to make the claim.

It had all been a mistake. A new guy had confused Naim's name with a suspect on their Alert List. But Naim's visa was in order. His record was clean.

"They saw that I'm Catholic," Naim said, tapping the cross around his neck. "I think they were even more happy that I have an English mother."

Liv snacked on hummus as she watched John make spaghetti and Naim make salad. When they sat down to eat, John lowered his head to pray, then so did Naim. Liv watched.

John's head came back up. "Naim's Catholic," he said. "He lived in an Armenian village near Beirut."

Naim's head came out of his prayers to look at Liv across the table. "My mother knew the Israelis would not bomb the Armenians," he said.

The men smiled at her. As if it's a prank, Liv thought. As if they had jumped out from behind the couch to shout, "Surprise! We're Catholic!" She had made a documentary about Muslims and Jews, and her leading man was neither. "You're Catholic?" Liv asked.

Naim nodded and unbuttoned his top button to show his cross.

Liv mimed holding a gun to her head to shoot herself.

Naim was out when Liv got up the next morning.

"He asked me how to get to the Circle Line. I gave him a map and a winter coat," John told her.

"Why aren't you at church?" Liv asked.

"It was more important that someone help our guest. He's a little lost, Liv."

"Okay, bad hostess," she said, pointing at herself. "But I'm still in shock. No, I'm pissed off. He played me. He totally played me. He wanted to be in the movie, and he played Mr. Muslim." Liv pulled back her hair and then let it fall to cover her face. "Shit, I never saw it coming. I should have." She shook the hair out of her eyes. The 14-year-old-in-love bubble had burst. "I was an idiot. I should have checked. I mean there are tons of Catholics over there," she said.

"Arafat's wife, for example," John said. "Come on. It's not that bad. Make sure he takes off his cross for the screening. He's not stupid. There's nothing in it for him if he messes this up for you."

"Did he say how long he was staying?" Liv asked.

"I don't know how he's going to do it, but he wants to stay for good. He's looking into computer classes. He's interested in some karaoke software."

"Karaoke?" Liv said.

"He said there's a club near his house with a karaoke scene. He works there, sometimes. He asked me about your movie."

"What did you say?" Liv asked.

"I told him that he looked very good. I didn't know his mother was English."

Liv pulled her hair back. Her luck was still holding. She wasn't going to have to lie about the English. Her father was right. Take off the cross and Naim would gladly be everyone's favorite Muslim.

"Liv, what about Peter?" John asked.

Liv watched her father rub his thumb over his other fingers. The hand was fleshy with pronounced veins. Like her veins. She noticed a liver spot. Her father was upset about a new boy in the house. And this one was too young.

"You know Naim's not my boyfriend," Liv said. "I've never slept with him."

Liv could see that her father was very relieved.

16

$\mathcal{S}$ara was finishing the fourth chapter of *Silas Marner* when a car alarm went off in the street below her apartment. "Step away from the car. Step away from the car," the electronic voice blared against a chorus of whooping yelps. When the alarm stopped with an electronic chirp, Sara got out of bed. I'll make vegetarian chili, she decided. It was noon on a workday.

At the grocery store, she threw a bag of beans into her cart and thought, I'm provisioning. I'm prepping to be Silas Marner, the recluse. No, I'll be George Eliot, she decided. I'll retire from the world to critique its sad state. She threw two more bags of beans into her cart, and then another one for the pleasure of throwing.

The mail was there when she got home with the groceries. The *New Yorker* and something from J-Films.

She checked her voicemail: one message: "It's Sandy. There's a meeting tomorrow morning to talk about your, uh, departure. They'll fucking plotz if you kept anything."

Sara deleted the message and opened the J-Films envelope. An invitation to Liv's film screening. Sara rinsed the beans and picked out the weird ones. Beth Meisner would probably like the film, Sara thought. Serious and topical. Beth would probably like Liv.

Sara picked up the phone, coaching herself: Just fucking dial. She quickly punched in Beth Meisner's number. The voicemail picked up with a long outgoing message containing fax and cell phone numbers. There was a way to page her or to have more "op-tions." Sara simply kept hold of the receiver, waiting for a beep. It's coming. Hold on. No big deal. You're just leaving a message, Sara told herself. The beep came.

"Hi, it's Sara. I got an invitation to a screening of a documentary that I thought you'd like. It's on the 18th and I was wondering if you wanted to go." She hung up.

That was easy, she thought, and then she thought about doing it again just to verify how simple it was to leave a message in a superior person's voice mailbox. But only a crazy person leaves the same message twice in a row, Sara thought.

She picked up the phone again and dialed Linus. His voicemail: an outgoing message about what constituted an emergency and how to page him in the event that you were truly having one. Sara had done this only once, and that was years ago.

"Hi, it's Sara. Could you call me back this afternoon? I'm back home."

When Sara stopped going to work the week before last, she hadn't been ready to tell Linus. Instead, she canceled her upcoming appointments, telling him that she was going out of town. On business. To Kansas City. The one in Missouri, she had told him.

Sara turned off the phone ringer and read *Silas Marner* at the kitchen table. The windows fogged from the simmering chili, and she rubbed a porthole through the steam. It was snowing again, and kids coming home from school had their faces to the sky to catch it with their mouths. Sara wondered how much particulate matter was mixed in with the snow. A woman ran from a brownstone across the street in a robe and loafers to her car. Sara checked her voicemail. Three messages:

"Sandy, here. We're very worried." There was nothing at all worried in her voice.

"This is Dr. Kezian. I'll be at my phone from 5:00 to 5:20." It was 4:45.

"Hi, it's Beth. Call me on the cell."

Sara called Beth on the cell. In only a few hours, dialing Beth Meisner was almost as easy as calling her own Verizon voice mailbox.

Beth took Sara's call from the back seat of an Audi on her way to a windowless televideo conferencing center. This would be Beth's final interview with the board of the Hamburg investment fund that would determine her high-profile, high-risk deal involving making up to five pictures a year for the next five years. If all went as she told herself she wanted it to go, she would soon be the head of the fund's new international film production entity called Media Capital Group. She knew her performance in today's video interview would finally make the Germans realize that it was she, above all the other candidates, who could best smell out talent to make their money grow with international hits. But Beth was nervous because she knew the truth, and the truth was that she had nothing—zero, zip, nada—in her pocket, not one script, not one fresh director. The only reason she had gotten this far was because the Germans couldn't yet recognize that Beth was suffering from studio executive disease, a syndrome that sets in after too many years accommodating the vagaries of the market to protect the studio's bottom line. Beth Meisner had no creative point of view. She was effectively good for nothing. *Nichtsnutzig,* to the Germans.

"I got the same invitation," Beth said. Her teeth were chattering, and she hoped the call's delay and garble would mask the sound.

The Audi was stuck behind a garbage truck, and Beth watched a young mother push her twin stroller into a Starbucks. I should just get inseminated and become a mom, she thought. A runner stretched at the corner. Or maybe I should devote myself to becoming an athlete, an Ironman. Ironwoman? Why the hell not?

Because I was a *scholar*, that's why the hell not, Beth thought. Because I published at 19. Because I deconstructed signs. Because I was supposed to have become the next Susan Sontag.

"Oh, I should have figured you'd get one, too," Sara said.

Beth could hear Sara's disappointment. "It doesn't matter. I still want to go together," Beth said.

"The next Susan Sontag" thing had never happened for Beth, and she was certain that it was only a matter of time before she finally and totally failed at her latest venture. Soon everyone would know that she was a loser. In a year or maybe eighteen months, her contract would be terminated. *Beth Meisner: Nichtsnutzig.*

"Maybe we could meet before for a drink," Beth said.

A waitress hurried into a coffee shop, looking up at the snow, hunching into her coat collar. Why not waitress and maybe write a book on the side? Beth thought. Maybe it's not too late to get back on track. Point of view couldn't be lost forever.

"Okay," Sara said. "Where?"

"I don't know. We'll figure it out," Beth said. "There's supposed to be a dinner after. But if it's okay, with you, I'd like to go someplace else together, by ourselves. Unless you want to go to the dinner."

The garbage truck moved, and Beth's driver finally made the left. Beth made herself picture Sara's unruffled Hampshire calm. There it was: Sara giggling with her boyfriend, eating chocolate cookies across the student cafeteria. Beth's hand relaxed its grip on the phone. Her breathing slowed as she knew it would with this image of Sara in her head.

"Dinner together would be good," Sara said. "Really good."

Beth's teeth stopped chattering. She sounds so happy, Beth thought.

"Okay, great. Wish me luck. I'm about to go into an incredibly stressful meeting."

"Good luck. I'm sure you'll be great," Sara said.

The driver was pulling into the parking garage. Beth was losing signal. "Thank you for saying that, Sara," Beth said, rolling down the backseat's tinted windows to see the valet reaching to open her door. "You make me feel good. Really." She was sincere.

Sara hung up. A corner had been turned. The fever had broken. Life was different, because it was hers. She had accepted a one-on-one dinner with Beth Meisner. She had told her that she'd be great in her meeting. She had heard Beth Meisner shaking, and then said something that made the shaking stop. I made Beth Meisner feel good, Sara thought.

Sara called Linus.

"How was Kansas?" he said.

"Missouri. I want to go off Paxil," Sara said.

Linus leaned back and thought about how movies showed people going off drugs. He imagined Frank Sinatra shaking and sweating in *The Man with the Golden Arm* and that young actor—what was his name and what was the drug?—sweating in *Rush*. Paxil wasn't heroin, but kicking was kicking, and Sara had been on one kind of antidepressant or another for ten years. Over ten years. And before that, she had spent a year of frozen inactivity, unable to look for work, almost unable to take a shower. Linus had come close to hospitalizing her, but Sara's mother had stepped in, moving her daughter back home, forcing her to get into the bath and to open the paper to the want ads every morning.

"It's not an easy thing, Sara," he said.

"That's why I'm asking how to do it."

"Sara, why do you want to do it?"

"Because I don't need it. I asked Bob Nascent to lunch. Remember him? I did exactly what you said I should do. Well, what you implied, anyway. I was proactive. But then I had to get away from him because, guess what? He's an idiot. I went home from work, and I haven't gone back. I wasn't out of town. I've been rereading George Eliot. I called Beth Meisner and we're going to dinner. I'm making vegetarian chili. I'm my own woman, the captain of my ship. The architect of my destiny. All that stuff," Sara said. I am La Pasionaria, she thought.

"You sound manic. You're going to have to come back to the real world, Sara."

"What's real or normal about sitting in a cubicle and working on a second-rate trade journal? Not one thing. It's unnatural and unhealthy. Remember *Brave New World* and Soma—that drug that everyone took so they could do their awful jobs?"

Linus made himself focus on what she was saying. This wasn't a movie, and she wasn't a character. He was there to help people deal with lives spent working in cubicles.

"I don't think you're ready, Sara," he said.

"Why do you keep saying my name?"

"What?"

"You always end or begin a sentence with my name. I don't keep saying your name. When I use your name, it's for emphasis. I mean I'm sure you can remember your own name without me saying it over and over. I don't get why you keep saying my name."

Linus couldn't answer the question. Was he saying her name because he had once learned that the patient feels special and more rooted when the therapist frequently says his or her name? Was it because he was afraid that he'd forget and slip up—calling Sara by a wrong name, and *really* making a mess of everything? "Why does it bother you?" he asked, consciously not saying "Sara."

"Because I know my name."

Linus couldn't remember Sara ever criticizing him before.

"I stopped taking it yesterday."

"You can't just quit cold turkey like that."

"If you won't tell me how to go off it, I'll go online and check out some forums. I'm sure there's a shitload of activity out there about antidepressant weaning. I'll see you on Tuesday with an update."

"You're being aggressive."

"Maybe. We can talk about that, too," she said. "My chili's sticking, and I have to stir."

"You can stir and talk on the phone," Linus said, hearing himself whine. We're breaking up, he thought.

"No, really. I can't," she said. "I'll see you." She hung up.

"Yeah, yeah," Linus said, hearing himself sound like a pissed-off adolescent.

Sara took the chili off the heat and wondered if she should call Sandy. Why bother? I'm never going back there, so what's the point of calling? she wondered. "Let them call me back," she said to her stove.

She had enough padding to last six months. Maybe eight months if she cut the cable package, the gym membership that she never used anyway, took fewer cabs, and ate out less. Her mother could kick in some money. In another month, she would consider her next move.

She heard shouting below her window, and she saw six teenagers racing on skateboards. Their kicking legs swung high. The back of one guy's sweatshirt had "Goofy" written in reflective tape. A guy with dreadlocks rammed the curb, tucked, and solidly planted himself back on his board. Sara could see his chest heaving. His friends slapped his hands. And then they were gone, banking around a building to head down the promenade. She heard their wheels grinding, and then that was gone, too.

There was a Paxil withdrawal support site with a "Bye-Bye Paxil" FAQ. Sara could look forward to insomnia, exceptionally vivid dreams, a feeling that she existed outside of herself, panic attacks, serious mood swings, a feeling that she was going insane, confusion during her waking hours, suicidal thoughts. All this could last for two to six weeks. What the fuck, she thought. How bad can it be?

"Fuck Linus," she said aloud.

17

"I said simple. Japanese. Minimal," Liv said to the florist as they both stared at big flowers in big vases. Birds of paradise. Waxy anthuriums with flamboyant stamen. Sprays of giant green fern. "This is not simple," Liv said.

Tables, glasses, napkins, bottles, and trays were being loaded into the lobby for the cocktail party that was to follow the screening of Liv's documentary. Liv's hands were sweating. In only a few hours, they—each guest plus one—could be saying *anything* about her film. About her. These flowers were awful.

"But we used a similar arrangement at a big studio party last week," the caterer said.

Liv wanted to say 'Fuck your studio party,' but she needed the florist to fix the arrangements. These flowers belonged on the set of a 1980s prime-time soap opera where people wore giant shoulder pads and said catty things. The huge tropical messes in the swollen ginger jar vases would create a biosphere in which toxic criticisms of her movie could flourish. She imagined stuffing these flowers into the alley dumpsters and then burning sage in the lobby to exorcise their bad vibes. She thought about the Ativan in her pocket.

"Look, I hate red, okay?" Liv said, touching a red anthurium.

"Why?" the florist asked.

Liv thought, I hate red because I saw a 4-year-old in a red T-shirt disappear in a cow pasture. I saw bloody corpses. Red is aggressive and mean.

"It's not important," Liv said. "I know you can do something to make them look totally great."

An hour later, the florist was petulantly reworking the arrangements with a load of white hyacinths. The three bars were set up. Glasses were being stacked into pyramids. Waiters were arriving, clean white shirts on hangers draped over their shoulders.

Liv's cell phone rang.

"Can I see the movie?" It was Naim.

Liv had seen him only sporadically since his arrival ten days ago, always very late at night when he told her about his visits to the Met, Ellis Island, the Museum of Tolerance, the Bronx Zoo. He told her that he ate dinner at a coffee shop "somewhere."

"But what do you do between dinner and when you come home?" Liv always asked.

Naim always shrugged. Liv, the resentful mom; Naim, the sullen teenager.

"Of course," Liv said. You *have* to see it. I'm reserving a seat for you tonight. You remember there's a dinner afterward, right?"

"I want to see it now," Naim said.

The film ran ninety-nine minutes. Liv looked at her watch; there was barely enough time before the crowd would start arriving. She could say no, but then she'd risk his absence at the screening and the dinner.

"Okay. But where are you? There isn't a lot of time."

She'd definitely have to sit with him while he watched it, which meant that she wouldn't have time to wash her hair in the ladies' room sink.

"I'm across the street."

She looked through the lobby doors, and there he was: watching her from a pay phone.

She took the Ativan.

Liv sat beside Naim in the middle of the empty screening room, keeping him in her peripheral vision to check his reaction. She watched for a leg recross, a shift to lean on an armrest, a smile. But he didn't move. Not for ninety-nine minutes.

As soon as the last credit rolled, Naim asked, "Why are people interested in this?"

Liv's hunch was that the film would appeal to an audience that would never cop to the guilty pleasure of cheesy reality TV. But Arabs and Jews stuck in a bus together—now *that* reality was interesting. Not cheesy, but timely and *important*. Identifying with the people on the bus could stand in for real emotion. She expected that much of the audience would probably be Arab-phobic, which meant that any emotional identification was going to be doubly packed with frisson. All that would only make her movie better. Weren't meaning and emotions the very things missing from most people's lives? Here she was offering it to them in one hour and thirty-nine minutes.

"It's history. You're part of one of the most important groups in the world right now, and people want to know about you. You and the Jews."

One hundred and seventy-five people were showing up to watch her movie, and Liv really couldn't say anymore why she had made it. She wanted to go home and read a book.

"Why did you come here, Naim?" she asked.

He turned in his seat to face her. Liv saw something flutter at the corner of his eye. An eyelash? A tic?

"If I stayed home, it would mean that the trip was only a two-week vacation. I came to New York because I need it to mean something. The trip to California was the most important thing I ever did. Really."

Liv reached to touch the corner of his eye, and he ducked away.

"I'm not crying," he said.

Liv nodded. She heard the projectionist rewinding the reels.

Naim unhooked his cross, pocketed it, and smiled at Liv. "I will wait here. I want to see it again with an audience," he said.

Naim took her hand and kissed it and then turned to face the screen.

Liv hesitated before getting up.

"Go," he said. "You probably have a dress or something. You want to change."

"Yes, I do," she said.

Peter was sitting on the editing console when she rushed in to get dressed.

"I look like shit. I don't have time to wash my hair, the flowers are cheesy, and the Ativan better kick in soon," she said, ripping the dry-cleaning plastic off the dress hanging on the back of the door. "Do you think I should take a second one?"

"No. It looks bad when the director sleeps through her own screening."

"Look at this," she said, holding out her hands. "It's a *movie*, and I'm fucking shaking."

Peter put his arms around her.

She dropped her head onto his chest. I'm going to break up with him. I'm going to end it. This isn't going to last, Liv thought. It's not right to let him comfort me.

"You have to get dressed," Peter whispered, letting go of her.

She took off her T-shirt and jeans and let Peter help her slide the dress over the head. For a second Liv forgot his name.

"Peter," she said, her head emerging from the neck hole.

"What?"

"I was just saying your name."

18

"*I* had to go to Brooklyn Heights to meet with a writer. Why don't I give you a ride?" It was Beth calling from her cell phone.

There was a fumbling with the phone, and Sara heard Beth ask someone how far it was to Sara's apartment. "We can be at your place in about fifteen minutes. If you're not ready, it's okay. I can wait."

Sara understood then that she would ride to the screening in a chauffeured car. "No, no, I'm ready. I'll be in the lobby."

Sara hung up, and the phone rang. She forgot about screening her calls, and she answered.

"They're going nuts. They think you're going to another journal or you broke a confidentiality clause or something." It was Bob.

"A confidentiality clause? It's a *trade* journal. Look, I'm not coming in. I haven't broken any confidentiality clause, because I never signed one. Can you tell them that?"

"I don't know," Bob said.

He sounded scared, and Sara was sure that other people were listening on the line.

"Try, Bob. Try to tell them that," Sara said, hanging up on him.

When the driver opened the backdoor of the Audi for Sara, Beth was piling scripts in the middle of the backseat to make room.

"Get in, get in. It's cool. There's room," Beth said.

Sara slid in and was surprised how dark it suddenly got outside. Tinted windows, she realized.

"I used to get sick reading in a car, but now I'm used to it," Beth said. "Too much time's wasted if I can't read. Of course, when you see what I'm reading, maybe I'm still wasting it." She was talking about the scripts.

Sara thought about how so many people would love to be as world-weary as Beth Meisner.

"How do you know the filmmaker?" Beth asked.

"She's my brother's girlfriend."

"Who's your brother?"

"Peter Koehl."

"Oh my God, of course," Beth said, digging through the stack of scripts, making her pile collapse.

Sara tried to straighten the mess, but Beth waved her away. "It's not worth it," Beth said, and she shoved the scripts onto the floor, her shoes already making footprints on the covers. "I can't believe I didn't make the connection. Why didn't I guess? Have you read it?" She held up Peter's *Bound Lover*.

Sara shook her head. "Our relationship is exclusively about dishing mom. I don't know shit about Peter's life outside of that. How is it?"

Beth was suddenly annoyed at herself. Why had she shown Sara the script? Now she was stuck. She had to say something. But what? If she complimented it—the easiest solution in the short term—it would get back to Peter, and he would expect something from her. If she were too negative, she'd be stuck with who knew what kind of weirdness all evening. "It's not bad," she said, realizing that Sara was too smart to accept such a vague answer. "But I think he was trying to please too many people when he wrote it," she added.

"He manages to make our mom happy. Maybe that's where the problem started," Sara said.

They were into this *way* too deeply, Beth thought.

"God, what I am doing being honest with his sister?" Beth said, asking for a sign from Sara that nothing would be held against her, that nothing would get back to her brother.

And Sara shrugged—just the way Beth remembered from Hampshire. The shrug that said, Who knows; why bother; who cares; *I* don't care. This was the sign Beth needed. Sara could be trusted.

"He shouldn't worry so much about what people like me are going to say. He should just trust his point of view," Beth said. She loved how she could talk with Sara, how nothing ever seemed like such a big deal.

"But what does that mean? I mean, concretely, in terms of writing a script," Sara asked.

The car jerked to a stop. Up ahead, a wall of skateboarders and cyclists, rollerbladers and people on kick scooters moved toward them from the Brooklyn Bridge.

Beth was stumped. What *did* it mean? Concretely. She had reached the limits of her opinion.

"Make crazier shit happen. I don't know. Something fresh," Beth said.

Sara rolled down her window and stuck out her head.

A pack of skateboarders swerved around the Audi. One of the boys slapped Sara's hand in a sort of high five.

"It's those people who want to get rid of cars in the city and replace them with bikes and stuff," Sara said to Beth. "I think the group's called 'Critical Mass.'"

Sara stuck her hand out further, and the rest of the skateboard group slapped it as they raced by. Slap. Slap. Slap. Slap. I'm with you, she thought. I'm not really in this Audi with a chauffer. I'm with *you*.

"It's sort of cool," she heard Beth say. "They're right. There really are too many cars."

I'll get my teaching credentials, Sara thought. I'll become a high school English teacher. That's what I'll do next, Sara decided.

19

*N*aim got up as the end credit roll began, and Liv grabbed his arm. He shook it off, and she started after him. He couldn't disappear now.

John put his hand on her shoulder. "A hundred dollars says he'll be in the lobby to greet his fans," he whispered.

Someone started clapping. Was it Linus? Other people joined in. Liv settled back in her seat. Naim better be in the lobby, she thought. She needed him tonight.

Someone whistled at her name on the screen. She thought it was Peter. Was Beth Meisner here? Was she clapping? There was a cheer when the bus passengers' names rolled down the screen. You can relax, Liv told herself.

The first thing Sara saw when the lights came up was Linus. Hugging Liv. I can't see this. Not him. Not like this, she thought, turning away to get her coat from the back of her chair. No problem, she told herself. Beth and I'll go out to eat. Linus'll never even know I was here.

"Introduce me to her," Beth said, grabbing Sara's arm.

And then her brother was coming up the side aisle. Waving at her. Cornered, Sara thought. They're closing in.

"Hey, Sara," Peter said.

His voice was bright. This must be her brother's "on" voice, she thought.

"Hi," Sara said. "This is Beth Meisner."

"Peter Koehl," he said, shaking Beth's hand. "Not to sound like an opportunistic pig, but I think you've got a script of mine."

He never breaks eye contact, Sara marveled.

"I do. But I haven't gotten to it. This weekend. I promise," Beth lied. Sara was entranced.

"It's a great film, isn't it?" Beth said.

"Yeah, she did a great job," Peter said, putting his arm around Sara and nudging her to turn toward Liv. No turning back, Sara thought. On "three" I'm going to have to turn and see Linus. One, two, three. Sara turned and the first eyes she saw were Linus's. He shrugged, his hands turned to the sky in an "Oh, well." He thinks it's weird, too, Sara thought. She shrugged back at Linus with her own "Oh, well," and walked with her brother and Beth down to the group around Liv.

Beth grabbed for Liv's hand. "I really enjoyed the film. It's exceptional," Beth said.

"This is Beth Meisner," Peter said to Liv.

Linus leaned close to Sara and said softly, "Don't worry about it."

Sara concentrated on his suit's carefully stitched collar. "So you're not a Paxil withdrawal hallucination?" she asked.

He smiled and put his hand on her shoulder. "No, we're both here. I'm her uncle," he said nodding at Liv. "It's funny, but I never made the connection with your name."

"But Linus, you're so good with names," Sara said.

"Ha ha, Sara," Linus said, getting the reference to their strange phone call.

"I hope you can join us for dinner. Both of you," Liv said to Beth, and by extension to Sara.

Sara opened her mouth to say something to Beth: *But what about the tête-à-tête dinner in a quiet restaurant?*

"That would be great," Beth said, still holding Liv's hand.

Sara closed her mouth.

Joy had arrived late to the screening. She never found Nick, and was forced to take a seat in the back corner, next to a crate of extra wine glasses. When the lights came up, she immediately started scanning the room for Nick as she also struggled to detach her coat which had gotten lodged in her chair's folding mechanism. She saw Beth Meisner talking to a tall woman who Joy guessed was the filmmaker, Liz. Liz? Liv. There was a dirty blond next to Beth whom Joy remembered as Sara, the woman from Beth's kitchen. The coat sleeve released from the chair, and Joy felt sick. She sat down, her coat bunched in her lap. What was she doing in the back row next to the caterer's boxes? What was she doing so far outside the circle of Beth and the filmmaker? It was embarrassing. She looked back at the circle and saw Liv reaching through a knot of people for a man: Peter. And Peter was talking to a man in a dark suit: Linus.

"Sorry I'm late," Nick said, rushing in the back door, snow still on his collar. "I tried to call, but you had your phone off."

Joy turned her face to the wall.

"Is the tall dark one Liv?" Joy asked, studying the wall's acoustical tile paneling.

Nick glanced across the theater. "Yeah," he said, unbuttoning his coat. "Do you want a glass of wine? I can grab two glasses now before everyone rushes the lobby."

Joy turned her head slightly to watch Liv go up the aisle to the lobby: Peter on one side, Beth Meisner on the other. Sara behind, trailed by Linus.

Joy's face was soft and a little slack. Nick noticed her breasts. For the first time since meeting her two years ago, he thought about her naked. She hadn't looked at him yet. Not one smile.

"Joy?" he said.

"She's with my shrink." Joy's voice was low and hoarse.

Nick squatted next to her. Joy's face tensed and shook; her breath caught.

"*I* should be with Beth Meisner, not that woman, Sara," she said, and she started to cry.

Nick put his hand on her waist, and he felt a softness he hadn't expected. He saw Joy's bra strap through her thin sweater. It was nice to see her distracted and lost.

He glanced at a side exit. The two of them could leave through that door and take a cab to his place. Joy probably parked in a garage, which meant they could leave the car there until tomorrow.

"We could get takeout and go to my place," he said, stroking her head, imagining that she was a disoriented stranger he had found wandering the streets. He didn't want her to smile. He wished he could forget her name, and he thought about his tongue on her clit.

Sara took a glass of champagne from a waiter and, from behind a large flower arrangement on one of the lobby bars, watched Linus talk to Beth. Specifically, she watched his hand. Was it going to touch Beth, like it had touched her? Was this something that Linus did when he was out socially? Touch women? His hand reached out to take a glass of wine from a passing waiter. No, he wasn't going to touch Beth.

Sara saw the Arab from the movie, the one with the video camera, break off from a clump of people that included Liv and Peter. Sara saw her brother take Liv's hand, and Sara could tell that Liv didn't like it—the public handholding. The Arab was walking toward her. He's going to the bar, she thought, wondering if there were any nonalcoholic drinks for teetotaling Muslims. He was looking at her, and she touched a hyacinth. He was smiling at her now like he knew her. Sara looked over her shoulder to see who was behind her. It was a wall.

"I was in the movie. My name is Naim," he said, holding his hand out to her.

Only foreigners can behave like this, Sara thought. Fearless. Guileless.

"Yes, I saw you," she said.

"You liked it?" Naim asked, reaching for a champagne flute.

They must have a different sense of personal space, Sara thought, backing closer to the wall.

She nodded. "I think it portrayed everyone on the bus respectfully."

"It's not boring?" Naim asked.

"No," Sara said. She thought that everyone in the film had come off as complicated as people should come off. Especially Naim, who was attractive and mysterious.

"What's your name?"

"Sara."

"Sara," he said. He pronounced her name so much better than Americans. "You sit next to me at dinner."

Was this a question or a statement? Sara wondered. Was Naim privy to the seating plan for dinner? She started to panic. What about Beth? Where would she sit? Did this guy like her or something?

"Here you are," Beth said, sidling up to Sara. She stuck her hand out to Naim. "I hope you're happy. It's an excellent film. My name's Beth Meisner."

Naim shook her hand. "I don't know who will be interested in the movie," he said.

Beth swept the crowd with her hand. "A lot of people. Look at them. They loved it."

What Beth really thought was that the film was interesting but had zero hope for an audience. Some distributor might eventually pick it up for a limited theatrical release but what was really important about the film was Liv. In the first twenty minutes of the film, Beth had her first plan for Media Capital: produce Liv's second movie. Not a documentary, but a feature. Surely there must be a script on the floor of the Audi that would bring in a solid, if not stellar opening weekend. By the end of tonight, Beth vowed to herself, she'd have Liv in her pocket.

The restaurant had set up a long table in a private room. Candles were the only light, and it felt like the family feast for which everyone is nostalgic, even though they had only experienced such feasts in European movies. Liv was at the center of the table, flanked by Linus and John. She wanted Beth Meisner to be seated across from her, maybe Peter too. Definitely Naim. But what about Sara? Would she have to let Sara sit in the center too, just because she was with Beth?

Naim, Beth, and Sara entered the room and Liv watched Naim pull out the first chair at the table's far end. He motioned for Sara to sit. Then he sat next to her, turning his back to Liv. Beth hovered, unsure of where to sit. No chairs were being pulled out for her. This is so high school cafeteria, Liv thought, starting to get up to rescue Beth.

"Down here." It was Peter, coming into the room, touching Beth lightly on her elbow to direct her to the center of the table.

Liv sat back down. At least Beth would be in the right chair.

"I think the star of the movie is trying to sweep your sister off her feet," Beth said as Peter pulled out a chair across from Liv.

"Liv, tell Beth that my sister isn't easily swept," Peter said.

Liv scanned the room: there were darting eyes, nervous fluttering hands, self-conscious tugs at clothes with less-than-flattering cuts. She looked at Naim, relaxed and settled in his chair, every piece of himself directed at Sara. Has anyone else at this table ever been as clear about their desire as Naim is being right now? Liv wondered.

"He's not easy," Liv said. "I mean *she's* not. Easy. To sweep off her feet."

"Well, easy or not, there's something going on down there," Beth said, arranging her pashmina over the chair back.

Naim passed Sara the breadbasket and then dished tapenade onto her bread plate. He waved a waiter over and ordered a bottle of champagne. "To go with this," he said to Sara, spreading the olive paste onto a slice of bread for her. And then he was quiet.

Sara waited for her reaction. Like an MRI, Sara scanned herself: *Disassociation. Anxiety. The shakes. Suicidal thoughts.*

She's got to stop staring at the Arab, Peter thought. The two lines between Liv's eyes were deepening. Why doesn't she understand that no one likes a scowler? What the hell was the Arab doing in New York, anyway?

He scooted in his chair and reached under the table to put his hand between Liv's legs, but the table was too wide, and he could only reach her kneecaps. Liv was startled by his touch, and she turned away from Naim to face Peter. That's better, he thought. She was back with important people at the center of the table. He smiled at her. She shrugged. She's shrugging? He was appalled. What's that? Doesn't she get it? It's time to start chatting up Beth Meisner. He touched Liv's knees again, and she closed her legs. Peter straightened back up. He couldn't remember seeing Liv sit with her knees together. Ever.

Their lives were supposed to turn corners because of this dinner, and Liv was fucking up, Peter thought. He wanted to scream: *Beth Meisner is talking to your father about double-knit clothing production. That is not good for either of us.* Peter finally saw just how bad

Liv's hair looked. How could she be so disorganized as to have dirty hair? he thought.

"I think Liv's ability to see into people is a talent that a lot of immigrants have," Peter said, interrupting John and Beth's conversation. "They're always on the outside, no matter how well integrated they become. When I did a doc on Bosnian refugees in Germany, it was amazing how clear their point of view was about the society around them after only a few months. That kind of insight is a survival skill, I think."

Beth turned slowly away from John, to Peter. "You don't talk like a romantic comedy writer. I'm intrigued," she said.

Is she trying to be seductive? Peter wondered. *Intrigued*?

Beth's head kept moving—past Peter and on to Liv where her eyes stayed locked.

"Peter's right, you know," Beth said to Liv. "Point of view is everything. I'm not just talking about what you want to say with the material, but your filmmaking style, too. It's all of a piece."

She read my script, Peter realized. He felt his eyelid flutter. He blinked. Was it a tic or a piece of hair? He brushed back his hair. The eyelid fluttered again. It was a tic. Beth Meisner had lied to him. She *had* read his script, and she didn't like it.

"Have you thought about directing a feature film?" Beth asked Liv. Peter's teeth felt cakey.

"I really think that should be your next step," Beth said to Liv. "A feature. You know I'm with Media Capital Group now."

"I'm not sure. I mean, I've thought about it, but I don't have a script or anything ready," Liv said.

Why isn't she saying that *I'm* the feature director? Peter wondered. Why isn't she mentioning that *I* have a script that *I'm* going to direct? He looked for water. His glass was empty while everyone else around him had full ones.

He waved to a waiter. "Can I get some water?" he asked.

"In just a minute, sir," the waiter said.

"Why don't you take on Peter's script and direct that one?" Beth asked Liv.

Peter smelled everyone's sweat: Campbell's chicken soup in a badly ventilated school cafeteria. The candles burned higher, their wisps of black smoke shooting to the vaulted ceiling, sucking out more of the room's oxygen. The sound of the ceramic salad plates grating against the glass chargers hurt his ears. His shirt cuffs were too tight. His collar choked. His socks were sliding into his shoes, filling up the space below the arches. *I'm the future feature film director at the table*, he wanted to scream.

"I don't know anything about romantic comedies," Liv said. "Romance is never funny, is it?"

She's *joking* about my script? Peter thought. She doesn't mention my experience—far, far greater than hers—but she manages to make my project into a joke.

Six waiters came into the room with plates of mesclun salad.

"But you have such a light touch," Beth insisted to Liv. "That sensibility could work so well with Peter's script."

Peter slammed himself away from the table, the hem of the tablecloth catching on the chair. A centerpiece slid and tipped over, his fork fell to the floor. A candlestick tipped, and a waiter lunged for it, knocking over Peter's chair. Another caught his heel on the ladder-back of Peter's chair; he fell, the plates of mesclun salad with him.

The room was quiet. Peter stared at a shard of broken glass that had wound up in a breadbasket. He let go of his napkin and watched it float to the floor. There was lettuce stuck to Beth's pashmina shawl.

"Sir, if you could move. We'll clean this up in a jiffy." It was the headwaiter with a phony British accent.

"Fuck you. I don't have to move," Peter said loudly. "It's *my* script. *I'm* the director. She's made one fucking documentary." He squeezed himself behind the long row of diners, toward the side door.

Sara pushed her chair away from the table, but Naim put his hand around her wrist like a bracelet.

"He'll be okay. Men do that," Naim said.

"I've never seen my brother do that."

Naim shrugged. "He's still a man."

Sara sat back down.

Peter was gone from the room.

More waiters rushed in with brooms, and the only sound was broken crockery being swept from the floor.

Liv started to get up. Linus held her hand and thought, if you catch up with Peter, all you'll wind up with is Peter, so sit down. He was transmitting the command psychically. Liv sat back down and smiled at Beth. Good girl. She's going to be a director, Linus thought. She knows what she's got to do.

"He does that sometimes. He'll be fine," Linus said to the table. "I'll go talk to him." With that, the guests started talking again. The party was salvaged because a shrink had let them know that Peter's outburst was nothing that could hurt them.

Sara started to eat another piece of bread with tapenade. Her brother was gone in an embarrassing cloud. Beth Meisner had abandoned her. A strange man who talked as little as Bob Nascent—maybe less—leaned very close to her. Still, no panic.

"I like you," Naim said.

Come on, panic; show yourself, Sara thought. He was younger. By a lot. Foreign. She hadn't been with anyone for a long time. Everything was stacked against her. Sara felt fine.

"Can I stay with you? Do you have a place I could sleep?"

Now Sara waited for the tape loop to begin: (1) What does he mean? (2) Does he want to sleep with me? (3) In my bed? (4) Should I sleep with him? (5) How do I say no? (6) Should I say no? And then back to the beginning: (1) What does he mean? (2) Does he want to sleep with me? And so on, and so on. She kept waiting. The loop never even began.

"I have a mattress that you blow up. Some friends who were visiting said it's comfortable."

Liv watched Naim and Sara leave the room. They had never even touched their salad.

"I told you. It's the real thing. I was standing with them after the movie, and I felt it: love at first sight," Beth said.

Beth wrote off Liv's silence as the behavior of someone with bigger things than dinner gossip on her mind. Creative things. She knew she was sitting on a major directing talent. With Liv in tow, Beth thought she might just last through her contract and possibly into contract renewal.

Linus disappeared into the men's room. He washed his hands and straightened the towel roll, picturing how Sara looked with the Arab. *Quivering with anticipation* was the fitting cliché, Linus decided. He smoothed the part of his hair that always stuck out over his left ear. I could be jealous of the Arab, he thought.

Linus was playing the character of "the Shrink" for the table. He checked his watch. He had been gone for ten minutes. Was this enough time for "the audience" at the table to believe that "the Shrink" had caught up with Peter on the street and calmed him down? Sure, Linus decided; ten minutes was sufficient.

He washed his hands again and carefully dried them. He checked himself in the mirror. He looked good, his cheekbones defined, the dark shadows under his eyes not so dark tonight. He turned to catch his profile. Not quite aquiline, but the nose was noble. The cloddish Peter was, no doubt, out of Liv's life, and Linus felt himself moving in to fill the gap. This dinner with all these movie people was exciting. Linus was having fun.

"He's embarrassed, but he'll live," Linus announced to the table. He sat down and leaned close to Beth to say, "Liv's too shy to mention anything, so I will. She has a script that she's been working on."

Linus touched Liv's back, a gesture that meant: go with this, don't say anything; it's time for "the understanding" to kick in, "the understanding" being that in public you shut up and roll with whatever the other members of the family were dishing out. It had been a survival strategy for living in Armenia—a code of behavior that remained in place long after Liv, Linus, and John had snuck out of the country. "Secrets" was not a dirty word in this family. It was the blabbing to Joe Blow that was inappropriate. So if Linus said that Liv had a script, Liv knew to act as if she had a script. She would find out the details later, privately.

"It's a thriller about an art heist and the cat-and-mouse game between a refined art thief and a female Europol investigator," Linus said.

Two sentences and Liv knew the script would be a veiled retelling of what Linus and John had done to get out of Armenia. In the Hollywood version, Linus was a refined art thief, not a desperate young doctor. Liv watched her father dissect his salad. This script's news to him, too, Liv realized.

20

*F*rom Nick's sofa, Joy could see down the long hall to the back of the apartment. Three bedrooms. A maid's room off the kitchen. Balconies running on two sides. It was an apartment for a family of four.

Nick brought her a glass of Bordeaux. "Are you okay?"

"Does Liv have a boyfriend?" Joy asked.

"Yeah, for a couple of years. Some guy. Peter, I think," Nick answered.

Joy didn't cry. Of course Peter's girlfriend was a pretty and talented filmmaker that someone like Beth Meisner would want to talk to. But why the hell was Linus there?

"Who was the older guy she was with?"

"Which one? There are always two. Her father and her uncle."

"The one in the Agnes b. clothes."

Nick sat down on the couch and took off Joy's shoes. Joy remembered that she hadn't waxed for weeks and that her toes were rough, the baby toenail cracked. Fuck it. I don't care, she thought.

"Her uncle," Nick said.

Joy made herself think the words: *Linus is the beautiful, talented filmmaker's uncle.* She waited to see if she'd feel betrayed. Would she cry? *My shrink is the uncle of the beautiful, talented filmmaker.* Was she humiliated, embarrassed, angry, sad, depressed? Nothing. There were no tears. Nothing. *Linus is the beautiful, talented filmmaker's uncle*, she thought, chasing after the pain like a child worrying a scab.

Joy wasn't smiling at Nick. She wasn't even looking at him, and Nick liked it. He wanted her, and she didn't even notice. And that made him want her more. He pulled her leg, and she slid onto her back. He pressed her feet into his crotch. He took off his jacket, pushed her legs apart and looked at her panties in the streetlight. He put his fingers under the elastic and watched her eyes close. "Yes," he whispered.

He had one hand between her legs, the other hand at her face, finding her lips. He saw it all like a movie, like he was taking her. This wasn't a movie; he knew that. But watching himself move more quickly and roughly amplified what he was feeling. It was better as a movie.

"Take off my clothes," she whispered.

Before his present job with the city of New York's building permit department, Nick worked for a U.S. senator from New York. He began as an intern, then an aide, then *the* aide for the senator.

His decision to quit the senator came after a campaign stop at a Park Slope synagogue where the senator ate a pastrami sandwich with a men's group in the temple's multipurpose room, joked about cholesterol, and posed for photos. Much of Nick's job was about gently touching the senator's elbow to direct him toward the right person, the correct chair, the best exit. It was Nick's responsibility to position the senator to look into the right eyes in any given room. Nick wasn't employed to be seen himself; he was employed to hang back. At the temple he took calls from the office and made sure the driver knew which door he should be parked at when the senator finally made his exit.

As Nick and the senator moved to leave the temple, a fat man in a blue cardigan blocked their way. "You're both going to die without ever knowing your greatness, or even getting close to knowing the greatness of God," the man said.

Nick waited for the senator to rub his thumb across his lips, the sign that Nick was to deal with this, which meant, "Get me out of here." But the senator did nothing. Nick timed the silence on the wall clock: two minutes. Two minutes in a campaign can lose the election. "He's the rabbi," the president of the Hadassah whispered to Nick.

The fat man said, "Please, stay for services."

The senator put the yarmulke back on his head, and it seemed to Nick that the light in the all-purpose room went suddenly dim, as if the fat man had personally brought down the sun for Shabbat.

The rabbi talked about waste and truth, distraction and focus. He warned of the finality of death and that there are no second chances. He talked about the wandering Jews of New York, and Nick thought that the rabbi was looking at him when he welcomed all the new faces in the room.

The next week Nick bought three new suits. Black, not Italian. At the farmers' market near his apartment, he watched a couple wheel their twins in a doublewide stroller. The man chose the produce; the woman packed the bags into the stroller's storage rack. Nick jealously thought about how the man got to have this woman every time he wanted it. He followed the family for five blocks.

The next evening, he went back to the temple in Park Slope and watched men hurrying in for Torah study, quickly slapping yarmulkes on their heads before crossing the front door's threshold. They wore dark overcoats and carried leather briefcases. They had cellphone earpieces. God gives them an edge, Nick thought.

At the office next morning, the senator's foreign-affairs consultant was late for a meeting because his 7-year-old had been up all night with a fever. "You know how it is," he said to Nick.

"I don't," Nick said.

"Well you will," the consultant said. "A guy like you. You're a catch. Only a matter of time before you're under the *chuppah*."

Nick cried in the men's room during a morning break. He cried again in an empty vending-machine room at the end of the day. And then that night, while Nick and the senator worked out the details of a trip upstate, Nick cried again. He claimed to be trying to control himself, but he was lying. Nick liked seeing himself weeping real tears in this heavily paneled office with a senior senator who wore suits well and had a great head of silver hair.

"What is it?" the senator asked.

He told the senator that he was crying because he was afraid that he'd die without experiencing family and faith. He wanted the senator to put a hand on his shoulder, and the senator did.

"This job is a killer on family life," the senator said. "Look at me. Second marriage as disastrous as the first."

We're men, Nick thought. Men talking about meaty things.

The senator said that if Nick were serious about family, he couldn't continue working in politics.

Three weeks later, the senator got Nick the job with the building permit department of the Borough of Manhattan, and Nick started looking for a Jewish wife. At the last fundraiser Nick attended for the senator, he met Joy. He knew that the building permit department would offer few—probably zero—invitations to openings and screenings—the stomping ground for sexy Jewish girls. So, pegging Joy Brundage as someone who got all the invitations, he decided to make her his "find a Jewish wife search engine." Win-win: she would always have a date, and his pool of future wife candidates would stay large.

But what he found—date after date with her tight sweaters, her contrived excuses to get him up to her apartment, the way she rubbed his neck in public, her teary confessions about old boyfriends that somehow became dirty stories—was that Joy repulsed him. She was a desperate lap dancer using every trick to make him see that she was the girl who should be his future half. After two years, their arrangement had stopped feeling so "win-win" to Nick.

But now, on his couch, with Joy not giving a shit about looking good, behaving right, or caring what the rest of the world thought you should have when you were a 38-year-old upper-middle-class New Yorker, everything felt different.

Nick heard something rip. Had he torn her shirt? She didn't notice. He kept going. Should he mention a condom?

Her hand reached for his prick. She moaned and her legs tightened. Her back arched. It took a long time for her body to relax, and he could see that she didn't know where she was. He wondered if she even knew his name.

21

Sara inflated her guest mattress, the loud electric pump making conversation impossible. She felt Naim staring at her as she dutifully pressed each section to test for firmness.

She dug out a pair of sweatpants. "These should fit," she said, handing them to Naim. Then she piled the mattress with a blanket and comforter.

"Thank you," he said.

"I don't have to be up at any particular time tomorrow. Do you need an alarm clock?" she asked.

Naim shook his head. "I am a Catholic, Sara," he said.

Sara laughed and then so did Naim.

"You play Muslim well," she said.

"Yes. Thank you," he said. "I am so happy to meet you."

He reached for her and kissed her on both cheeks, placing his lips solidly on the skin, keeping them there long enough for Sara to feel their warmth.

She lay in her bed and listened to the blow-up mattress squeak against the living-room floor as Naim crawled in. Then the apartment was quiet. He's young and an Arab, she thought. She felt no panic. He's Catholic, but he pretended to be a Muslim. Still no panic. None of it worried her as she lay watching the ceiling. Paxil withdrawal: _insomnia_.

22

$\mathcal{L}$iv and Beth finished the night at a bar filled with men dressed like women in a way that biological women no longer dressed: bouffants, Chanel-ish suits, pumps, and nylons. During the lingerie fashion show, Beth tried to find out more about Liv's script.

Liv said, "It's late; I've had too much to drink, and the script isn't done, so it's too early to talk about casting."

A model came out in a bra made from a mink pelt, the mink's teeth acting as a clasp in front.

"Would you ever wear a bra like that?" Liv asked.

Beth told Liv that she respected not wanting to discuss the un-finished script. "It's right to protect the creative process," Beth said.

"I have to pee," Liv said, heading to the toilets.

Liv called Peter from a filthy stall. "Are you okay?" she asked when Peter picked up.

"I feel like shit. I was an asshole." He was at Donald's.

"It all happened so fast. Suddenly you were just gone," she said, studying the initials and hearts drawn in magic marker on the metal stall walls: TL + BB, SU + CT 4evr. She imagined the men in the bar making sure to pack magic markers in their purses before going out.

"Are you saying that it happened so fast that no one noticed?" Peter asked.

"No, of course people noticed. It's just that it might not be as big a deal as you think. You were acting like the *enfant terrible artiste*, and that's not such a bad thing."

"Yeah, right," Peter scoffed, pouring his third whiskey. "Be careful with that Beth Meisner. She's a total opportunist."

Liv tried to remember if she had ever written her initials along with another's inside a heart. LJ + who? "Of course she's an opportunist," Liv said. "She's a producer."

"That Arab is a weird one."

"He left the dinner with your sister," she said.

"You're kidding."

"No."

"That guy's going to have a rough row to hoe," Peter said.

"Oh yeah?"

"Yeah. Sara's terrified of men."

Liv relaxed. Sara wouldn't sleep with Naim.

"Liv, what's going on with us? I asked you to marry me, and you said yes. Usually that means we talk about the future, and we pick out a ring or something."

Liv took a breath and held it. She had to say whatever she had to say, fast. In one breath. "I don't want to get married." There, she said it.

Peter was quiet.

Was the phone dead? Was the cell down? How long should she wait before saying something? Liv left the stall to stand next to the window. Maybe the stall had become a cell-phone dead zone. A man came in to re-gel his Marcel waves.

"Bitch," Peter said.

Liv waited. Count to ten before responding, she told herself. One, two, three, four, five, six, seven, eight, nine, ten. Eleven.

"You're a self-serving bitch." Peter said, and then he hung up.

Liv washed her hands and studied her face in the mirror. She was calm. It wasn't pretty, but, the thing Peter said, well, it was reassuring to be recognized.

Liv lay back on the Audi's seat, pretending to be exhausted and on the edge of sleep, because she was tired of being with Beth. Beth's driver was careful not to slam the door, and Liv could feel, from under closed eyes, that the uptown traffic was light. She had to withstand Beth's company for only a few more minutes.

She remembered that her father had sent an Audi like this one to pick her up from JFK when she finally came home from Azerbaijan and Paris. That car had had Iranian fashion magazines in the pockets behind the front seat, and that driver had also driven well and been respectful of her need for quiet. Liv remembered that he simply nodded at her when she went into her building, and that he didn't pull away from the curb until he saw that she had passed by the doorman and reached the elevator. An hour later he appeared at the apartment door, because she had left her bag in the backseat.

"You don't want to forget this, Madame," he said.

"No," Liv said, taking the bag and closing the door.

In the apartment, she slid the bag into the back of a closet where it still sat, still packed. Then she pulled on one of her father's old running T-shirts, and a pair of cutoff sweatpants. She dragged an overstuffed chair to the front window and watched the light change. For weeks.

In the first month back from Azerbaijan she left the apartment only twice. The first time was to get her legs waxed. She made it only as far as the park where she sat on a bench with a woman who smelled like a wet dog. The second time was to go to church where her father helped her light candles for the people she saw shot and one for Artur, wherever he was. She raised her hands to catch the dripping wax, and she smelled the hair burning on her arms.

Weeks later Peter rang from the lobby. He came up with a bag of pot, and they watched the film that he had sold to Arte. They went out to dinner, but Liv had to leave before the meal came. "Too much life," she said, sliding out of the booth.

Liv never submitted a story about Nagorno Karabagh to the *New York Times*. Reporting made no sense at all.

Linus made her take some pills because he said Liv had to "function." Then there was a decision to assist on an independent feature film, and then another film. There was a flirtation with translation, an interview with the U.N. translation program. And then a year or two after that, there was the article she read about a bus tour with Arabs and Jews and how it made Liv imagine the men with guns, sitting on a bus in California with Marina and Artur and the rest of her family. Liv thought that change might be possible on a trip like that.

It was after reading this article that Liv saw Peter again. She was looking for advice about making a documentary about the bus trip. They met at a coffee shop in Brooklyn where Peter stepped her through the whole process, since now he was an expert, having made other films since they had last seen each other.

They went back to his apartment where they had sex, both of them laughing at the retarded inevitability of it.

He's gone now, Liv thought, and she opened her eyes in the Audi.

"Do you think Peter could direct his script?" Beth asked.

She was staring at Liv, as if she had been waiting for her to wake up.

Liv nodded.

"It might be a good idea for me to include a romantic comedy like Peter's on the slate," Beth said.

"Yeah, it's an excellent idea," Liv said. He's a good director.

23

*B*y four a.m. Peter and Donald had smoked all of Donald's hash.

"Fuck her," Donald said.

"Which one?"

"Both of them. They can't take your script away from you. Meisner was only there because you put her on the list. She's a cunt who's never going to make good on her contract with New Media. In six months they're going to realize they've been ripped off. They want an entrée to the American market, and they bring on Beth Meisner as their secret weapon? Give me a break."

Peter thought that maybe he should read *Variety* more closely, so he could be as informed as Donald.

"Fuck Beth Meisner, the poser. Fuck Liv Johansson, the wanna-be director. Fuck 'em all," Peter said.

At dawn, Peter lay on Donald's couch imagining the thirty people at dinner gossiping about how he had flipped out. Peter imagined phone lines clogging, and the thirty guests growing exponentially to become 900 and eventually 810,000—all of them laughing at Peter Koehl. He felt banished.

Then Peter remembered Joy, and he realized that she hadn't been at the screening. Maybe he wasn't totally shut out. Joy didn't hate him—not yet. He imagined the table again. Who did Joy know? Beth Meisner, but surely Joy wouldn't be the first person Beth called this morning, not at dawn. It might take hours or even days for the story to reach Joy. He had to see her immediately. He had to get to her before she heard that Peter Koehl was a loose cannon, someone unable to toe the line, a man with impulse control problems.

It was 7:45, and Joy wasn't in.

"I can wait. She's probably out running," Peter said, sitting on one of the lobby's couches, picking at the welting separating from its cushion.

"She hasn't been in all night," the doorman said.

Peter didn't like that. He didn't like that Joy had another man in her life. Maybe more than one. A producer should be totally on the director's team. Unconditional devotion. That's what it took. He felt the stitches give way between the welting cord and the cushion. What the hell was she doing fucking some other guy? Peter stormed out of the lobby, forcing the door to swing in rather than out.

24

*J*oy woke slowly, first only aware of the sheets. What were they? Five hundred thread count? One thousand? She saw the duvet next. White embroidery on white fabric. Chic in an indescribably old-world way. She noticed the velvet drapes. Then a rug from the Caucuses. Nick's bedroom felt protected, sacred.

The front-door buzzer rang, and she sat up to find a robe laid out at the foot of the bed. Silk. Long. Embroidered. Nick must have put it there. Was it his? Joy put it on. It was a woman's. Who had worn it before her?

Joy felt Nick's absence as she walked toward the door. Had he left her a note? Where would he have left it? Did he want her out of the apartment by the time he came back?

"Who is it?" Joy said to the closed door.

"Groceries."

Joy looked through the peephole: a young man with crates on a dolly.

"Is Mr. Gorelich in?"

"No," Joy said, realizing too late that you weren't supposed to tell a strange man at the door that there wasn't a man in the house.

"He's usually back by now," the deliveryman said.

Back from where? Joy wondered. Then she wondered if there was anything perishable in the crates. Nick might be upset with her if she didn't let this guy in. She opened the locks and held open the door.

"Sorry," the guy said as he wheeled the crates in. "Mr. Gorelich's usually back from temple by eleven o'clock. Do you want me to put this away?"

Joy nodded. "Does he always go to temple?"

"If it's Saturday."

There was a note on the refrigerator door:

Please don't go. I'll be back by 1:00.

The guy delivered fresh vegetables, some fish, and eggs. The refrigerator was full enough for a family. When did Nick eat all this? Didn't he eat out most nights? Was he having a dinner party? Joy saw two sinks. Two refrigerators. Nick kept kosher.

In the daylight, the living room looked larger than she remembered from last night. When it came to categorizing people with money, Joy made three columns: comfortable, well-off, and rich. She thought of herself as "comfortable." This apartment put Nick in the "rich" column.

She stood at the wide windows and watched a running group, all in matching polar-fleece overshirts, stream into the park. She made a mental calorie list of everything she had eaten yesterday. It wasn't much. She didn't really have to run today.

Her cell phone rang.

"Hi." It was Beth.

"Hi," Joy said, surprised. A call from Beth Meisner on a Saturday morning?

"Look, we're going to have to get Peter's script into shape. I mean, actually, it's pretty good, and I'm really only talking about a polish. But don't tell that to Peter. It's important that you keep him on his toes," Beth said. "It's easier if he's feeling a little nervous about his abilities."

Joy sifted through the *in medias res* chatter: *Peter's script. A polish. Important that you keep him on his toes. You* means *me*, Joy realized. She took a breath and sifted the information again. There was no doubt. *This* was the call. This was the call marking a new period in her life. *Keep him on his toes*. I'm *it*. A real producer—the creative kind, Joy thought.

"Of course I'll keep him on his toes," Joy said.

Being stuck in the back row of the screening room, seeing Linus, Peter, and that girl Sara, all grouped around the filmmaker: it no longer meant a thing. How could it, now that she had slept with Nick and had a movie to produce?

"We'll really need to keep his impulse control in check," Beth said. And then Beth told Joy about the dinner and about how Peter spit when he yelled at the waiter, and how he kicked chairs out of his way when he left the room.

Beth told Joy that Liv had been thinking about leaving Peter for a long time. "You know *la vie en couple*. She's really better off without him," Beth said. "Where were you last night?"

"I had other plans," Joy said. Then she agreed with Beth that Peter could be unpredictable. She said she would talk to him. "He trusts me, and he'll listen to me," she said, making herself invaluable.

"I just don't want to be stuck with a loose cannon, you know what I mean?" Beth said.

"Don't worry. I know I can keep him in line," Joy said, knowing that she wouldn't have to do anything at all, since Peter would do whatever it took to make a movie. He would toe the line as hard as Joy would toe it. The rewards were too delicious to make being a loose cannon anything but profoundly stupid.

Joy hung up. I'll make a frittata for lunch, she thought.

Nick came into the kitchen and put his arms around Joy from behind. He wore a black velvet yarmulke. His hair smelled like snow.

Joy wondered what happened to the girlfriend Nick had when they had first met—a tall black woman who Joy had once glimpsed eating lunch with Nick in a crowded deli. It was the same woman Joy saw again at a party six months ago—alone, never taking off her trench coat and smoking in the apartment of a virulently antismoking film financier.

"Did you ever sleep with Liv?" Joy asked.

"No. I only met her once, and she was pretty fucked up, then," Nick said.

"Why?"

"Supposedly, she saw some bad stuff in Nagorno Karabach during the war. Why are you so interested?"

"I want to know about you," Joy said.

"Why? I don't want to know about men you've been with."

Joy started to cry. "Whose robe is this?" she whispered into his neck.

"It was my aunt's," he said.

"How can you afford this apartment?" she asked.

"A trust," he whispered. "Stop crying."

Joy did.

With the first money available from his grandfather's trust, Nick bought this apartment because it was within walking distance of the rabbi's temple. He rehabbed and decorated it and, until last night, had never brought a woman home to it. Until last night, he fucked exclusively outside the neighborhood, usually the same Nigerian prostitute at lunch. He had kept the apartment pure—a place for his future wife and children. He had bought the embroidered silk robe Joy was wearing at a Soho antique store.

"What does *la vie en couple* mean?" Joy asked.

"The life of a couple," Nick whispered, loosening the robe's belt.

25

$\mathscr{L}$iv stayed in bed all morning. She scanned her luck: abandoned by a mother, but rescued by a father; meager beginnings in Armenia, but brought up in comfort in Manhattan; she made it through a violent hold-up in a cow pasture; she was able to take drugs without getting hooked; she always managed to have a man nearby; a powerful movie producer wanted her; she had an uncle who could pull a script out of the air.

She heard her father come in, talking on the cell phone to Linus. She knew they'd be talking about her. She waited until she heard her father get off the phone before finally getting out of bed to go see him in the kitchen where he rummaged in the refrigerator for food.

"What do you know about the script Linus was talking about? If he doesn't have something concrete, I'm fucked," Liv said. "Beth is really hot for the story he told her."

John put out a plate of yogurt with honey and toast. "He says he's in the third act. It's two hundred pages."

Liv heard the shut-off switch click on the tea kettle.

"Two hundred pages, and he's not done?" Liv laughed, but John shrugged. "Dad, a script's usually 120 pages, max. It's about us, isn't it?"

"Probably. I haven't read it yet," John said, pouring the boiling water into a pot, over a tightly packed tea ball. "We did this incredible thing, and all he does with it is write a stupid script."

"It's over thirty years ago, now. Why not write a movie?"

"Because there are other responses to what we did, that's why." He poured two cups of tea, handing one to Liv.

"Like what? Repent?"

"For example," John said.

John crossed himself, kissed his thumb, touched the cross around his neck, and dropped a sugar cube into his tea. Why is she trying to impress those people—especially that producer? he wondered. Why does she want to make a product that wastes people's time and keeps them from God? You can't pray at the movies.

John knew that it was possible to argue that his clothes were too revealing, too sexy, but John also knew that wearing spandex never prevented a person from getting down on his knees and praying. Why did Liv think he was a boring businessman with an obsessive relationship to God, but that her uncle was God's gift because he was writing a film script? John understood why Peter had thrown the salad plates.

"I'm sure you'll be able to use the script. I'm sure it's fine," he said, turning on the oven to preheat.

Liv heard the dismissal in her father's voice. "Why do you even bother with him if he annoys you so much?"

"He's my brother. There's no better reason to be annoyed by someone."

"Sometimes it sounds like you hate him," she said.

"He's got a big head."

Liv felt for a second that he was talking about her. The oven fan kicked on.

26

Sara woke up two hours and fifteen minutes after finally falling asleep. She didn't want to creep around the blow-up mattress on her way to the kitchen for coffee, so she stayed in bed to start Trollope's *The Way We Live Now*.

Yeah, the way we live now, Sara thought: me in my room, him on a blow-up mattress in the living room. She heard the front door click; Naim was gone. It was the first sound she had heard him make.

The mattress was shoved into a corner, the blankets and sweatpants carefully folded. In the kitchen, she found a plate of yogurt swimming in honey, a spoon, and a folded napkin next to it. He's staying, Sara thought. There was no note on the refrigerator. But she knew he was staying.

She sat in the kitchen, drank coffee, and wondered whom she could call to tell about last night. There was Beth, but she already knew half the story.

A woman salted the front steps of the building across the street. With whom could she speculate about the possible cultural reasons for Naim's behavior? To whom could Sara admit, "I like him. He's serious and respects me"? The answer was no one. No girlfriend with whom to share the details of the screening and the chaste way in which the night had ended with Naim. There's always Verizon Communications' reminder call option, Sara thought, smiling at her old insane self.

A grocery delivery truck double-parked across the street. Sara called her mother.

"I met someone," she said as soon as her mother picked up.

"Oh," her mother said. "At work?"

Sara remembered that her mother still thought she was employed. She was going to have to tell her she didn't have a job anymore, but not right now.

"No, at a screening. That movie that Liv was making," Sara said. "Peter's girlfriend."

"Is he in the movies, too?"

"Not really. He's one of the Arabs in the documentary."

Sara wanted to make her mother sit up and take notice. An Arab.

"Oh. Is he visiting?" her mother asked.

"I think he's staying."

"Does he have a job?"

"I don't think so."

Sara could hear her mother running water. Coffee? The dishes? Rinsing out the wine glass from last night?

"You sound tired. Are you okay?" her mother asked.

Why doesn't she just say, "How's your emotional state? Maybe you should increase your dosage," Sara wondered.

"I'm not tired. I'm fine." She wouldn't tell her mother about the Paxil. Not yet. "I really like this guy, mom."

The water was off. Sara had her attention.

"He's quiet. A little like Thumper. Remember how quiet Thumper was?" Sara said.

"Yeah." Her mother's voice always got low and soft when talking about Thumper.

Since the summer Nancy hired Thumper to build shelves in her apartment, Sara had always thought her mother was slightly in love with him. Every day that summer, Nancy and Thumper shared beer and deli sandwiches at lunch, and Nancy bought ice-cream bars from the truck that passed at five o'clock.

"I thought I saw him at the drugstore," her mother said.

"I know, Mom." It hadn't happened to Sara for years, but she knew what that felt like, that glimpse of pale hair disappearing around the end of a store aisle.

David Roper/White Rabbit/Thumper had disappeared eleven years ago after an eco-tour of the Galapagos. The eco-tour had been a Christmas present to Sara and Thumper from his father, an envelope of tickets and brochures they opened Christmas morning.

Thumper and Sara bought new luggage and binoculars. Sara read some Darwin. On the morning of the day they were to leave, Thumper told Sara about the woman he had been sleeping with. He said the woman didn't matter, because from now on he was going to be a faithful and truthful boyfriend. The woman was a stripper with redone tits and collagen cheeks. Thumper called her a dancer. Sara was devastated by the cliché.

"I could maybe get over the sex. But, Jesus, a stripper. Does it have to be so fucking typical?" Sara said, slamming the bedroom door.

She listened to him finish packing, all the while considering calling out from the bedroom, "I'm pregnant." But she didn't do it. Mainly because she wasn't yet absolutely sure, and she didn't wanted to stoop to the most soap opera of lines, especially after having accused him of being a cliché with his stripper.

He told her through the closed bedroom door that the cab was there. When she didn't answer, he said, "So you're not coming?"

She didn't answer.

He said, "Sara."

And she still didn't answer.

She listened to him leave the apartment and then imagined racing to the street to stop him from going.

On the way home after the tour, the group had a free day in Quito before an early morning flight back to the U.S. Thumper never showed up for the airport shuttle, and the tour guide learned from the front desk that he had checked out the night before.

His family hired investigators. There were interviews of the hotel workers, of Sara, even of Sara's mother. In the final report, the investigators said it happened all the time: people want to "escape" to start a new life.

Sara got her period.

"He really loves his mother. She lives in Bahrain," Sara said to her mother.

"Do you want me to meet him?" her mother asked.

"I don't know. Yes," Sara answered. "I don't know when. It's all very new."

"Well, just let me know, honey."

Sara was a child the last time her mother had called her honey. Eight years old, Sara thought. I was 8, and I had a fever. *Honey.*

27

"*Yoga*," Joy said, sitting up from the couch where she was reading the paper. "My yoga teacher's coming over at four o'clock." It was three o'clock.

Nick shifted in his chair across the room so that he could see Joy's thigh rolling out from under the robe. "Cancel it."

"I can't."

"Why not?" Nick asked.

"We're making progress. I don't want to fall back."

"What's one lesson?"

"It's important."

She started for the bedroom to get dressed, and Nick knew that once she left, he couldn't be sure when he'd see her again, or how long it would take to get her back into this state. What was the state? Relaxed. Unconcerned. Pliant. Sloppy.

"Tell her to come here. You can do yoga in the back bedroom. It's as big as your living room, right?"

"Yeah. Where will you be?"

Nick shrugged. "I can stay here or go out for a while. Will it bother you if I'm here? How long's the lesson?"

"An hour. Sometimes she goes over. It won't bother me if you're here."

During the class, Nick heard the yoga teacher tell Joy that her upper back was really opening up, and that that was a sign that the heart chakra was also expanding.

After the yoga teacher left, he and Joy fucked, and then Nick rolled Joy onto her stomach to slowly trace his finger up her spine. He kissed her between her shoulder blades, pulled the blankets up, rolled her on her side, and entered her from behind. "Let's make a baby," he whispered.

She lifted her ass slightly, and he thought he heard her say, "Yes."

28

*E*ven before stepping through the back kitchen door, Naim could tell from the accent that they were from Bekka. The River Café had been their first job upon arriving in America. Two of them had gotten legal. The other two had girls lined up to marry. They thought that the manager could be convinced to take on someone two days a week for private parties. They told Naim it was "prep work"—peeling potatoes, hard-boiling eggs, and making sure that the bins were full of sprigs of parsley. If anyone showed up—immigration, police, *anyone*—he'd have to say that he had shown his manager false papers. If he didn't do this, the guys told Naim that the manager's guys would fuck him up, and then he'd be really fucked. No one wanted Arabs these days, but this owner kept them working. He had lowered their hourly rate by twenty-five cents, and the guys told Naim that even though it sounded like the manager and owner were real hard-asses, they were okay once you knew what to expect. Naim could hope to make two dollars an hour, and sometimes his checks would be late by a month.

It was dark and windy when Naim left the hot kitchen. John's parka was too big and drafts of air blew up under it. The bridge arched above him, the traffic grinding on the metal grating. He heard a squeak, and something darted between the plastic grocery bags stuck in the embankment's frozen ivy. Naim waited for it again. He held the parka tight to keep out the wind. Squeak. There it was. A kitten.

The kitten stopped and froze, and then darted for the bags. Naim grabbed for it. Shaking and wet, it was the size of his hand. Naim knew it was motherless. He unzipped the parka and held the animal inside his shirt.

By the time he reached the subway entrance, the kitten was purring. He would give it to Liv. Life with Liv and her father would be good for this gray kitten.

29

$\mathscr{L}$iv couldn't stop reading Linus's script. An hour ago, she took it with her to the toilet. The half hour before that, she kept reading as she let in the grocery delivery guy. The groceries still sat in bags on the kitchen floor, the milk going warm, the cheese starting to smell.

People said and did surprising things, and the plot kept moving. Liv knew it would fly with Beth. But that wasn't why she couldn't put it down. No. It was seductive because it was about her family. The brothers and Liv, their millions and how they had gotten them.

Although Liv had been only 4 years old, when she combined her father's and uncle's versions with what she could remember for herself, the story was clear and complete. It was the family's Event. An event that started simply enough in Armenia with Linus saying at dinner, "Guess what I found out? Omar has been stealing church statues and religious icons."

Omar, a local heavy-machinery factory chief, had been stealing religious relics and stashing them in a recently shut-down abattoir. Linus had confirmed the gossip and found out that the relics were sitting in the abandoned building, waiting for Omar to return from a farm expo in Yerevan. Omar's plan was to truck the religious stuff to Istanbul where an auction house was ready to move it all for great profit.

At three in the morning, after hours of discussion, Linus's simple piece of local gossip ended with the brothers making a plan. (1) We steal Omar's cache before he gets back from Yerevan. (2) We get

out of Armenia, and (3) we sell it all. This dinnertime chit-chat—
Guess what I found out? Omar has been stealing church statues and icons—
changed their lives.

Linus and John broke into the abattoir, and for four nights they
filled a twenty-ton truck with stolen goods. There were stacks of
silver and gold gospel covers that Omar had hidden inside fifty-
gallon oil drums; there were crosses and statuary; there was a marble
dome from a fifteenth-century altar, a life-sized gold crèche, and a
massive parade of icons leaning against the stone walls tinged red
from the building's forty years of animal slaughter.

The whole operation went smoothly, except for when Linus
slipped on a frozen puddle while toting a stone hand of St. Thaddeus
to the truck. Linus moaned and complained, and John told him to
shut up and keep moving. The injury slowed them down, and they
were still loading after sunrise. John kept muttering, "Shit, shit, shit,
this is bad," as the day got brighter, and he became more convinced
that they'd be caught before they could hide their loaded truck in
the spot he had found at a muddy auto-scrap yard.

But no one stopped them, and the loaded truck sat hidden in
the scrap yard for weeks. John and Linus went about their days,
acting normally while they waited for the right moment to drive the
truck out of the country. Every day after his shift at the hospital,
Linus checked to see that the truck was still there, still loaded. Over
dinner, he enjoyed speculating about what must have happened when
Omar found his artifacts missing. John told him that he was being
immature. It was better to not think about it.

"Oh, is that what you call 'repression therapy'?" Linus asked.
John told him to shut up.

Both brothers heard rumors that Omar was beating his wife and
selling off his factory's equipment under the table. One day Linus
saw him fall in front of the train station and not bother to get up.

After five weeks of payoffs, bribes, promised percentages, and gifts, John finally bundled Liv out of bed at two a.m. It was the day. Time to go and they had to be fast, even on the roads made for goats that destroyed the truck's shocks in the first half day out of Spitak.

In two months, they were settled in a house outside Iraklion, Crete, the stolen goods packed in shipping containers at an abandoned fish-drying factory on the southwest tip of the island—a place accessible only by boat and a long hike around the rocky point. John and Linus would have made more money with guns, but Crete was the kind of place where almost any merchandise could be moved.

Linus studied to pass his Greek medical boards, and John showed potential buyers the goods. For John, the best part was watching the art dealers hobbling across the hot rock beach and then up a narrow ravine in their expensive Italian shoes. For Linus, the best part of Crete was leaving after the right papers for the U.S. could finally be bought.

Linus's script was about Robert, a world-weary debonair art thief, who outfoxes everyone but Brigitte, a Europol babe. While Brigitte starts out harshly judging Robert's criminality, she comes to join him. The stolen artwork is sold for a fortune to an art dealer with a religious wife who sees just how shady her husband's business practices are. Robert winds up rich, but happy only when he finally admits his love to Brigitte. Linus's script was by no means a verbatim retelling of the family's story, but Liv was compelled by the shared themes. Greed. Desperation. Obsession. Thieves' honor. Sneakiness.

Naim thought Liv had been sleeping when she opened the door, the script still in her hand. He even thought for a moment that she didn't recognize him.

"Is it cold outside?" she asked.

He pulled the gray kitten from the parka. "I think it's a girl, but I call her Yasser. It's for you."

Liv didn't want a cat.

"I found her. She peed in the coat. I will clean it for your father."

Naim went to the kitchen, found a baking pan and poured a whole bag of polenta into it. "For her to pee again," he said, stepping around the grocery bags.

"Where are you staying?" Liv asked.

"In Brooklyn. I found a job," he said, pouring a teacup of milk from the sweating carton.

Yasser sniffed at the milk. Naim stuck his finger into the cup, and the cat licked it dry.

"So who are you staying with in Brooklyn?" Liv asked.

"A nice girl from your party," he answered.

"You don't waste any time, do you?" Liv said.

Naim didn't know what she meant. He knew that she was mad at him, but he told himself that he couldn't help that. He didn't want to be with her, because she made him feel off balance. He thought she was sneaky, and he didn't like that in anyone, especially a woman. She was too sure of herself. Too much like a man. A cat like Yasser would help her. He held his finger very close to the top of the milk, and the kitten ducked her head to lick his finger. He moved his finger even closer to the milk, and she started to lap it directly. He took his hand away from the cup, and the cat kept drinking.

"See, she learns," Naim said, smiling at Liv.

He went back to the guest room to restuff his clothes into his gym bag, glad that he had sold the Handycam before coming to New York. He was down to one bag, which was good, considering how small Sara's apartment was.

"Does your mother know you're staying in New York?" Liv asked.

"No," Naim said, deciding not to tell Liv yet that his mother had died over two years ago.

The teacup crashed in the kitchen. Yasser.

Part Two

1

*J*ohn watched Linus stuff his face with peanuts in the bar at the Hilton out near the Meadowlands. "You're eating like a vacuum cleaner," John said. "They're going to make you sick, and then fat."

"I know," Linus said. He took a fresh bowl off the empty table next to them and balanced a peanut on the spire of the foam-core model of the new Spitak church sitting at John's feet.

"Don't. It'll leave a grease stain," John said, flicking the peanut onto the carpet.

Linus scooped up more nuts. His stomach hurt already.

"I don't know why you're so upset. It's my money," John said. "You don't have to be involved."

"Let me get this straight," Linus said. "You made me drive to New Jersey to meet an architect who specializes in 'sacred spaces,' and now you're saying I don't have to be involved? How old is he anyway, Mr. Sacred Spaces? Twelve?"

"He's won a lot of awards," John said.

Linus brushed the salt off his hands, letting it fall like dandruff from God onto the church roof.

"So what's your plan, exactly? Go on Armenian television and say, 'Gee, I'm sorry about ripping off your religious art during the black days of Soviet control, but hey, I'm a rich American now, and I'm making it all up to with you a factory and a church.' Is that how it's going to go?"

"Something like that," John said, maintaining his calm. "I thought we could do the apology part together."

Linus laughed, half-chewed peanuts spraying from his mouth. Shit, he thought, I'm going to choke and die on peanuts. My brother's going to have to Heimlich me in a cocktail lounge.

The waitress approaching to light their table candle stopped and went back to the bar. A busboy held back from clearing John's empty ginger ale glass. The Kezian brothers had a bad air about them right now, and it was better to stay clear.

Linus got hold of his choking.

"Well, this is me on Armenian TV," Linus said. "Hello, I'm Linus Kezian, and I admit it. I plundered national religious treasures with my brother. And let me tell you, I did it once, and I'd probably do it again. Sacred stuff for sacred spaces is not what the world needs."

"You're wrong," John said. "It's exactly what the world needs, and we violated that. Now I'm dealing with the guilt."

"Fine. Deal. But leave me out of it."

"The apology's important. I'm trying to move on with my life. Isn't that what you tell your patients to do?" John said.

"No. That's not what I tell my patients to do," Linus said. "If you really want to move on, send money with no return address. What you want is some twisted idea of fame and glory. First you cry on TV, and then everyone hugs you."

"I believe in confession," John said.

"You believe in your fifteen minutes."

"Fuck you."

"No, fuck you."

Linus grabbed his coat and headed for the exit, remembering only when he got to the parking lot that they had come in one car, and that it would be a nightmare to find a cab back to the city at this hour.

He went back and sat in the lobby where he watched his brother calmly pay the waitress, carefully put on his coat, and pick up the architectural model. John was slow and plodding because he wasn't reacting to every little belch and hiccup of the world around him. I'm the drama queen, not John, Linus thought. For John, life, death, and forgiveness were real enough; it wasn't necessary to add extra emotion to make things more exciting.

Linus woke up that night at his usual three a.m. Up until nine months ago, he had killed the hours between three and seven with his plans for Joy and his script. But the script was done, and Joy had conformed to Linus's design: married to an observant Jew, more or less an observant Jewish wife. If he was going to keep waking up at this hour, he needed a new project.

Linus padded to the window, imaging other agitated New Yorkers doing the same, everyone staring blankly out from great heights. The lights came on in the penthouse six blocks up, and Linus thought about getting binoculars, learning semaphore, and making a connection with other restless people. The lights went out, and Linus lit a joint. He considered taking up running, becoming lean and hungry—running ten miles before most of the city was even awake. There was probably a running club that met at 3 a.m.; this was New York, after all. Too obsessive, he decided. An activity for recovering substance abusers. The joint went out and he relit it. Maybe he should take these early morning hours to find Joy. She might have a baby by now. It could be fun to check in and see how her life as a Jewish wife was working out. He imagined catching her in the middle of frying matzo brei, a squalling kid in her arms. Then what? he wondered. Would he jump out from behind a door, take a snap shot, and run away? "Lame-o," Linus said out loud, imitating a suburban teenager's bored inflection. "I need a real project."

He picked up the three rocks sitting on his desk. I need a project with heft, he thought. He tossed his rock from Ellis Island into a bowl of tomatoes on the dining room table, and then the rock from Crete. He kept hold of the one from Armenia; my anchor, he thought. "Hyestan," he said, using the Armenian word for the country in which he was born. "Hyestan," he repeated, trying to *feel* Armenian, imagining a tourist board campaign: *Buy a rug. Watch some folk dancing. Go on, feel Hyestan!* He bounced the rock in his left hand.

What was Armenia, anyway? A piece of real estate run over by Romans, Persians, Sassanids, Byzantines, Mongols, Tartars, Seljiks, and Ottomoan Turks. "And don't forget the Russians," he said to his reflection in the window.

Linus remembered the nights loading the truck with stolen religious art. He remembered holding the stone hand of St. Thaddeus, the apostle who had brought the Church to the Armenian corner of the world. *That* was an Armenian Moment, he thought. My big A.M.

The hand of Thaddeus had been heavy and poorly sculpted, more like a swollen knob. Dull-mottled brown, black, and gray, the size of a human heart. Lumpy and old was what Linus had thought when, over three decades ago, he had grabbed its knuckles with his fingers, his hands forming a protective flesh envelope around it. He was so anxious to steal that hand that he never saw the frozen puddle before slipping and falling on the slaughterhouse floor. His ankle was sprained, and John had to finish loading the truck alone while Linus moaned in the corner, never letting the stone hand go.

Lumpy and old. Laughable and comfortable, Linus thought. He knew it was just second-rate religious art, but he missed it anyway. "It was my Armenian hand," he said. Linus closed his fingers around the rock from Armenia, and he heaved it across the room, knocking his new carbon-fiber bicycle helmet off the coffee table.

He licked his fingers to put out the joint. The ash hissed, and he suddenly knew what his next project must be. He'd find the stone hand of Thaddeus, that sculpted mitt of the saint that had nailed him to the floor of the old slaughterhouse. "Thaddeus, the Great Illuminator," he said to his apartment. John had sold the hand, along with everything else in Crete. "But that hand's mine," Linus said. There'd be Internet searches, e-Bay inquiries, phone calls to galleries and collectors; he'd find that hand and buy it back.

2

"God, what's happening to your body now?" Nick mumbled as he got out of bed, throwing off the soaked blankets. "You wet the bed."

Joy held her belly, waiting. Was this a cramp, a contraction, or a kick? Should she be worrying? There it was again. She tried doubling up, but she was too big in the middle.

"I think that's my water," she said to Nick, grabbing onto the nightstand to lift herself up. Nick stood in the doorway with a pile of clean sheets. It took him several seconds to say, "Oh, your water."

It was 5 a.m., January 9. Two weeks before Joy's due date, the first day of principal photography of *Bound Lover*.

The movie's location manager was already at the coffee shop across from the day's first location—a laundromat in Brooklyn. A grip truck came around the corner, and the location manager went outside to wave him to the parking spaces blocked off with orange cones.

"I think that's one of your trucks," Nick said as they crossed Atlantic Avenue. Joy didn't answer.

"Joy?" Nick said.

Joy looked at him, and Nick could see that she was confused. He knew that she didn't really know who he was at that moment. He smiled at her, and she laid her head back on the seat, staring at the Saab's ceiling.

"I won't be fat anymore," she said.

Nick sat next to the bed and stared at his sleeping wife and daughter, Sydney. His daughter's face was blotchy from the exertion of being born, his wife's pale and oily. He lifted up the sheet to look at Joy's body. She was wearing a new nightgown bought especially for her stay in the hospital, and Nick saw no trace of what he remembered were buckets of blood. He put the sheet back down, lowered his head, and prayed to give thanks that the birth had gone well, for mother and baby. He mouthed the words in Hebrew. After almost two years of classes twice a week, he wasn't half bad.

He waited to be washed in big emotions—the miracle of birth, the continuity of history. But pleased and relieved were as deep as he could get. He wanted Joy to wake up and take his hand. He needed her to see him praying. If she could see him like this, then he was sure he'd feel those big emotions.

When Joy woke up, Nick was sleeping in the bedside chair. The room was dim, the afternoon light cut off by the high-rise at the end of the block. Joy listened to Nick's steady breathing and to the nurses at the far end of the wing. A woman set a potted ficus tree onto the fire escape of a building across the airshaft.

Sydney stirred, and Joy lay very still. She couldn't wake up. Not yet. What would she do when her daughter started crying? She was too tired to face her. The ficus tree blew over in the wind gusting down the gangway. Its root ball stuck up in the air like a bare rear end. There was another gust, and the whole tree rolled off the ledge.

Joy had held back from telling Linus about Nick, determined to use the news about her relationship for its optimal effect.

Their sessions got quieter and quieter, with Joy choosing to spend more and more of her time staring at the upper branches of the tree outside Linus's office. She liked that from her angle on the couch she could see only the tree and the sky and nothing of Park Avenue around it. Sometimes she heard Linus crossing his leg. Once she heard him put down his notebook. She listened closely, but she never heard him pick it back up again. One day she dozed. Then, just before what would become her last session, she did a home pregnancy test in the ladies' room down the hall from his office. Negative, and she cried.

Joy was silent for forty minutes of that session. She stared at the tree outside Linus's window, imagining herself as a scrap of paper. She was a densely written note, so tightly folded that the paper was a hard morsel, no bigger than a chewing-gum wrapper. The note's words were folded on top of each other, all meaning lost in the paper's folds. She stretched on the couch, feeling every skin cell pulling taut. Her skin was the paper, and the note was finally unfolding. Her old mantra about becoming a First Lady as elegant as Jackie Kennedy seemed silly in the face of her real circumstances: she was mated, and she was a real producer. She told herself to not get too upset about one negative HPT. They had only just started trying. She had bought six tests. Take that, Dr. Linus Kezian, she thought.

A man with a chainsaw rode a lift to the tree's upper branches, his orange hard hat a stain in the sky. He yanked on the starter and went for a bare branch. There was a crack, and the branch fell to leave a raw stub. Joy sat up and spun to face Linus.

"I know your niece is, was—whatever—involved with Peter Koehl. I know that she's going to be a big director and has a deal with Beth Meisner and that she's going to make a movie using a script you wrote. You're not the only person who knows everything," Joy said in one breath.

Linus smiled, and Joy wondered if he was proud of himself. For what? For keeping his secrets from her? For being a know-it-all? For getting his first screenplay produced?

"I've been having sex with Nick Gorelich, who you said would never be interested in me. I've moved into his apartment in Brooklyn, and we're getting married by his friend, the rabbi of his temple," Joy said. "I'm going to get pregnant."

Joy had always imagined Linus's face going from distant to respectful, maybe even awestruck by this news, but his expression never changed. She got up and put on her coat.

"This is our last session," she said.

She hated him. She wondered why she had ever even started seeing him. She was too open and free with herself. No one should ever know as much about me as he does, she thought.

"Does this mean that you're giving up your apartment?" Linus asked.

Sydney settled, her head rolling to the side.

"Hi," Nick whispered from the chair.

"She looks like my mother," Joy whispered.

Nick studied his daughter's face more closely. "A little," he said.

"Did you call her?"

"She wants to come out next month, but I think she really wants you to come out there for vacation after the movie."

The phone call had been the first time Nick had spoken to his mother-in-law since calling her a self-hating Jew because she had ordered shrimp from Chinese takeout. "My Joy *loves* shrimp," Joy's mother said. "Where do you think she comes from, the shetl?" She went back to Coronado Del Mar two days early.

"She wanted to make sure that you had used an epidural. She said that nothing good comes from pain," Nick said.

Maybe it was the pregnancy hormones, but Joy felt her mother slipping into the comfortable general category of "someone I know." She was someone with whom Joy used to play tennis at the club.

"Did Peter call?" Joy whispered.

"No."

"Good," Joy said. That meant everything was under control.

"They sent that," Nick said, pointing at a massive flower arrangement, its sunflower larger than his daughter's head.

"Nick, it's a really stupid script," Joy said, staring at her daughter's swirl of red hair. It felt good to admit the truth. She was a mother. She had a husband. She had to be brave and admit that she had committed herself to making a piece-of-shit movie.

"It won't be the first stupid movie. It might actually make some money," Nick said.

"That won't be a first, either."

"There was so much blood," Nick said. "At first I thought that she was just a big blood clot. Were you scared?"

Joy shook her head. She had never been scared. She couldn't even remember if it hurt although she did remember asking for drugs but by that time it was too late, and she wound up doing the whole thing drug-free. He put his finger on her lips, and she slid it into her mouth and closed her eyes. Sydney stirred, and Nick took his finger out.

"It's okay," Joy whispered, taking Nick's finger in her mouth again.

"Is this all I am to you?" he whispered.

"Yes."

Nick had read enough about being a new father to know that he might feel jealous of the baby, that sexually things might be disrupted. Maybe he'd have to start seeing the Nigerian from time to time. He had seen her only twice during the last few months of the pregnancy, but with the baby around maybe he'd need her more.

Joy opened her nightgown and slid the baby to the dark nipple.

"The nurse said to wait until she came in before you tried feeding," Nick said, staring at the nipple, rubbing his finger over Joy's lips.

Joy knew that Sydney would have no problem feeding. There wouldn't yet be any real milk, but she knew that Sydney wanted to suck.

"Kiss me," Joy said as Sydney latched on to her.

Sydney stopped sucking. Joy's breath caught. Shit, she's going to cry, Joy thought. And Sydney did.

3

*P*eter was in the set's portable toilet throwing up for the second time in six hours. He pressed the button on the electric flush and washed his face in the tiny sink. Did the crew think he kept going to the toilet to snort lines like other directors they had worked with? he wondered. Did they think he had intestinal problems? Both, probably, he thought. Why did Joy have to have her baby *today*? Today was not the day to have a baby. Why couldn't she have induced labor two weeks ago? A *serious* producer would have induced labor. He had shot a half page. He had four more pages to finish today, and it was already one o'clock. His producer should be here for him.

Peter pushed his way out of the toilet and onto the street. The sky was bright blue. Why the fuck are we shooting in a laundromat today? he thought. Why the fuck had the assistant director scheduled the laundromat on a day when they should be taking advantage of the beautiful weather? This was the kind of day that he needed for the scene when the couple finally gets together and spends a happy New York day: shopping, coffee, lunch. A day culminating in fantastic sex.

"Sally, I think we should expand their walk and talk and get it today. This light is amazing," Peter said to his assistant director, a short, thick woman wearing a headset and a bulky jacket with a lot of pockets.

Sally had been the assistant to eight first-time directors. Although none of them had gone on to direct a second film, Sally had never stopped working. She was known as the assistant director who could bring a first-timer in on schedule and on budget. Her boy-friend told her that *she* should be directing, not those bozos, but Sally kept taking the jobs, because she liked being the hero. She liked how the producers complained to her about the director. She liked how she and the producers made up code names for the problem direc-tor and how, by the end of production, they could share jokes that were too complicated to explain if you weren't part of the inner circle. Sally liked being in the "us against him" club. This was only the first day of shooting, but after weeks of preproduction, Sally already had two official nicknames for Peter: the Confused Prince and the Fly Catcher.

"Peter, you wanted to try to shoot in at least an approximation of script order. That's why we're here. Plus, I don't have Alex until five, and he's not on call because he did that guest spot last night," Sally said. "This isn't a doc, you know."

It was the ultimate cut-down-to-size remark. *This isn't a doc.*

"We could send off a team to get some shots—street stuff," Peter tried.

"Where's the street stuff in the script?" she asked.

"I'll find a place for it. New York looks incredible today."

"You start throwing beauty shots that aren't scripted into dai-lies, and the studio will shit."

Peter knew enough to know that she was right.

"When Joy gets back we can talk about additional shots and a second unit. Maybe she can finesse it," Sally said.

"The light won't be the same when she gets back."

Sally touched her headset and listened to an incoming message, her eyes staring into the middle distance over Peter's shoulder.

It was the first day of shooting. Peter knew it wasn't the right time to start demanding second units or schedule changes. He should wait for Joy to do that. That's what a professional would do. What he needed to do now was concentrate on the next shot: a pull-back from the dryer as Julie bends down to open it.

"Copy that," Sally said into the walkie-talkie. "I'll go get Julie. She's ready for her walk-through," Sally said to Peter.

"Great," Peter said brightly.

Sally walked ahead of Julie, clearing the way of crewmembers so that the star could have the open, "safe" space she had demanded during preproduction meetings.

"Julie's here," Sally said quietly in Peter's ear as he watched the video playback of the last setup.

Peter looked up at his leading lady, and Sally was impressed. The Confused Prince's face changed on a dime, his attention becoming a bright spotlight that could only make Julie feel like the most loved and special woman in the world. Even with the sucky script, this kind of attention might get his B-level television actress to give more than she had ever given. It might be enough to allow Peter to direct a second picture. The Fly Catcher just might have a future, Sally thought.

Peter put his hand lightly on Julie's back. "Your look at the end of the last shot says it all. You're so comfortable in your skin that you have no idea how beautiful you look," Peter said.

Julie smiled.

"Don't tell me I'm beautiful," she said, putting her hand on his arm.

"Ever?"

"Ever."

4

$\mathcal{I}$n Los Angeles, Liv Johansson was pulling herself out of her director's chair to meet her assistant director at the back of the camera truck.

"We're going to start losing light, so I say we shoot out this whole angle, and then turn around and do the rest up against the house. We have to finish scene 16 today," the assistant director said, running his hands through his shoulder-length hair.

"She's freaking out," Liv said.

"I know that. But sometimes you got to say, 'Hey, you're making three million dollars. Deal with it.'"

"Where's Beth?"

"Talking with Germany."

"Shit," Liv said, taking off for Beth's trailer.

Everyone on the crew had been trained to know that *nothing* could ever interfere with Beth's calls to Germany, even though Beth claimed that *nothing* would please her more than hanging up on the FGs—the Fucking Germans.

Liv had only talked to the FGs once—a conference call about upping the budget to include more days with the camera crane. The main FG was Arno. He pronounced his R's too softly, interrupting Liv to say, "But you said you had enough cwane days."

Liv knew she was behaving badly, but she shouted into the speaker, "Ahno, things change. Now I'm saying I need more cwane days. Roll, I mean Woll, with it." She stormed out of the office, slamming the door behind her so Arno could hear her exit.

Later, Beth told Liv, "You can't break trust with financiers. Arno thinks you're very hard, and he doesn't like hard."

Liv wondered if Beth had any idea how lame "break trust with financiers" sounded. "But did we get more crane time?" Liv asked.

"Yes we did, but don't push it," Beth said. "I can't keep running interference for you."

That was the first time Liv imagined slapping Beth.

Liv stepped up onto Beth's trailer's stairs, a twinge in her thigh. She heard the chirp of Beth hanging up the cell phone, and Liv held on to the doorframe to pull herself into the dim trailer.

"You've got to help me with her," Liv said.

"She hates me."

"Yeah, she does. So let's use that. I think it's time for the principal to be stern with the naughty student."

Beth picked at her new manicure.

"You've got to say, 'Kim, you're getting paid three million dollars and that's all the motivation you need to do the next scene,'" Liv instructed.

"Why can't you just complete the scene she was doing this morning? She's in the mood. Shouldn't we milk it?"

Liv sagged. Yes, of course they should "milk" the actress's mood, but that wasn't the only factor in production. Why did she, the *director*, have to explain the demands of production to Beth, the *producer*? Why was it that her producer didn't seem to understand that production was scheduled around things like light, actors' schedules, union contracts, and rules imposed by the owners of the locations in which they were shooting? Beth had become the FP. The Fucking Producer.

"Because it would add a day, which we can't afford. That's why we can't 'milk' Kim's mood," Liv said, trying, but failing, to not sound bitchy.

"But we don't have a day," Beth said with a small voice.

Liv looked to see if Beth was smiling. This couldn't be serious, could it? Surely Beth's ridiculous comment was part of some trippy, anarchic Marx Brothers' logic.

Beth didn't smile.

Oh my God, Liv thought. Beth really is an idiot. Liv poured herself coffee from the kitchenette's coffee maker.

"It's cold," Beth said.

In the months leading up to production, Liv presented herself as if she and Beth were creative partners. Beth controlled the money, and Liv understood that it was in her best interest to act as if Beth was an equal. In preproduction, this act was fairly easy to maintain. Vague concepts and metaphors about film and "storytelling" could be thrown around with the only consequence being Beth's excited and flushed look, which was exactly what Liv wanted. But now, in the grind of production, the act was too hard to keep up. Beth could make deals; Liv would hand her that. But make a movie? Not really. Light, action, point of view, emotional beats and logic, continuity, color, visual coherence, a reasonable number of shots per day, meal penalties and overtime incurred by a lagging grip and electrical crew, rain days, actors with colds, a set that wasn't ready in time: concrete details overwhelmed Beth. And in production, it was these details, not concepts, metaphors, and passion, that constituted "creative."

Beth wasn't going to Kim's trailer to convince the star that she should be a trooper, not a diva. Liv knew that Beth was *never* going to Kim's trailer, for Beth was nothing more than a mouthpiece for a cabal of German investors.

"Shit," Liv said, taking the first step out the trailer door. Fucking socket joint, she thought, feeling her hip twinge with pain.

"Liv, you're the director. You're supposed to deal with the actors, and you're excellent at it," Beth said, defensive because she thought Liv's "Shit" had been directed at her.

I'm the one with the point of view. I'm the proactive one. I'm the reason anyone's even on this movie set, Liv thought. I'm the creative force at the helm of this ship, and my FP is dead weight. Demonizing Beth Meisner boosted Liv's waning strength.

"You don't know what pricks these German fuckers are," Beth said, and then went on to insist how Liv should be grateful that Beth protected her from the Krauts.

Liv turned sideways and slipped her foot down the last six inches between the trailer and the ground.

"You're not used to dealing with men like them. You've got the protective bubble of your father and your uncle. I'm the one who grew up with a pig for a father, so I'm the one who ends up equipped to deal with these FGs."

Liv knew Beth was right; Liv was indeed the lucky one, here.

"You should know how lucky you are to have it so easy with men."

"Yeah, yeah," Liv said quietly. Now Beth was onto something else—a refrain she had been chiming since preproduction when she finally understood that Liv was promiscuous.

"How many men have you slept with?" Beth had asked in the first week of shooting when she saw Liv arrive on the set with Michael, the director of photography.

"In my life?"

"No, since we got to Los Angeles."

"I don't know. Three."

"Three different men in eight weeks?"

"Yeah."

"You're amazing."

Liv could tell from Beth's face that it wasn't amazing good, but amazing "weird"—distaste being mixed with jealousy.

"What can I say, I'm a slut," Liv had said, going for a laugh. She would never tell Beth that the night before she had been with Michael *and* Cody, the craft service guy with whom she had been sleeping since the first production meeting. Cody was 19. Michael was 42.

Cody had left the house at five that morning to be on set by six with the coffee. Liv came to the set later with Michael, who asked if they could do it again, but maybe not with Cody.

"You didn't like it," Liv said.

"I didn't say that."

"It freaked you out."

"A little."

"You thought I liked it too much, right?" Liv asked and Michael nodded. "You know, I'm not a whore because I fuck a lot," Liv said, choosing the words "whore" and "fuck" to make Michael feel shitty about the judgments he was making.

"I know," Michael said.

"Okay, we can do it alone sometime," Liv said. Why complicate her life with two men while she was shooting? she thought.

Cody had nodded and kissed Liv on the forehead when she told him that she and Michael were going to try to work something out. Liv said that she still wanted Cody to come to the house on the weekends to watch tapes of the week's dailies. "You're the only one who has an overview. I swear you're the only one who knows how this thing should be shot," she had insisted. This was real, not just something said to make Cody feel better.

"You're doing an incredible job," Beth called from inside the trailer—the collegial producer.

"Fuck you," Liv muttered.

The caterers were closing up the kitchen from lunch, the folding chairs tipped up against the long tables. Cody was laying cut vegetables and egg salad sandwiches for the afternoon snack on his craft service table. When he saw Liv, he reached into a cooler and brought out a plate of yogurt and honey.

"I can't eat it now. Save it for me," she said.

"What's going on?"

"I've got to go talk to our leading lady, and I'm tense," Liv said, wondering if Cody ever got tense.

"You should be more like the Cody Man."

"I know. You should bottle some of that 'Cody Man' stuff; you could make a fortune."

It had been a mistake to have chosen Michael over Cody. Choosing a director of photography over the craft service guy was too obvious and, with Michael's endless digressions about his ex-wife, so boring.

As she approached Kim's trailer, Liv relaxed her face to look more like the Cody Man. A little vacant. Slightly stoned. Happy, never manic. She felt her hip sag again. Only a couple more weeks of shooting. After that, she could replace the whole goddamn joint, or even sit in a wheelchair the rest of her life—whatever. She'd have the production office send a masseuse to her house tonight after dailies.

"I know what you're going to ask, and I'm fucking sick of it," Kim said, her voice shrill, on the verge of a shriek. The kind of voice that comes before a woman throws a plate at the wall above her lover's head. It was the voice she had used in the last shot.

"What can I say? I have to finish the scene today. You want to finish the scene, don't you?" Liv asked.

"Of course I do, but I want to get it right. If that means taking an extra day. Fuck it."

"We don't have an extra day, Kim."

"We have a day. The studio just says you don't," Kim said, her voice lowering. "You're a first-time director, so they think they can intimidate you." She held out a cigarette to Liv.

Liv suspected that Kim was probably right about the studio, but wasn't sure what to do about it. Call their bluff and go over schedule anyway? Liv took the cigarette. Kim would acquiesce more quickly if she had someone to smoke with.

"I think you can do it, Kim. I really do. You've nailed the scene. You could do *Singing in the Rain* now and still come back to the place you got to before lunch," Liv said, looking Kim straight in her trademark huge green eyes.

"You think so?"

Liv wondered how Kim could be so sharp one minute and then so gullible to Liv's half-baked compliment the next. She should be sent to a place where they pound suspicion into her brain, Liv thought. A reeducation camp.

"I know you can," Liv said. "I'll let you run the shot long, so you can build. Liv thought about how she'd let Kim do the entire scene in this one shot to give her the opportunity to build to her emotional climax. In editing, Liv knew she'd only use the thirty seconds of the emotional high point, but Kim needed to feel that her director was respecting her process. "You have your process, and I respect that," Liv said.

"Thanks, but I don't want Michael watching."

Liv waited to see the flicker of the joke on Kim's face. Nothing.

"Kim, he's the director of photography," Liv said. "He's paid to watch."

"I don't care. I heard what he said," Kim said.

"He said you were stunning."

"He said that for such a babe, I sure had dark circles in the morning."

Liv put out the cigarette. She squirted some of Kim's SPF 60 into her palm and rubbed it on her nose.

"Kim, Kim, Kim. Didn't anyone ever tell you that men are pricks? They look like shit. Their hair's a mess. They have fucking food in their teeth. Their guts spill over their pants and their shirts are torn. But we, us women, have to look good at all times," Liv's voice was getting louder. "Fuck that, Kim. I say fuck that. I want you to tell Michael that he smells. I mean it." Liv was shouting.

"Shh, he'll hear you," Kim whispered.

"So what? You heard *him*. He shouldn't be able to get away with that shit," Liv screamed.

At the end of the day, while Liv was waiting in the backseat of her car for her driver, Michael leaned into the window and asked her if he really smelled.

"Sometimes."

"Do you want me to come over?"

Liv shook her head. Tonight was reserved for her hip.

5

$\mathscr{I}$t wasn't the socket joint. It was something that needed an MRI. Liv made an appointment for two days after the last day of shooting. The lady at the imaging center told Liv to bring a CD. Music, it seemed, was important during an MRI.

The film's music supervisor gave Liv seventy-five CDs. Reggae, hip-hop, French baroque, bluegrass, west coast jazz, indie guitar rock, Bollywood soundtracks, and more.

The house the production company had rented for Liv was in the hills above Sunset Boulevard. Two thousand square feet. Ten thousand dollars a month. Post and beam, cantilevered out over the hill. A courtyard that a maid swept twice a week, a pergola, teak patio furniture. Furnished down to the special long matches to light the fireplace, a stocked bar, a full rack of wine, a 10-CD player.

Liv started listening to the CDs at lunch. At midnight she was still listening, two bottles of Bordeaux, empty. She put a CD on repeat and built a fire in the fireplace, using old call sheets and scripts for kindling.

It looks like a coffin, but it's just a tube that hums, Liv thought, imaging the MRI machine. You've seen people shot, but you lived. You're lucky. You're alive. Don't even *think* the word "coffin," Liv told herself. The CD was a woman's choir. Language unknown. Complicated ululations and clapping.

Yasser sniffed Liv's mouth and then stretched out along Liv's side.

"I ate dog," Liv said to the cat. "But you don't care. You probably think that's a good thing," She was extremely drunk. "But it's not a good thing. Eating a pet is bad."

It's going to be loud, she remembered. Magnetic *resonance* imaging.

"What the fuck is good MRI cancer-screening music?" Liv screamed, heaving a jewel case at the living-room wall. It was 4 a.m.; her appointment was for seven o'clock.

Yasser jumped onto the back of a chair, ready to spring and run if Liv moved again.

Liv wondered if the cowherds had cremated the dead bodies in the pasture. How about Artur? No, Liv thought. Catholic or Muslim, the cowherds would've dug a hole for the bodies. She imagined worms and plant life crawling through the little boy.

Liv sat in a dusty-pink and beige hospital office. A woman had a file opened on her desk; behind her, small porcelain figurines of dogs and angel-like children were lined up on the windowsill. Liv had to work hard to understand what the woman was saying to her. There was a brief history of MRI technology, how long Liv would be in the tube, where the results would be sent.

"Your job today is to relax," the woman said.

The woman's name was Angela, and Liv needed her to slow down.

Liv straightened the cancer informational brochures on Angela's desk and put them in the empty Plexiglas brochure holder.

"Since you didn't bring your own CD, you can choose from one of ours." Angela said, pointing at a CD shelf.

Liv told Angela that they had used the same shelf on the set of her movie. "But it got in the way of every shot, so the set decorator brought in another one that worked better. The character's a music lover, so we couldn't just yank the CDs out of the set, even though this thing was a pain in the ass, you know?" Liv said, wondering if she should explain to Angela what a set decorator was.

"A lot of film people use this facility," Angela said.

She knows what a set decorator is, Liv thought.

"Most people choose classical. Handel or Bach," Angela said.

Liv turned the desk clock to face into the room. It read 6:45. Her watch read 6:43. Liv used her fingernail to press the tiny button on the back of the clock to adjust the minutes.

"We have some New Age music too," Angela said.

Liv's watch and the desk clock changed to 6:44 at exactly the same moment. "Please don't make me decide," Liv said quietly.

Angela took Handel's *Water Music* from the shelf and opened the case to make sure there was a disc inside. She had nice hands. Coral pink with long fingers. No nail polish. No rings. The pinky finger stuck out delicately.

"My luck isn't holding. It's not holding," Liv whispered.

"What?" Angela said.

"Would you hold my hand?"

Angela opened her mouth and then closed it. She placed Liv's hand between her hands as if she were trying to reverse frostbite. Angela's hands were slightly moist and warm. Like a pod, Liv thought.

"Are you ready?"

Liv looked up. The clock turned to 7:00.

They gave her Valium, and she liked how the orderly or technician, or whatever he was, wrapped her gown around her and pushed the hair from her face. He's so nice, Liv thought. Just like Angela.

"What's your name?" Liv asked.

"Josh," he said.

"It should be Angelo," she said.

Liv didn't have to close her eyes, but she did. She heard a clicking sound. Hard soles on tile. Who was coming? she wondered, imagining a man in dress shoes walking up the MRI tube. She opened her jaw wide, and there was a crack behind her ear.

"Keep still, now," a woman said over the intercom, and Liv steadied herself. Lie like a baby, she thought. She heard rain now, and Liv thought how nice it was to be in a warm tube when it's raining. I'm hallucinating, Liv thought.

The blanket made her cheeks hot. But I don't have a blanket, Liv corrected herself. I'm wearing a hospital gown. I got Valium, but no blanket. The clicking came back. Maybe there's a flamenco dancer in here with me, Liv thought.

"You don't have to hold your breath, but keep yourself as still as possible. No talking. No singing. Here we go," the woman said.

The first movement came over the speakers. The loud banging began.

This isn't so bad, Liv thought. There was music, banging, a hallucinated blanket, clicking heels, and rain. Orange clouds began swirling behind her eyelids and then she saw psychedelic cows in pinks and greens. Artur's hair had been in her mouth when she carried him. Could a dead boy remember her hair? *Mitt golv*, Liv mouthed, wondering why she was remembering two Swedish words, and how many milligrams of Valium they had given her. "*Mitt golv*," she heard a woman on a Swedish floor-cleaning commercial squeal.

It was non-Hodgkin's lymphoma. Caught early. An indolent tumor. Low grade. Some prefer to keep to normal routines. Others want to go on vacation or spend time on a hobby. Did Liv have a hobby? Liv remembered everything that Sandra, her oncologist, told her as bullet points.

Sparkle Life

Liv was one of those patients who wanted to disrupt the normal rhythms as little as possible. Chemo for eight to ten weeks if Liv could tolerate cytotoxic drugs, and there was every reason to believe she could since she was in such good health. Prognosis: good on a scale that went from poor to excellent. The bullet points were piling up. Reproduction would no longer be a possibility.

6

"$\mathcal{I}$was in orange clouds, but it was a tube," Liv was shouting into the phone. "It was loud, but I heard rain." She had taken two Ativan with a martini and had been speed dialing her father for three hours. She couldn't feel her lips.

"Talk slower. The connection's bad," John shouted. He had just turned the phone back on after a four-hour meeting in New Jersey with his architect and general contractor, recently back from Spitak where the church was nearing completion—three months late.

John was concerned about what were becoming near-daily protests by the local building trades over what they saw as the project's overreliance on German equipment. John didn't want the protesters to sniff out his other project—the Sparkle Life factory, up and running for six months now. It would be disastrous if the protestors found out just how much profit John was making at the new factory.

"It was weird, but I remembered a stupid Swedish commercial," Liv said. "I understood Swedish. *Mitt golv*, my floor. Can you hear me?"

"Yes, but there's an echo," John said.

It was raining and dark in New York. The barometric pressure had forced a headache behind his eyes, and he smelled the highway's diesel fumes even inside the Range Rover. The shiny Exxon tanker truck ahead of him sped up and then braked. John was too close to the truck's back bumper.

"I have cancer," Liv shouted.

John's thighs got hot. He smelled something like burning hair. The tanker's emergency flashers started blinking, and John pumped his brakes. There were concrete K-rails to his left, a United Van Line truck to his right. The guy behind him was in a pickup, leafing through a magazine.

"I'm coming out there," he yelled into the phone.

The phone connection was disturbed by what sounded like metal rods dropping into an empty swimming pool.

"Daddy?" Liv said. The signal was gone.

John eased over to the narrow shoulder. He opened his door, smashing it into a K-rail. Diesel and moisture. The roar of cars and trucks moving no faster than fifteen miles per hour. John dropped to his knees and touched his head to the concrete. He watched the traffic move from under his car. An oil spot swelled as tires smashed it. He heard growling and a gasp for air. He kept his forehead on the ground, and he saw his butt riding up like a Muslim man at prayer. The highway lights flickered on, and he pictured how the light must be gleaming on his bald spot.

Then John found himself in Chelsea, standing at a table where his brother sat reading *The Principles of Physical Geology*. Was Linus interested in rocks? When had that started?

"Sit down. I ordered oysters," Linus said.

"It's the wrong month."

"No, it's not," Linus said. And then he jumped up, his arm out to catch his brother. "Whoa, there. Steady. You okay?"

John shook his head and grabbed Linus's hand. It felt so different from the last time he had held it. When was that? How long had it been since they had touched each other? "Liv has cancer," John said.

Linus tried to pull away, but John tightened his grip. John touched the cross around his neck, lowered his head, and prayed. A waiter put a plate of fines de claire on the table.

7

*N*aim was pacing, coming down hard on his heels—deliberately, Sara thought—aiming for the parquet. "You fucking Jews are always showing off. You buy another sofa. Why? To impress people. Look at me, here with you and then out working for an Israeli peacock who buys five hundred dollar shoes. And where does he wear them? To clubs where it's so dark, you can only see his head. He could wear the shoeboxes, and no one would notice. You people just consume. You consume land, people, things."

"And water. Don't forget how much water we consume, while Palestinians are stuck licking dripping pipes," Sara yelled as Naim disappeared into the bedroom.

"Where are my gray pants?" Naim shouted.

"Hanging in the closet. I'm not Jewish. It's just my mother."

"Don't keep saying that. You're Jewish. I know Jewish law," he said, coming into the kitchen, buttoning the shirt her mother had given him for Christmas, his pants draped over his shoulder.

"Do these go together?" he asked, pointing to the pants and the shirt.

Sara nodded. "Look, if you don't want to do the party, don't do it," Sara said.

Naim had become a karaoke DJ, playing mainly Arab and Indian weddings in New Jersey, for Jules, an Israeli who wore five hundred dollar shoes. Life had turned out ridiculous. No wonder he yells, Sara thought.

"I have to do it," Naim said.

"Did you tell Jules about the disc player?" Sara asked.

"Yeah. I had a big talk with him. I told him about expanding the stock. Do you know we don't even have 'Rock the Kasbah'? People always want 'Rock the Kasbah,'" Naim said. "How much did the fucking sofa cost, anyway?" he asked.

"My mother bought it for us."

Naim stopped, smiled, and put on his pants. "I'm an idiot," he said.

"Yep," Sara said.

"Do you work tonight?" he asked.

"Not tonight," Sara answered.

To make extra money while getting her teaching credentials, Sara had taken a restaurant job, which she still had, even after nearly a semester teaching in a Bronx high school. Now, most days, from five until ten, or whenever the last customer left, she waitressed, and from ten until midnight, she sat in bed with papers and lesson plans. She had lost fifteen pounds, and her ankles were starting to swell. The sixty-hour-a-week schedule was the only thing keeping her off antidepressants.

"The party's in Short Hills," Naim said.

Now Sara understood why today's panic attack had been worse than usual; Naim was going to do a Jewish party.

"You're going to fit right in," she said.

"That's what Jules said," Naim said. "You know what I found out? He has other equipment for Jewish parties. Really. There's a whole separate storage space for it. The equipment's all new. There's a better van to haul it, too," he said.

"Fucking Jews," Sara said.

Naim kissed her. Did Naim know she was kidding about the "fucking Jews" thing? Sara wondered. This was the intermarriage, cross-cultural gray zone, and she would never know for sure.

She waited until he was out the door before going back to the lesson plan. *Catcher in the Rye.*

Sara stood absolutely still at the front of the classroom, waiting for her thirty-three students to sit down. "Sit down," she had said three minutes ago, before freezing herself into this ramrod position, her eyes theatrically fixed on the wall clock. They did this every day—her students and Sara. The students stole every second they could away from their desks. And Sara let them, up to three minutes. Sometimes she sent the students who wouldn't settle out of the room, but most of the students had their internal clock set and were seated in three minutes. Sara knew that within twenty minutes many of the fidgety students would be dozing, their heads in their hands, sometimes buried in crossed arms on their desks.

"When have we seen other walks like Holden Caulfield's?" Sara asked, breaking her stillness with a step.

She could almost see the question suspended over the students, and she knew that in their heads they were hissing: *Why can't you just tell us the answer? Why make us suffer? Hasn't someone already done the interpretation? Movie previews tell us everything, so where do you get off making us guess? Suffering doesn't help us, can't you see that? Why bother? Aren't you supposed to help us prepare for the real world? Get real.*

"I'm looking for other examples of long walks. They can be from literature or movies or TV. Whatever. When is a walk or a run or even a swim important to a person's development?" Sara was pacing, now.

While Holden was off on his existential adventure, developing and changing, his teachers were stuck back at school, standing in classrooms, facing bored students, Sara realized. She pictured the teachers facing full classrooms, idly noticing that Holden was absent. There was still no response from the class. Sara wasn't surprised, but she was still new enough to teaching to be resentful. No one had told her how boring students could be.

"When characters are troubled, well, when many of us are troubled, a walk is a common antidote," Sara said. "Where have we seen that in other literary works? Lucia?"

Lucia flinched, and Sara stopped walking to stare at her student's braids pulling the scalp taut in at least a hundred points.

"Jesus in the desert."

Cyrus was at the door, holding up his hall pass.

"Jesus in the desert," Sara repeated.

"He was trying to escape the phonies, too," Cyrus said, sitting at a desk near the door. "There he is in Jerusalem, or wherever, with all these followers, and he's saying to himself, what kind of club can this be if *I'm* a member? Like Woody Allen said."

"Actually, it was Groucho Marx," Sara added.

"Oh, yeah?"

Sara nodded. As usual, when Cyrus was in class, "class discussion," was a one-on-one conversation between him and his teacher. When this had happened at the beginning of the year, Sara had tried to include the other students. But that was before she understood that they were as articulate as parsley. Recently, Cyrus has gotten a job on the night shift at Dunkin' Donuts, and he showed up less and less for class. So, now, when he was there, Sara didn't even bother with the pretense of including other students. If they want to act like vegetables, that's their choice, Sara decided. She had a crush on Cyrus.

"So, Jesus is taking time out from the phonies to examine his motives. He's asking himself, 'What is it that I *really* want to do? Do I really want to be a charismatic leader?'" he said, pronouncing charismatic, "chair-is-matic."

"Charismatic," Sara said.

"Oh, yeah?"

Sara nodded. Faulty pronunciation was the price of reading above grade level while always hearing below-grade-level talk.

"So, Jesus was setting something up, and he needed some time away to give the whole thing a long glance. Holden, on the other hand, isn't questioning his motives. He's just reacting," Cyrus said.

"Okay, so project into the future. Holden is now more together; what's he doing?" Sara asked. "Let's say ten years later he's taking another long walk."

"Easy. He's in L.A. He finally gets that he was wrong about his brother D.B. being in Hollywood. The best thing to be is a movie director, because that's the only way you can get the suckers out there to behave. If they don't see it on TV or at the movies, they don't know how to act," Cyrus said, waving his hand across the room, talking about his classmates, the suckers.

8

On the security monitor, Liv watched a Town Car pull up to the house. She was relieved to see that there was a driver: Tommy, the film's transportation captain, in charge of the movie's vehicles and drivers. At least Liv wouldn't have to be alone with Beth in the car. She glanced at the front-hall mirror, checking to see that her under-eye concealer was holding and then let herself out the front door, forcing a smile.

"I think you're so smart to jump right into it. Always stay active and focused, right?" Beth said, making room to share the backseat with Liv.

She's not going to ask how I'm feeling, Liv thought. "Right," Liv said.

"The assembly's almost done, and it's got to be the best assembly I've ever seen, Liv," Beth said as Tommy headed down the hill toward Sunset.

"Yeah, but how many have you seen?" Liv asked. Her throat stung when she swallowed, and she asked Tommy for gum.

Beth turned to the side window. She knew she was overdoing the "sunny outlook" thing. It was way too obvious how much the cancer was scaring her shitless. The truth was that she had little experience with an assembly edit, that early part of the editing process when the editor simply linked up the shots with little thought given to pacing. It was true: Beth had no idea what made an assembly "the best" or shit. She knew she should ask Liv how she was feeling, but she couldn't do it. She was scared, and so she babbled.

They were stuck in a back-up at La Cienega. Liv sunk down in the seat and leaned against the door.

A forty-foot truck stacked with I-beams backed slowly out of a construction site, taking up three lanes. Beth opened her door and got into the front seat next to Tommy.

"Now you can stretch out," Beth said, happy to have the opportunity to show how sensitive she was to Liv's condition, happy to have Tommy as an audience for her empathy.

Liv curled up on the seat and put her hand over her eyes. It was nice in the dark where she could better feel the leather on her cheek and hear the car's engine.

Two Lincoln Continentals had been waiting for Liv, John, and Linus when they arrived from Crete, over three decades ago. One of the cars was for all of their possessions—three trunks and seven suitcases; the other was for the family. Linus sprawled on the backseat. John sat up front with the driver, so he could begin to understand the roads in Manhattan. Liv sat in a jump seat, eating nuts from the bar on the center hump, playing with the electric windows, and watching the luggage-Lincoln trail them.

"I know this car, Tommy," Liv said.

"Oh yeah?"

"Yeah. It used to be called a Lincoln Continental, right?" Liv asked.

"That's right," Tommy said. "JFK was in one when he got shot."

"It's a good car," Liv said before falling asleep at Fairfax.

She woke up on the Hollywood Way off-ramp, 30 minutes later.

Tommy dropped Liv and Beth at the postproduction facility entrance, where Liv managed only ten steps before taking Beth's arm. She was repulsed by its boniness. Where's the muscle tone in this bitch? Liv thought.

Beth smiled at Liv.

If she pats my arm, I'll scream, Liv thought.

Beth patted Liv's arm. Liv didn't scream.

Liv held on to the edge of the editing table to keep herself upright as Brian, the editor, rolled the assembly edit.

"It's too loud," Liv whispered.

"No, it isn't," Beth said.

Kim laughed on the soundtrack, and Liv felt her sinuses reverberate. "It hurts," Liv said. Brian turned down the volume.

Liv fell asleep at minute fifty-three. She woke up at minute seventy-five. At minute ninety-two, she walked out of the editing suite. She heard Beth say, "Pause it."

Liv was almost to the exit door. She could see Tommy smoking a cigarette next to the Town Car.

"What's wrong?" Beth asked, hurrying into the lobby.

Liv leaned her forehead on the glass door. It was only now at this exact moment that Liv finally understood Beth. Producing a picture that could kill the competition in its opening weekend was the foundation of Beth's identity. It was here—only here—where Beth found meaning.

"Get Cody over here," Liv said.

"Oh, Jesus. Is this an addiction with you?" Beth said. "It's okay at night, but we've got work. I have Germany calling me in an hour, and I can't say that my director isn't available, because she's being 'serviced.'"

Liv laughed. Serviced.

"What's so funny?" Beth said.

A palm branch scuttled across the parking lot and got caught in a Range Rover's grill.

"I can't walk more than ten steps without a rest, but you called me a sex addict. That's funny," Liv said. "Please send a car to get Cody."

"The character's not likable," Cody said. "I think you're probably okay with Robert, but we don't really like Brigitte. She's the moral center of the film, and we have to root for her. I think you should reconstruct the performance from the beginning of the second act when Robert first lets her into the warehouse of stolen paintings. You've got the footage," Cody said.

Liv squeezed his hand. She was going to owe him. With money? With a credit? Probably both. "Why don't you and Brian go through the takes?" Liv said.

Brian had been editing for fifteen years, and he knew enough not to raise an eye at any request made by a director. If Liv wanted him to watch the takes with her cocker spaniel, he would. Watching them with her 19-year-old boyfriend, who was also the craft service guy and seemed like a stoner, didn't seem so scandalous.

"Can you start today?" Liv asked Cody.

"Time belongs to the Cody Man," Cody replied.

9

*T*hree days later, Liv watched John and Linus's arrival on her security monitor. Tommy, who had met their plane, let them out of the car. John shaded his eyes and looked up at the sheer cliff wall across the street from her house; Linus pointed to her gate, and the buzzer. She read his lips, "It's here."

Liv hurried through the courtyard, under the pergola, past the teak outdoor furniture and threw herself into John's arms. She couldn't look at his face.

Over her father's shoulder she watched Tommy carry their bags into the courtyard. John's Gucci. Linus's Patagonia. She let John go, and Linus approached, taking her face with his hands to stare into her eyes.

"Are you judging my prognosis, doctor?" she asked.

"Just your beauty, Liv," Linus said. His voice cracked.

Liv was in bed when Cody showed up. She heard her father say, "She's very tired."

"Send him in," Liv called from her room, and Cody appeared at her bedroom door with a bag of cassettes of the takes he thought she should consider for a major scene at the end of the second act. "I brought some pot," he said.

"Maybe it'll make me hungry," she replied.

Cody put in the first cassette and rolled a joint. Scene 52, shot 14. Brigitte was confronting the art thief in his lair/warehouse. It was here where Brigitte, the crack Europol investigator was supposed to face off with the master thief's cunning. It was here where her tough veneer would crack and vulnerability would seep out. Kim had had a hell of a day that day.

"Mark," the camera assistant said on the sound track. The clap sounded, and Liv heard herself say, "Action."

"Look at her face here," Cody said as he lit the joint. Liv froze the image. Kim's eyes were nervous and scared.

Liv let go of the image to let the scene run. She sucked hard at the joint, and Cody handed her a bottle of water. Brigitte was circling Robert, the thief, questioning his motives. Had he ever considered the consequences of his actions?

"Look at her," Cody said. "A perfect lamb to slaughter."

"The girl does do victim well," Liv said.

Linus came into the room and sat at the edge of her bed to watch. Cody handed him the joint. The thief told Brigitte that he hadn't expected an ethics course. He thought he was there to talk money. Linus sucked on the joint. Liv froze the image. "What's the reverse?"

"It's good. He looks cool, and matter of fact. There's nothing telegraphed," Cody said.

Liv let the shot run to the end. John came into the room as Brigitte, still talking, was stepping slowly away from Robert as the camera closed in on them. The shot was designed to make visual their intense but still undeclared and highly inappropriate mutual attraction.

Liv, John, Linus, and Cody watched three hours of takes, and then Cody made sandwiches and found three forgotten chocolate bars at the back of the freezer. John thought the way Kim said "consequences" was sexy, and it made him want to save her. He mimicked her, and he looked like a female impersonator. Linus couldn't stop laughing at John's show, banging his hand against John's shoulder to make him stop.

Cody slept on the couch and was out of the house by eight to be in the editing suite by nine. The list of great takes, good takes, and shit takes was smeared with mustard from their dinner.

The next night Cody called from the freeway on his way home, and John went out for takeout: Mexican from Poquito Mas. At eight, Cody was in the door. By eight-fifteen, a new scene was playing.

10

$\mathscr{F}$or the next four weeks, this was the routine: John ran in the morning, starting with the sharp hill down to the Strip, then an easy lope west into Beverly Hills and sometimes up Wilshire into Westwood. He went to mass at the Church of the Good Shepherd in Beverly Hills. Roman Catholic, not Armenian, but with very clean toilets, which he usually used before heading back into West Hollywood and the grueling run up the hill back home.

Once home, he took a tray to Liv's room where he sat and told her about the people fast-walking and jogging down Sunset, the man who did a Vegas dance routine in the park across from the Beverly Hills Hotel, the guy who waved a "Honk for Peace" sign at the corner of Wilshire and Santa Monica, the kids who sold star maps, and the small vans of tourists prowling Canyon Drive looking for the stars' homes. One day he was sure he had seen Jack Nicholson coming down Benedict Canyon.

I'm scared, so I *prattle*, he thought. What he wanted to do was to shut up and be dead if that was the deal necessary to keep Liv alive.

From lunch until sunset Liv watched the day's light outside her bedroom window—the white haze going to evening pink, then to gray, and then to the glaring street lights on the Strip. She tried to understand the pamphlets and articles that the oncologist had given her to read, about how the cancerous cells express more or different cell surface antigens, and that if the chemo didn't work, they'd try launching monoclonal antibodies into her system so they could attach to these tumor cells and tag them for demolition. Liv pictured a bomb squad blowing up an abandoned suitcase in an airport. Monoclonal antibodies: boom, cancer cells demolished. She thought this image was "positive thinking," an important aspect of the healing process, she had read.

Linus spent his daylight hours at the movies. One day he visited the Writers' Guild of America headquarters, because, with the sale of his script, he was now a member, and he wanted to see what the place was like. The lounge had a coffee urn, a couple of sofas, and three men arguing about when the horses ran at Del Mar. In the late afternoons he came home to sit on the deck overlooking West Hollywood to write his new script on Liv's laptop—a thriller about a misanthropic shrink.

Cody's call from the freeway was the wake-up call to go to work. Shepherding Liv's movie to completion was now a family affair, Cody being the first person to ever be included in what had always been a troika.

Only Mondays were different, because Monday was chemo day, which meant that John and Linus sat on a sofa in the hospital waiting room while Liv sat in a bulky recliner listening to a Discman while the poison flooded in. Cody stayed away.

Tommy picked them up from the hospital, Linus and John sitting up front, Liv sleeping in back. At home, Liv crawled to the bathroom to throw up and sometimes to fall asleep on the tile floor while John held his daughter's hand, and Linus paced the bathroom door.

"I hate this," John whispered to Linus on the fourth chemo day. "Nothing's happening."

"You don't know that," Linus whispered back, squatting on the other side of Liv, who was sleeping soundly on the floor.

"I feel like I'm stuck in a bus station," John said. "It's never going to change. The bus isn't coming."

"It'll change," Linus said. "The chemo could be working."

John looked away from Liv to Linus. When had his brother ever been so encouraging? When had his tone ever been so optimistic?

In the middle of the fifth week, when John reached Liv's gate after his four-mile run, he swung around and went back down the hill. After weeks of running hills, John no longer minced his stride on the declines; he no longer stopped to walk the sharp inclines. He could run from Hustler's World on Sunset Boulevard straight to his daughter's gate in one burst, his heart rate returning to resting in a fast five minutes. In his prayers, John was ready to make the deal: I die; she lives. But the deal was meaningless, for John had never before been so healthy.

The intersection at La Cienega was clogged with a beer delivery truck, a gardener's pickup, and two SUVs squeezing through the light. Guards were emptying a row of bank machines. John bounced up and down, maintaining his run, but after three minutes of no vehicular movement, he stopped, suddenly tired and distracted by the shiny reproduction 1950s diner dominating the area. I'll get Liv ice cream, he thought, knowing he could run fast enough back up the hill to beat its melting. What did she like? Chocolate? Vanilla?

John got himself a vanilla milkshake, still considering what Liv might like. You eat ice cream at the zoo, he thought. Had he ever taken her to the zoo? He remembered Liv feeding peacocks and then realized it was Liv feeding pigeons in front of their building. He squeezed his eyes shut and searched for ice-cream memories. What about picnics? He remembered going to Shakespeare in the park. There had been a picnic basket. Wine. No ice cream.

"Smile, brother." It was a young man in a polo shirt with a stretched-out collar at the next table. *Milk fed* was how John thought the young man looked. "Smiling leads to the Lord," the young man said.

John was Eastern European and then a New Yorker. He talked to strangers only to share whispered cracks about bumbling clerks and inefficient bureaucrats. John scouted the terrace, looking for another table. There were no empty tables.

"I'd like to think, quietly," John said, looking down at the dome of whipped cream on his vanilla shake.

"You can pray anywhere. Sometimes it's good to pray with others." The young man lowered his head.

"Don't do that," John said. His throat stung, bile cutting through the milk.

The young man kept his head bowed.

"I said don't do that." A waitress looked over.

The man looked up at the sky.

"My daughter's dying," John said. "Please leave me alone."

"Then she will be close to God soon," the man said, smiling.

John shoved himself away from his table. He heard his aluminum chair fall and saw his milkshake splat on the ground. He smashed the young man in the face.

The young man curled silently on the cement, and a woman knelt down to help him. John looked dumbly at his fist; it should be bigger, he thought.

There was a scrambling, and John was suddenly aware of people shouting, "Hey, hey!"

John heard his face crack. How can it *crack*? he wondered as he fell to the ground, hitting a chair on his way down, seeing a pigeon fly up out of his way.

The young man stood over John. He punched me, John thought, still incredulous, even after touching his bloody nose.

The woman who had tried to help the young man now kneeled next to John. "Stop it!" she screamed, holding her arms out stiffly, her hands held like traffic cops at John and the young man. "Just stop!"

"Call my brother," John said to the woman.

He managed to make the woman take his cell phone. Speed dial number 1: Linus.

The young man helped John to his feet. "You okay?" the young man asked.

John nodded. "You?"

"Yeah," the young man said. His forehead was bleeding. His cheek was puffy.

John gave the young man all the cash he had on him, seventy-three dollars, because the man said he didn't have insurance. "My brother will have more," John said to the young man.

But when Linus came and offered the young man what was in his wallet—a hundred and twenty—the young man wouldn't take it. "It's okay," he said. He left before the police showed up.

The West Hollywood police came, and John bought them milkshakes. Neither he nor the restaurant wanted to file a report. Since the young man was gone, the officers went away.

There was blood on the pants of the woman who had kneeled to help both the young man and John. He offered to buy her a new pair of pants, and she said, "Sure, why not."

She was Marilyn from New York, in Los Angeles to visit a son. John wanted to go home. It was Liv's lunchtime, and he hadn't yet prepared the tray. Could the drive-in make a fresh salad for him to take to her? She needed her vegetables. Antioxidants. Ice cream was a bad idea. Too processed.

"What happened to you?" Liv asked, when John delivered her lunch tray.

"I got into a fistfight with a born-again Christian," John said, regretting it. It was too flip. He touched his cross.

"Oh yeah?" Liv said. She liked flip. "How'd that happen?"

John tried to remember if he had ever lied to his daughter. There was *not* telling her about closing the factory, but *not* telling something wasn't the same as fabricating an untruth. No, he had never lied in the face of any direct question from Liv. Not when she was 6 and had asked him what Linus was doing with a woman on the kitchen floor at 3 a.m. Not when she had asked about her own conception or about Inga. He had always answered with dispassion: Linus was a libertine. Inga was a drug addict. But to answer the truth now—*I hit a man because he thought it wasn't so awful that you're dying*—that was an obscenity.

"I went nuts. You know how those people press my buttons," John lied.

"That's not what happened," Liv said.

"Yes it is." He insisted. "Your old man's getting funny," he said.

"Don't play the old-age card, dad," Liv said.

"Do you like ice cream?" John asked.

"Not really," Liv said. "You didn't punch the guy because he pressed your buttons. You punched him because of something else. Something about me."

John shrugged.

"I feel really crappy today," Liv said. "I want to blame someone. I mean really lay the blame on thick. I want to put someone on the hook for how I feel, and I feel like shit. I want to hold the Republicans or someone like that responsible."

"Blame the Born Agains," John said. "Go ahead and blame them."

Cody called Liv from the 405 freeway. He had a very rough cut for everyone to look at. It was two hours and fifteen minutes. "Let's have Italian, okay?" he said.

Liv wanted to tell Cody about how her father was getting into brawls. She wanted to say that maybe having family around wasn't the best thing. Maybe the proximity to her cancer was poisoning her father and making him "weird." But Liv knew Cody wouldn't want to hear this stuff. Too messy for the Cody Man.

"Italian's fine, but we eat after the film. I don't want distractions," she said.

Cody made popcorn, and they drank Coke. Liv insisted that no one talk while the rough cut ran. "Can we smoke dope?" Cody asked.

"After, with dinner," Liv said.

John kept an ice pack on his cheek during the screening. Linus made him dissolve a stream of arnica pills under his tongue.

The five of them were quiet for two hours and fifteen minutes.

Linus thought they had lost some of the forger's backstory. Liv thought the movie was moving closer to what it should be; was there too much nudity? Cody already knew how they could cut thirty minutes without even thinking too hard.

"I like how the girl's vulnerable even though she tries to be tough," John said, his face wet from the melting ice.

"Dude, that's exactly the right thing to say," Cody said, wrapping his arms around Liv's father. "Have you rubbed vitamin E cream on this?" Cody was stroking John's face like a father soothing a young son.

Why was Cody all over her father? Liv wondered.

Linus jumped up to get the food. Liv rewound the tape to watch a chase sequence again. Cody went to his car to dig out the vitamin E cream that he was sure was in the glove compartment.

"He's such a nice boy," John said.

"He has his moments," Liv said.

"What does that mean?" John asked.

"It means don't talk about him like he's perfect," Liv said.

Their family unit was three, not four. John and Linus were hers,

Liv thought. Why wasn't her father acting normal and making boundaries clear with Cody?

Cody came back with the vitamin E cream, and when he started to rub it into her father's cheek, Liv reached over and kissed Cody for a long time.

Later that night Liv asked him what she had tasted like.

"Popcorn," he said.

"Not like metal?" she asked.

"No," he said.

"Good, because my mouth tastes like aluminum all the time."

"I think it's going to be a good movie," he said.

"Can you stay here tonight?" she asked. "No sex." She pointed at the bed. "Just sleep."

"Yeah, sure. What's the thing with your father?"

"I told you. He's getting weird. He got into a fight."

"Not that. Between you two," Cody said. "You're curt, and he's nervous."

She didn't like the accuracy of Cody's observation. This was *her* troika. Liv, Linus, John. A troika meant three, not four.

"It's just a father–daughter thing, you know?" Liv said.

Linus went to his room. Liv and Cody closed her door. John walked through the living room, out onto the deck and then back through the dining area. He dissolved more arnica under his tongue. He lit the roach he saw in the ashtray on the hearth and continued pacing the house. It was his first time smoking pot since an afternoon in 1980 with Linus after someone named Gunner had called to say that Inga had died on a layover in Papetee. There was a life insurance policy for Liv that worked out to be $100,000.

John finished the roach. He tried to remember Inga, but all he got was Marilyn, the woman who had helped him that afternoon.

He wondered why Linus liked pot so much. "Marilyn," he said out loud.

Hannah and Her Sisters was in the DVD player, and John fast-forwarded through it, watching New York. All golden light and familiar. Marilyn, he thought. He got to a party scene, and he let the movie play. He watched the couches, the bookshelves, the lamps and paintings in the sisters' family's gracious apartment. He thought about knocking through the far wall of his kitchen, expanding into Liv's room so he could have an island counter area. People would be able to hang around the island, eating crudités and aioli while he prepared dinner. People liked to stand around in the kitchen at parties, John thought. He would hang the wine glass rack he had recently seen in a catalog. Marilyn. She'd be at his dinner parties.

He choked off the fantasy and lowered his head in a prayer. I'm sorry, John told God. I don't want to take over Liv's room, his prayer continued. Liv'll get well, and we'll pack up and go back to New York. Liv lives with her daddy. I can have dinner parties in the kitchen as it is. I don't need Liv's room. I'm so sorry, he repeated to God.

He turned off the movie. A coyote ran across the deck, and he slid the doors shut. He'd send Marilyn a dozen of his street-wear pants to replace the pants with blood on them. "Size eight," he said out loud. "She's a perfect size eight."

The door buzzer woke John. He had slept on the living room's leather couch, the smooth hide a relief against his battered face. The door buzzed again. It was UPS. A package for Linus, from Israel.

It was the hand of Thaddeus, tracked down through Drouot, the French auction house, to a private collector in Tel Aviv. And now it sat on a pile of apples in the fruit bowl as Linus and John ate their cereal.

"How do you feel?" Linus asked, staring at the hand.

"How much?" John asked, staring at the hand.

"Twenty-five thousand euros," Linus said.

"You overpaid," John said, pouring more cereal. "I think the arnica's helping."

"It's not for the church, you know," Linus said. He kept himself from touching it even though all he wanted was to hold the hand under his shirt next to his skin. He imagined eating it. He wanted it *in* him.

"Suit yourself. Keep the stone. It's too small for the church, anyway," John said. "You're a selfish asshole, but you already know that. Think of what twenty-five thousand euros would have meant for the church."

Linus grabbed the stone hand and put it in his lap. "You bought all those saint statues and icons. You've spent a fortune. Fine, it's what you want, so you should have it. But I went out and got this hand back, because I missed it. So what if I spent twenty-five thousand euros? Your church isn't going to miss that. That's small change. This stone makes me happy, okay?" Linus's voice cracked.

"You're not going to cry about this, are you?" John asked.

"I might," Linus said. "You're not the only one with a corner on spirituality." He knew he was going too far. The stone hand had nothing to do with spirituality. What Linus would cry about was having no one in his life—his brother included—who would kiss the top of his head and say, "You're so great, Linus. I love you."

11

*T*he next Monday after chemo, Liv said, "You don't have to all squeeze in front. I don't feel so bad today."

It was the second to last chemo session, and she felt good enough to sit upright, good enough to share the backseat.

The family was superstitious enough not to cheer this first victory in Liv's treatment, and everyone got into the car—Linus and Tommy in front, John and Liv in back—without a word.

"Did I ever tell you that the first car we rode in in America was a Lincoln?" Liv asked Tommy as they pulled out of the hospital parking structure.

"No, you didn't," Tommy said. "You just said that you liked it."

"We love this car, don't we?" Liv asked, looking at her father.

"Yes, we do," John said.

Liv could hear that he was close to crying. She could see that he was holding himself very still, as if too much movement might upset whatever good health she was feeling.

At home, Linus went directly to his room to hold Thaddeus's stone hand. John was right behind him.

"It's the hand, you know," John said. "The hand made her better."

"Maybe," Linus said. "Probably not."

The men stood with their heads bowed, their attention on the lumpy stone sitting on Linus's dresser.

"Yes, the hand made her better. I thought the same thing when we were in the car," Linus said.

"Armenia," John said, touching the stone. "I'm glad you found it."

Linus noticed that John's bruises were fading. His saw that his brother's arm looked more muscled and that his face was lean, his eyes clear. "You know, you look good," Linus said.

"Oh yeah?" John said. "Thanks." He rolled up his pants to show off his calf. Then he undid his pants to show Linus his defined thighs. "I'm getting a six-pack," John said, exposing his torso and abdomen muscles. "It's all the hill work."

"You're cut," Linus said.

They kept the house dim and quiet, all of them acting as if it were like any other chemo day even though it wasn't. Liv never threw up. She ate some lunch, and slept. When she woke up to the sound of the leaf blowers next door, she didn't go back to sleep. Instead, she got up, stretched, and touched her toes. The backs of her legs hurt, and she breathed to make the pain go away. She lifted up and stretched to the ceiling. Her hair had never fallen out. There was still some muscle tone in her arms. She hadn't gagged once today. It was time to start thinking about her next project.

Liv sat on the deck and made a list:

Agent
Linus, script?
Beth. Re: future
Cody, future?

She thought about calling Sandra for her latest counts. She thought about how the operator would ask for her patient I.D. before transferring her to Sandra, who would be busy with another patient. Sandra's nurse would ask Liv if she wanted to hold or leave a message. If she chose "hold," she'd be stuck with the Classic Rock station, and she couldn't face that quite yet.

The leaf blowers stopped, and Liv heard wooden wind chimes clap their hollow sounds. I could write a script, she thought. A love story, maybe. She'd ask Linus to return her laptop. This is what it feels like to feel better, she thought.

There was rustling in the chaparral. Maybe it's a coyote, she thought, leaning over the deck railing. No, not a coyote, Liv thought. Not at this time of day. It's probably rats.

Liv pocketed the to-do list, climbed over the deck rail and jumped down onto the slope.

Unlike in summer and fall when the hillside was dry enough to see the litter of plastic grocery bags and liter soft drink bottles, the brush was now green and thick enough to mask all garbage.

The gardeners at the house below were taking a break. "Exitos, Exitos, Exitos," a radio announcer shouted from their transistor. What am I doing? Liv wondered. Trapping rats? With what? My hands?

The rustling turned out to be a plastic bag caught in the ivy. Liv picked up the bag and saw a dead kitten, no larger than a rat.

She had heard a cat get killed by a coyote two nights ago. Cody had been changing the cassettes when they all heard the scream. "Another one bites the dust," Linus had sung as Yasser pounced on a half-empty carton of sushi.

She leaned close to look for puncture holes. Had this one been the coyote's prey? But there were no holes, no dried blood. No, this kitten had been born dead, Liv realized. Her nose was running. She was crying for the dead cat.

The phone was ringing in the house. Stop crying, she told herself. It's a kitten that had never been alive, period. There are other things to cry about.

She heard her uncle walk onto the deck above her. She heard the computer's boot-up chord as she wrapped the grocery bag around her hand to pick up the stiff corpse. She then heard ice in a glass, and she knew Linus had the laptop on his lap, a Diet Coke on the low table at his side.

What was Linus doing out here in California? Liv wondered. How could he stay away from his patients for so long? Liv tried to remember if she had ever asked her uncle about his life. She knew things about him: his affair with her nanny, and how her nanny's sudden flight back to England was somehow tied to that; how Linus knew all the best restaurants and saw every movie; how Linus had gone to Studio 54 and CBGBs, preferring CBGBs; how David Byrne had been a patient. These were things she had learned—gleaned— over the years. But had she ever, herself, asked Linus for information? Had she ever said, How's work? Are you happy that you chose psychiatry over another specialty? Do you ever think about paths not taken?

"Liv?" It was Linus hanging over the deck rail.

Liv walked into the sun to look up at her uncle. It doesn't hurt, she thought. Putting weight on her right hip hadn't hurt when she climbed over the rail or when she jumped to the ground.

"Your doctor called," Linus said.

"I found a dead kitten. I think it was stillborn," Liv said. It was suddenly very important to bury this kitten out here on the hillside. She'd dig a hole deep enough to keep it protected from coyotes and dogs.

"The cancer's gone," Linus said. "She said 'remission.'"

The sun was behind Catalina. The gardeners' radio was off, and she heard a car door slam. "I know," Liv said. "I felt it. Can you bring a shovel down? And a shoebox. There's one in my closet."

Liv put the kitten into a shoebox and Linus dug a deep hole.

"Why does he keep crying?" Liv asked. She could hear her father sobbing in the living room.

"Because he's normal, and when normal people are very happy, they cry."

"I don't."

"Neither do I," Linus said.

"I wish the kitten hadn't been born," Liv said. "I wish all the protoplasm had just burst and dissipated, so its mother hadn't had to give birth to it. That's my prayer." Liv threw dirt on the shoebox.

"What do you think about Chin Chin for dinner?" Linus asked.

"Get that tuna thing Yasser likes," Liv said.

Linus pulled his cell phone from his pocket and placed the order. "Twenty minutes," he said, hanging up.

"You've got to get your own laptop, Linus," Liv said.

"I'm trying to write a script about a misanthropic shrink."

"Write what you know," Liv said.

"I know I should get my own," Linus said.

"Is it a comedy?"

"Parts of it are funny," he said. "Are you going to write a script?"

Liv shrugged. "Yeah. Maybe. Why don't I know what's going on with your practice? Like how are your patients dealing with this two-month hiatus?"

"I closed it up," he said.

"You did? Just like that." Liv said. "Why?"

"Because they can't do it. Therapy," Linus said. "And it's pretty boring sitting there watching people bounce around like pinballs. I got tired of pretending that we're anything more than goats and fishes, so I closed it up."

"But what about plumbing the depths of consciousness? You became a shrink for some reason."

"It was sexier than working in a lousy hospital. The problem was that by the time I found out that people weren't really up to therapy, I was too far in. The truth is that when someone gets close to personal understanding or a breakthrough, he just freaks out. The most anyone can really do when they're in that state is keep their appointment."

Liv laughed, imagining New York filled with staggering basket cases capable only of rushing to their shrink appointments.

"It's true," Linus said. "Personal growth is overrated. All people really want are constraints. Jobs, children, religion, the army, jail—whatever works. They have to be told how to act because they can't figure it out on their own."

Liv's stomach clenched. Shit, she *was* going to vomit today. Tears came to her eyes. Goddamn it. She was in remission, but the chemo was still going to get her. She cupped her hands over her mouth, but the feeling passed. Liv calmed her breathing. She thought about crossing herself.

"A religious person, like Dad, is ahead of the curve then. He always knows how to act," she said.

"Yep," Linus said.

"Then why do you always give him grief?"

"Come on—think," Linus said. "I'm jealous."

He sat next to his niece, looking out over West Hollywood and then further toward the smudge on the horizon that was supposed to be Catalina Island. Liv wondered if her uncle would become a full-time screenwriter, knocking off TV series episodes, making a ton of money, working hard to keep his tan up and his gut off. Maybe he'd have a boat. He would warrant an obituary in Variety:

Deceased, Linus Kezian, writer/producer, who worked on several hit TV series, garnered two Emmy nominations, and was the originator of the short-lived but critically acclaimed series for the WB network, The Shrink, *in his Newport Beach, California, home, as the result of a fall.*

If her uncle wasn't careful, he would die alone. Liv took his hand. Linus started and pulled away. She held on. His hands were small and sweaty.

"What?" he asked, trying to pull away again.

"Sit here," Liv said.

He stopped pulling. Her uncle had been a shrink who never learned compassion, Liv thought. She put her arms around him and rubbed the back of his neck. He sat facing forward as if enduring a punishment. She turned and leaned close to his ear where she whispered, "It'll be okay, Uncle Linus," over and over until she felt his shoulders relax.

Linus woke from a vaguely sexual dream with a blond teen movie star. There was a pierced navel. He sat up quickly, hoping the sudden movement would push down the coming wave of thoughts about Liv and what happened yesterday.

It didn't work, and he felt yesterday coming back, no way to avoid it. His feet were on the floor, but he knew he couldn't walk. It would be too taxing; his body wasn't up to the coordination necessary for walking and thinking.

He let himself slide from the bed to the slate tile floor. The muscles just below the skin were trembling. There was help in the medicine chest if he could just get there.

Crawl, one knee after another, he thought. The body didn't respond. Just slide the leg, he thought. Still no movement. The muscles were twitching fast, now.

"Relax," he whispered to himself, trying to mimic how Liv had sounded yesterday, the last time he remembered feeling warm.

It was Liv's voice and her warm breath in his ear that he wanted, now; that's what had made him feel like warm soup yesterday, and that's what would make him feel better today. Then this fantasy about warmth and Liv's voice disappeared, and he was left with what had really happened: he had reached out and put his hand between his niece's legs.

"Jesus fucking Christ," she had yelled.

He remembered how she had jerked herself to standing. He could tell that she had wanted to hit him with the shovel, but instead had stormed up the hill, tearing up ground cover and trash, letting it slide onto his back. "Say a prayer for the dead kitten," she yelled.

Now on the tile floor, midway to the bathroom, Linus wished his niece had taken that shovel and beaten the shit out of him. He wanted to sob at her feet, beg for forgiveness, and then crawl to his brother to ask him what to do.

He heard Cody getting up in Liv's room. Cody would know what to do. He always knew how to behave, and Linus imagined following Cody as his acolyte, learning everything Cody knew.

He heard Cody and John leave the house, and he pictured Liv alone in her bed in her undershirt and baggy shorts. Yasser would be on the pillow above her head. He thought about the lines between Liv's eyes, the two slashes from worry and myopia getting deeper with each year. He thought about sitting beside her and stroking her hair. He imagined how she would open her eyes, smile at him, and pull him under the covers, because that's what Liv did with men.

Linus was able to reach into his dresser to pull out the stone hand of St. Thaddeus. The stone felt warmer than his skin, and he sat with it pressed to his stomach. He was starting to feel better. "Hornfels," he said. This was the geological name of the stone. A rock formed through contact metamorphism. Although Linus had learned that this geological process was commonplace—slates and shales in contact with granite, change happening through migrating fluids and heat—he found the word *metamorphism* rich.

How the hell was he going to face his niece? "I put my hand between her legs," he forced himself to say out loud. He felt sick to his stomach. Maybe if I throw up, I'll feel better. *I put my hand between my niece's legs.* "Jesus fucking Christ," he said.

Shame was not an everyday feeling for Linus Kezian.

Linus had the cab go east on Sunset Boulevard until the road ran out near the highrise downtown prison with its narrow slit windows. He then told the driver to head back west on the freeway.

Linus had the driver exit at Gower and then head up into the hills to wind through the narrow roads where the asphalt was broken and cracked from earthquakes and aggressive tree roots. The driver turned, and Linus saw they were approaching Franklin Avenue.

"Stay in the hills," Linus said. He couldn't go back home without a plan. Why hadn't anyone ever told him how *embarrassed* he was going to be by his life?

The driver turned off onto a very narrow street to head back up the hill, and Linus noticed a long wrought-iron fence surrounding a parking lot, gardens, and a white stucco building with onion-dome turrets, the sun just starting to flare against them. He asked the driver to pull into the parking area, and Linus saw a sign; this was the Vedanta Center.

Linus paid the driver, walked through the gardens and into a courtyard. A man approached and said, "Can I help you?"

"Yes, definitely," Linus said.

The man gave Linus a tour and then asked him if he'd like to try "sitting." Linus said he would, and he sat in a room with fourteen others.

It was dark when Linus left the room.

12

$\mathcal{T}$here was a call from the camera department on Sally's walkie-talkie; they were ready for the next shot, fifteen minutes earlier than estimated. "A few more days like today and the Confused Prince just might bring this movie in on time and on budget," Sally said to Joy, who was finishing breast-feeding Sydney in the production trailer.

Joy handed the baby off to the nanny. "Do you think I could go home early tonight?" Joy asked the assistant director.

"Definitely," Sally said. "We'll wrap by seven, so if you want to sneak home at four, go for it. I think we can manage without you for a few hours."

Since Sydney's birth, Joy had started wearing longish skirts and long-sleeve blouses. She had Binnsinger's All-Kosher deliver dinner, so she and Nick could more or less keep kosher even during her grueling production schedule. On Fridays Joy tried to observe Shabbat dinner, which this time of year meant being home by 4:45. She rarely made it: one Friday, she hadn't gotten home until 6 a.m. the next morning. But today looked like it would be an exception.

Joy got home at 4:30. The apartment was dark, and Binnsinger's delivery service had left a note in the box: *Unable to access apartment.*

Joy gave Sydney a bottle, called Nick's cell phone and got voicemail. She called his office. Voicemail there, too: "This is Nick Gorelich. I'll be out of the office until Tuesday, but I'll be checking in for messages." Joy called the number again: "I'll be out of the office until Tuesday." Was this an old message from the business trip he took last month to Boston? Had he come back on a Tuesday? Joy couldn't remember.

"It's me. Do you know your message says you'll be out of the office until Tuesday?" she said on his voicemail.

Joy called out for pizza and told the nanny to help herself. Joy wasn't hungry. She sat in the dark living room and felt her heart beating hard. Breathe, she told herself. The blood was coursing like a racehorse.

I'll be out of the office until Tuesday.

Joy tried to think of people she could call who might know where he was. There was the rabbi, but Joy didn't want to call him, yet. There were the two guys from Nick's office who moonlighted on the weekends as handymen. They had come over recently to reglaze the living-room windows and when they were done, Nick had poured them each a shot of single malt scotch that Joy hadn't known was in the house. "For the road," Joy remembered Nick saying to them. What were their names? Joy wondered. She had seen them before at Nick's year-end office party. Fleshy faces in button-down shirts. One of them had brought her punch as Nick had passed out grab-bag gifts and uncorked the champagne.

Joy found the bottle of scotch and poured herself a glass. *For the road.* She remembered the guys standing at the sink with Nick as they drank their shots. She remembered that one of them had extended his glass for a second shot, but that Nick was already screwing on the top.

These were the only two people from work that Nick had ever invited home. His parents came once from Wisconsin for a weekend. There was one night with his college roommate, a programmer living in San Diego. Nick said that the apartment was a sanctuary, a place where the outside should definitely be kept out.

It was a place for a wife and children, occasionally the rabbi. Boundaries were important. "They tell us who we are," he said once when talking about Israel's claim to the West Bank.

She called the police to ask about any car accidents. There was nothing involving Nick. They told her a missing person report could be filed when the person had been gone for forty-eight hours.

Joy had to be on set on Saturday morning. She pumped milk for Sydney and knocked on the nanny's door. "Don't bother with lunch. Nick won't be going to temple. He has to work today," Joy lied to the closed door. Nick hadn't missed temple in years. "I'll try to be home as early as I can," Joy said.

"Okay," the nanny said, muffled behind the door.

On the set, Joy comforted Julie about what she thought was her premenstrual puffy face, had a production assistant bring Peter a freshly squeezed orange juice, and rubbed the dolly grip's neck after the fourth take of a very long dolly shot. She told Sally she was doing a great job and should really think about becoming a production manager. She called Nick's cell phone fifteen times.

On Sunday Joy waited, filling the hours with Sydney's feedings, the Sunday Times, and a nap. She counted off each hour. Forty-six. Forty-seven. At forty-eight hours, she was at her local police precinct office with a photo of Nick. The policewoman typed Joy's answers to: What did she and Nick do for a living? How long had Nick lived in the apartment? Was he depressed? On medication? On drugs of any type? A drinker? Did he have a life insurance policy? Were there mental problems? Illness of any kind? How about in his family? Money problems? Were there old debts, grudges, jealous girlfriends? Did Joy have enemies? Joy answered that he didn't seem depressed. He worked in a city department that granted construction permits. No marital problems. No money problems. No enemies that she knew of. She was a movie producer.

The policewoman wanted to know if Joy had produced anything she might have seen.

Joy told her to watch for *Bound Lover* next year.

The policewoman gave Joy the card of a private detective. "We only have so many resources available," she said.

Joy went from the police station to Stop and Shop and bought the week's Pampers and groceries. Not kosher.

She ate potato chips for dinner and watched the empty park from the living room window.

13

*U*nder the basic contract of the Directors' Guild of America, Beth, the producer, was obliged to give Liv, the director, ten weeks to turn in an edited film. This could happen with or without the producer in the editing room—director's choice. However, if, after the ten weeks, Beth deemed the film terrible, she could take it away from Liv, have it recut and rescored, and even bring in a new director to reshoot problem scenes.

Since the day Liv kicked Beth out of the editing room, Beth was working on a plan for saving the film. Who knew what kinds of awful side effects the cancer drugs were having on Liv's judgment? Who knew what the stoner craft service boy was adding to the mix? Beth was convinced that Liv could only be making an unreleasable twenty-five million dollar piece of shit. My career-ending movie, Beth thought.

Beth began interviewing replacement editors and directors. The interviewees were all enthusiastic and ready to sympathize with Beth's position. They said they weren't surprised by Beth's problem, given that Liv was a first-time director. They said that Beth had a reputation for being a genius with story and craft. Beth was frantic to find a savior for her film, but the interviewees' desperate flattery repulsed her. She was sure that one was a pedophile. Then, the plan that should've been obvious from the start got very obvious: have *Peter* save the film. As soon as photography was completed on Peter's film, she'd bring him out to L.A. to save Liv's movie. The Germans would never know how close to disaster they had come.

Beth grew calmer. She was a fixer, a smoother over. Neither chaos nor disaster would ever be possible, because Beth Meisner covered.

"Hello," Peter answered the phone.

"Hi, it's me."

"Beth?"

"Yeah, it's Beth."

"Oh, hi." Had Beth Meisner ever called him before? Peter wondered. Why now? On a Sunday?

"I wanted to talk to you about what you're doing after principal photography wraps."

She's firing me, he thought. Can she do that? Does Joy know? "I have postproduction," he said. She can't fire me, he thought. There's a contract. She has to let me have a crack at editing my film.

"I have a problem, and I need your help. Liv's very sick, and she's really not able to finish the film," Beth said.

"What do you mean?"

"It's cancer, but the prognosis is good, very good. Her family's here, and her spirits are very, very good. That counts for almost everything, doesn't it?"

Peter crumpled the foil around his falafel, imaging Liv sick. He pictured her in Paris; she was very thin then, her eyes bulging from her face. She must look like that now, but worse, he thought. Why hadn't he been in touch with her? Why was *Beth* telling him this? He pressed the pedal on the trashcan, its metal lid banging against the wall.

"What was that?" Beth asked.

"My trash can."

"I think your movie's genius," Beth said.

"You do?" Peter said.

"Yes. Before you start post on *Bound Lover*, I want you to finish the postproduction on Liv's film. I saw an assembly edit of your film, and I think it's very good, maybe the best assembly I've seen."

How the hell had she seen an assembly? Peter wondered. Had Sally gone behind his back to send the executive producer the assembly edit that he, the *director*, hadn't yet had the time to watch? Could his assistant director do that? Did Joy know about this? But Beth said his movie was genius. How much could he really complain? The phone clicked.

"That's the other line. I'll be right back," Peter said. He looked at caller ID. It was Joy.

"Hi, it's me." Joy's voice was level. Peter could tell she was covering something.

"Beth's on the other line," he said.

"Beth?"

Why was Beth calling Peter on a Sunday night? Joy wondered. She had to keep her voice steady. Don't let on about Nick, she told herself. Pretend you're just calling to discuss what Peter thinks of the set for Monday. If Peter suspected anything, his suspicion would be transmitted to Beth, and that wouldn't be good for Joy. Boundaries define who we are.

"I'll call you right back," Peter said.

"Don't tell her I called," Joy said as he clicked off.

"I'm back," Peter said to Beth. "It was Joy."

"Is it an emergency?" Beth asked.

"No, she just wanted to chat."

Since when do a director and producer "just chat" when they don't absolutely need to? Beth wondered. She had never called Liv "to chat."

"Look, I want to concretize the plans for getting you out here. I really want to get the film done before the Cannes deadline," Beth said.

What should he say? Peter wondered. Why wasn't *Liv* calling him up to ask for his help? How could Beth say that his film was genius when he knew it was mediocre?

"You can imagine the kind of drugs she's on, and she has the craft service guy in the editing room with her. Peter, it's a piece of dreck."

She's fucking the craft service guy, Peter thought, picking a stray farfalle noodle off the counter. He needed a cleaning lady and an assistant. It was time to take his life seriously. He needed a rack for all his DVDs.

"So what do you think?" Beth asked.

Peter thought about Liv's father. He pictured him touching the cross around his neck, kissing his fingers, and praying for his daughter to get well. Peter wondered if John had ever prayed for him. It was suddenly important to know.

"I should talk to Joy about it. My first loyalty is to my film," Peter said.

"Can you let me know tomorrow?" Beth asked.

"The next few days are crazy," Peter said. "I'll call by Wednesday for sure."

Why wasn't he making this easy? Beth wondered. Didn't he understand that she was the only reason he had a semblance of a career? Didn't he realize that she was the only reason that *Joy* had a career?

"Okay," Beth said, forcing brightness. "So how's Joy doing with the baby and everything?" Beth knew that she should end this call talking about other stuff. That way Peter would remember the call as friendly and not mercenary. People remember endings.

"She's doing okay. She brings the baby to the set a lot, and that makes things more human or something."

At first Peter had hated having Sydney around, because she took Joy's attention away from him. But then Julie had had a bad wardrobe day, unwilling to work because she thought the clothes made her look fat, and Peter watched his producer wrap her arms around his star. He put on his headphones and heard over Julie's radio mic:

"I want to make it good for him, but I can't tell if he respects me. Does he really *see* me, or am I just a means to an end?"

"You're not a means to an end. You're an actress," Joy had whispered into Julie's ear, the words coming in loud and sharp over Peter's headphones.

The way Joy said "actress" had produced a compliant star who delivered the scene. Joy had turned a miracle. Peter saw a long future with her, and he bought a designer high chair for Sydney.

"I have to send a baby present. She doesn't really play yet, does she?" Beth said.

"Not yet," Peter said. "She's only 6 weeks old."

He slid down the wall and squatted on the kitchen floor. His nose was running. Why the hell were he and Beth chatting about Joy and her baby? Why weren't they talking slowly and profoundly about Liv's prognosis and her treatment protocols? Why was it that all he could think about were Liv's hands unbuttoning his pants and whether her father ever prayed for him?

The door buzzed. It was Julie. They'd have Chinese takeout for dinner. Maybe later they would have sex like they did last week.

"I have to go," he said to Beth. "I'll talk to you tomorrow, okay?"

"Right. Have a great rest of the evening."

"You, too. And, Beth?"

"Yes?"

"My movie is a formulaic story starring a television actress on hiatus," he said, suddenly so tired. He sagged, all his muscles relaxing. Telling the truth was a relief. Keeping up the enthusiastic front required too much energy. "But, hey, we're trying our best," Peter said.

Beth flushed. Peter wasn't smart enough to talk like this. When and how had he acquired a point of view? She opened her mouth and her jaw cracked.

"Peter, your movie's going to rule opening weekend," Beth said.

14

*O*n Monday morning, Joy went to Nick's office and talked to the young men who had reglazed the living-room windows. Their names were Ted and Quent, and they said Nick had been coming in late for the last month. It wasn't yet ten o'clock, and they thought Nick would be in soon.

Joy told them that Nick had been missing since Friday, and that she didn't think he'd be in today or even the rest of the week. "So, tell me anything you know," Joy said. "Has anything been different?"

Ted and Quent were nervous about answering, but finally it came out that Nick had told them that Joy was having health problems.

"You were in the hospital, and that's why he was late," Quent said.

"He said it was really serious. I thought she—you—were going to die," Ted said.

Joy talked to other people in the office. All of them thought she had been very sick, and they made a point of saying, "Nick was worried sick about her—you."

Joy made an appointment with Connie Owens, the private detective recommended by the policewoman.

"Connie's short for Conrad," the private investigator said when they met at a bar next to his downtown office. He was thin, with a high forehead, wispy white-blond hair, designer wire-rim glasses. He wore a copper bracelet. Around 55, maybe 60. He drank tonic water. He wanted Joy to make a list of all the people she knew in Nick's life.

Joy started writing names on a placemat. The senator, Ted, Quent, the black girl she had seen with Nick, Liv's father, maybe Linus, the rabbi. "I don't know the black girl's name," she said. "I saw her at a party once."

"If you know the name of the host of the party, I can get her name," Connie said.

Connie cost a hundred and fifty dollars a day. He suggested that he work for ten days; they could reassess then.

Connie waited until Joy's second glass of wine came before he asked, "Why do you think Nick left?"

She ran her finger around the rim of her glass and made a stab at imagining Nick on a beach. Isn't that where people go to disappear? But a beach didn't fit with the candles they lit on Friday nights—beautiful beeswax candles that Nick insisted on using even if they splattered wax and burned down too quickly. No, a beach was too bright—not Nick at all. She saw herself, Nick, and Sydney as a black-and-white photo with rich blacks and high-contrast light in a coffee-table book about middle-European Jewish life. She saw the smooth-running household, the cleaning lady that Nick had trained to polish the maple woodwork correctly, the weekly grocery order— all kosher, all organic—the temple charity dinner invitations that Nick RSVP'd.

"Shit," she said. "He planned it, didn't he?"

"They usually do," Connie said.

Joy knew Nick wasn't going to let himself be found by Connie Owens. I'm going to cry, she thought, looking past Connie to a table of stock traders in the back booth. Hugo Boss suits. One wore Hugo Boss socks.

"Nick was trying to live this Orthodox Jewish family life, but he was making it up out of whole cloth. It wasn't how he was raised at all," she said. "It was like a role he took on," she said. Nick had finally realized that the suit didn't fit, she thought.

Connie signaled the waitress for more pretzels.

"I think one day he must have gotten some perspective, and he probably thought, What am I doing working for the city, keeping kosher, and hanging on some fat rabbi's every word?" Joy said. She wasn't going to cry anymore. "That's what I think."

"That's what *you* think of Nick's life, or that's what you think *Nick* thinks of his life?"

"You sound like my old shrink," Joy said. "I don't think you'll find Nick."

After drinks with Connie, Joy had dinner at The Odeon, happy it was so dark because no one could see her skirt. She ordered shrimp, had another glass of wine, and smiled at a man who caught her eye when the girl he was with leaned over to get her cell phone from her bag. What would Linus say about her now? Joy wondered. Probably that she was doing just fine. Joy told herself that she had given it her all with Nick, but sometimes people are just crazy, and, in the end, Nick was probably crazy.

Joy crossed the river and was back in Brooklyn by eleven. At 11:30, she was pumping a bottle. She was too jittery to stay in the apartment, and by 12:45, she was back on the street, in her car. By 1:30 a.m., she was sitting in a Brooklyn coffee shop where a man at the counter poured so much syrup onto his French toast that it spilled over the plate and onto the counter, then over the counter and onto his pants. The ends of his long hair swirled in the shiny sticky mess.

"He does that all the time," the grill cook said to Joy, talking about the syrup man. "I charge him extra for all the syrup, but he pays it, no problem."

Joy smiled at the cute grill cook. He held up a pitcher of coffee, and Joy shook her head. She had had enough. The cook went back to his book—*Granta*.

"I used to read that," Joy said. The grill cook looked up, gave her a tiny smile, and went back to reading. Joy wondered why she had let her *Granta* subscription run out. How long had it been since she had read even a *New Yorker*? The French toast man raised his head and shook his hair, beads of syrup spattering onto the counter, floor, his shirt and face. How the hell did I ever wind up in Brooklyn? Joy wondered. She called Peter.

"What did Beth want?"

"Joy?"

"When she called yesterday. You never told me today what she wanted."

"Nothing. I'll tell you later," he said. "I was sleeping."

"Can I come over?" she asked.

"Julie's here. What time is it?"

"It's two."

Peter was in sweat pants and a T-shirt when he answered the door. It was 3:00. He had to be on the set in four hours. Julie had to be in hair and makeup in three.

"I just need a blanket. Go back to bed," Joy said.

Joy stretched out on his couch and surveyed Peter's living room. She smelled cigarette smoke. DVDs were strewn. There was a pile of scripts and a long shelf of *Granta*s. She turned her head to the right and then to the left. She heard bones crunch and she tried to breathe through it. I really need to start doing yoga again, she thought. She sat up, her gray skirt billowing in front of her. My Orthodox Jewish woman costume, she thought.

"I'm wearing a fucking burqua," she said out loud. She lifted the skirt up over her face, exposing her panties and tights to the room. "I'm wearing a fucking burqua," she repeated.

She unveiled herself and lay back down. What had she been thinking? The Brooklyn apartment with highly polished floors and oriental rugs. The embroidered robe. None of that was Joy. She was a Conran's girl.

She kept her eyes closed when Julie left in the morning. When Peter came into the living room a half hour later, she opened her eyes. "Hi," she said.

"My driver's waiting outside," he said, looking at his watch.

"I know. I'll be at the set very soon. Tell Sally not to worry. I'll explain later, okay?"

Peter nodded. "Sorry, but there isn't any coffee," he said.

"Can I borrow some clothes?"

"If there's anything clean," Peter said.

She found a pair of very worn jeans. Tight. She was going to have to lose the weight she had put on since Sydney. Still, it wasn't bad how she filled them out. She ran her hands down the legs. It was nice how the old denim felt against her skin. She found a T-shirt and a black turtleneck. An old parka. She even found a pair of sneakers that fit—probably an old girlfriend's, maybe Liv's. She zipped the parka and studied herself in a mirror. She'd slip away from the set today to go to Barneys.

She called the nanny from her car and told her to take a cab to the set. She clicked off the phone and merged onto the bridge traffic. Joy thought about crying, but she understood that if she cried now, it would be out of nostalgia for some home life that had turned out to be fake. Nick was gone, but it turned out he had never been there. Hadn't Linus told her she couldn't really long for something she had never known?

Traffic was moving, and she turned on NPR. She'd start looking for a place today. Maybe something in Battery Park. The high chair Peter had given her would go perfectly in her new apartment. She pictured Sydney chasing after ducks at the Battery Park pond. There would be a ring of attentive nannies, each one with a hand resting on her respective stroller.

Maybe she'd call Linus and start therapy again. Then she remembered his card: *Dr. Linus Kezian announces the closing of his practice*. There was a referral number. She could call the number, or she could just ask around. She knew so many people. She'd look for a woman therapist. That's what she needed now. A woman would understand better. After all, she was a mother now. Practically a widow.

Joy spotted the catering truck. The transportation captain would have her space marked off with an orange cone. Unlike almost anyone in New York, Joy could glide into a parking space only a few feet from where she wanted to be. Joy was a creative producer. She had a child. She was working with Beth Meisner, who had one of the most lucrative deals in the industry. Joy's first film would do very well. Her next film even better. She would start putting Sydney's name on Manhattan school lists. She might consider a week in California to visit her mother. "I'm at the next place," Joy said proudly out loud in the car. I'm ready for the next thing, she thought.

15

During his first week at the Vedanta Center, Linus read the center's texts that explained how he, like everyone else, had a divinity more luminous than the sun, moon, and stars. He thought the metaphor was lame (how was he supposed to picture "brighter" than the sun?), but he understood that it was an attempt to illustrate the idea that all of us, Linus included, were linked in our divinity. He liked the idea, even though it was a hard one to swallow. It was one thing to feel connected to people like Jung, Freud, Joe Strummer, Vaclav Havel, Albert Camus, or Roman Polanski, his A-list. However, to embrace scum, people like Omar in Spitak, the Christian Right, Henry Kissinger, Radovan Karadzic, Robert Mugabe—that was quite a different thing.

He made himself meditate on the two lists, focusing so hard on the names, that the columns started to blur. He wasn't yet sure about "divinity," but he was starting to understand that everyone might be stuck in the same soup.

He signed up with a rental agency to find an apartment in the hills for himself. He got himself invited to a Vedanta Center party. He managed to avoid ever being alone with Liv.

"Where are you going?" John asked as Linus started out the front door on his way to the Center's party. He hadn't seen them: John and Liv eating dinner in the dark living room, about to start watching *The Double Life of Veronique*.

"There's a screening of *The Decalogue* at the Cinematheque," Linus said, realizing too late that it was a stupid lie. *The Decalogue*?

On the same night as they were watching *The Double Life of Veronique*? "Can you believe I've never seen it?" Linus asked.

Liv looked him in the eye, the first time since the afternoon on the hillside. "I guess it's a Kieslowski kind of night," she said.

Linus knew she didn't believe him, but she smiled anyway, and Linus felt warm. Not warm as in hot and excited, but warm like he might someday be rescued from exile.

The Vedanta Center was bright with string lights and candles. A band was playing spacey world music in the courtyard. The women wore saris or clingy skirts. The men wore shirts cut like the ones Nelson Mandela wore. But Mandela looked elegant and these men looked clunky.

Linus was standing at the tea samovar when he saw the young man John had beaten up walk into the courtyard. His face bore no scars from the fight. He wore a button-down shirt and khaki pants. His hair looked freshly cut. It was the first time Linus ever remembered being impressed by a man's skin. It's *dewy*, he thought.

The young man drifted shyly through the party, and then, when he spotted Linus, he came over, his hand extended. "Hi, do you remember me?" the young man asked, as if he and Linus were colleagues meeting at a convention after many years.

"I do," Linus said.

The young man's name was Miles. He was from Idaho, in Los Angeles for the last eight months. He worked as a landscaper.

"What are you doing here? I thought you were a Christian," Linus said.

"I'm a seeker," Miles said.

He told Linus that he had grown up in a Christian home in rural Idaho. "Do you know I met my first Jewish person only three months ago?" Miles said. "I went to a Jewish service, and it was real interesting."

It was when he started working on a Beverly Hills home that he first heard about the Vedanta Center. "The woman in Beverly Hills, the owner—she's calm, and she smiles a lot," Miles said. "She told me this place helped her, and I was feeling sort of, I don't know, lost, you know?"

Linus thought about the Unibomber. Miles seemed capable of anything.

"I'm not mad at your brother, you know," Miles said.

Linus waited for Miles to ask about John's injuries, but he didn't. "Do you understand why he did what he did?" Linus asked.

"Yes," Miles said. "His daughter's dying or something."

The candle burning nearby should've been reflected in Miles's eyes, but it wasn't. Instead, the eyes looked filmy, as if a slow-moving mold was making its way across the iris. It was such a contrast to his beautiful, alive skin. Miles never asked Linus what he was doing at the Vedanta Center.

Don't judge him, Linus thought. You're no one to judge anyone.

Linus watched a blond woman in a green sari drape herself around a young man wearing a neck brace. Linus could see the woman's ribs flare out when she laughed. She ran her hand through another woman's hair, her bracelets jangling. Linus saw that Miles was watching the blond, too.

"I wanted to have sex with my niece," Linus blurted out, holding his teacup too tightly. He felt like he could explode, his skin, gas, and liquids spraying the guests, collecting in viscous puddles at the low end of the garden.

"Your niece is the dying one?" Miles asked.

Linus felt his face flush. He stepped toward Miles, a part of him wanting to beat the shit out of this boy with glowing skin who could toss Liv off as "the dying one."

"Watch your tea," Miles said.

Linus stepped back. Christ, I'm an overheated hysteric, he thought, putting down his teacup, looking for spills on his pants.

"How old is she?" Miles asked.

"Thirty-eight," Linus said. "Nothing really happened. But a line was crossed, you know?"

Linus wondered if he was becoming the kind of American who could only feel connected to someone if he confessed the worst, even if the confessor was this strange boy from Idaho.

Why isn't he asking me if I'm here because of what I felt about Liv? Linus wondered. Why isn't he curious about me? Linus wanted to tell Miles—tell anyone—about how he had found the Vedanta Center, about how he was trying to *find a new way of behaving in the world*. He wanted to tell Miles about how Liv had smiled at him tonight, and about how that made him think for the first time in a long time that everything was going to be okay.

"There's the woman," Miles said, pointing at a brunette near the band's speakers. "The Beverly Hills woman." With that, Miles walked away from Linus and toward the woman.

Linus was clenching a fist; there was a lump in his throat. I'm repulsive, he thought. No one can stand to be near me, not even Miles, the freak.

Linus left the party and drove west on Sunset Boulevard, all the way to the ocean where he turned around and drove back east.

I'm pacing, he thought. Sunset Boulevard is my living room, and I'm wearing down the carpet. West, east, west, east.

He knew he should be with people, but going home wasn't an option. John would be in bed, and he couldn't risk seeing Liv alone. He decided to go to Canter's Deli.

At two a.m., Linus was drinking coffee and eating poppy-seed danish at Canter's counter. In the booth next to him, two boys and a girl, each with Maori-style tattoos around their upper arms, drank coffee and picked at four orders of onion rings. The boys were moping. The girl held her face in her hands, tapping her nail against the stud in her chin. Linus stared openly at the group, and they didn't seem to mind. He thought the light in the room got suddenly brighter as if there had been a power surge. Linus thought of the word "luminous." This light is their divinity showing itself, Linus thought.

His waitress's hair was dry, a mottled blond. He stared at her, and she self-consciously put her hand to her scalp.

"I know. It looks like a pelt. I'm going to the hair colorist this week," she said.

Linus touched her hand. The waitress started, and then she relaxed. I see her divinity, too, Linus thought.

He swiveled on his stool to face the crowded room. Overhead lights with orange and blue plastic shades made hot pools on the terrazzo floor. Everyone looked tired. Many looked high or drunk. They're all divine. There is no A-list or shit-list, Linus thought. I see it. I see them. Divine.

"Here you go," the waitress said, refilling his coffee. "Hey, what's that?" she asked, her hand reaching to touch his face.

"What?" he said, leaning away from her hand, swiping at his face. He must have danish stuck to his chin. Linus felt wet skin. Was he crying?

"Are you going to be okay?" she asked.

Linus nodded. He knew that she had just seen his divinity, too.

16

$\mathscr{P}$eter came into the restaurant where Sara worked to pick up his to-go falafel and Turkish salad.

"How many more days?" Sara asked, putting a jalab down on the counter.

"Fourteen."

"And?"

"And it'll be a 'product.' Some people think it'll make a lot of money."

The production schedule had exhausted Peter, and he had no spare energy with which to shellac the world with an enthusiastic patina. He was becoming more like Sara, and Sara wondered if her mother now found both her children to be bummers.

The couple at the last table left the restaurant. Sara lowered the window blinds and turned off the front lights.

"Have you seen Mom lately?" Sara asked.

"She came to the set last week before she left town. I think she was bored." Peter scooped out the pine nuts from his date drink. "You remember Liv Johansson?" he asked.

"Of course."

"She has cancer."

"Shit," Sara said, staring at the Mediterranean coast painted on the wide wall between the windows looking onto Clinton Street. She imagined Liv, bald, thin, and pale, wearing a scarf like the Lebanese women in the prints of Beirut hanging over the booths. The chemotherapy scarf wearer keeps her baldness a secret; the Lebanese scarf wearer protects the secret of her hair. Sara thought about the relief of removing the scarves in the bedroom. She and Liv had had only one conversation, but Liv had seen her passion.

"It doesn't sound like she's going to die or anything," Peter said.

Sara put her hand on her heart the way Naim did when he said hello. "Thank God," she said.

"Yeah," Peter said. "Beth thinks Liv's movie is going to be a piece of shit because of all the drugs she's on, and she wants me to take over the postproduction. Her new boyfriend is helping with the editing, now. He's like 19 or something."

"*Beth's* new boyfriend?" Sara asked.

"No, Liv's," Peter said. "He usually does craft service, you know the guy who makes the snacks for the crew. It seems pretty sleazy."

"Being with the craft service guy?"

"No. Well, maybe, but I wasn't talking about that. I think it's sleazy for Beth to ask me to do post on Liv's film."

The last time Sara had seen Beth Meisner was at Liv's dinner. She remembered Beth staring at Liv, her mouth open, unaware that her hair was dragging in her salad's vinaigrette. She remembered how Beth's mouth opened wider as if to speak, but how she was cut off by someone's interjection.

"Maybe Beth's opinion has more to do with her personal frustrations than with the actual film," Sara said.

"You can't approach this like character motivation in a book, Sara. This is about protecting an investment by making a releasable film. We're talking about twenty-five million dollars. With P and A, that's almost fifty million. Beth has every right to be worried about that kind of money. P and A are prints and advertising."

"I'm not a moron, Peter. I know this isn't a novel, but Beth isn't just a 150 million dollar line of credit. The film's released, money's made and all that stuff, but then what? It has to happen in a context—emotional, psychological, whatever. We all have context, Peter. There's always *stuff* going on. Personal stuff. Even Beth Meisner."

Peter saw that his sister's cheekbones were sharper. She was pretty—no, intense. Was her hair straighter or thinner since the last time he noticed? Why was it so hard for him to notice stuff about people? Why couldn't he see that Beth Meisner had *stuff* and that she wasn't just a line of credit? If he couldn't see the stuff, how could his films ever be really good?

"What do you think I should do?" he asked.

"Call Liv up and say 'Hey, is your film shit?'" Sara said. "Be direct. There's nothing to lose."

"Were you always this smart?" Peter asked.

"Yes." She put her hand on Peter's. When had she touched her brother last? "It's cozy in here, isn't it?"

Peter looked at the wooden booths carved like benches on a boat, the lights that looked like ship lanterns casting a yellow glow. "Yeah," he said. "It's nice."

"Are you looking for a personal assistant?" Sara asked.

"I might be," Peter said. "Yeah, I am."

"I know a guy." Sara said. "He's working at Dunkin' Donuts right now, but he's really smart." Sara wasn't sure that Cyrus really needed to finish high school, but she knew he had to do something more than make donuts.

"Hi. Beth said your film's no good," Peter said in a rush as soon as Liv answered. He knew it wasn't what Sara meant by "be direct," but that's how he did it.

"Wow, that's quite a line reading, Peter. Did you work on that a long time?" Liv asked. "From one director to another, I think I would have chosen to pause between 'Hi,' and 'Beth said your film's no good.'"

"She wants me to come out and edit it as soon as you deliver your cut," Peter said, avoiding Liv's sarcasm.

"She's a bitch."

Peter relaxed. Why had he wound himself up to do Beth's bidding? Why had he allowed Beth to rattle him? Liv was right. Beth was a bitch. Why hadn't he been able to see this for himself?

"How is it?"

"Maybe you'd like to first ask me some polite questions about my cancer," Liv said. "I'm sure she mentioned that, right?"

What Peter wanted to ask was whether her father ever prayed for him. "Yeah, she told me. How are you doing?" He softened his voice and slowed everything down.

"The film's going to be very good. The cancer has decided to disappear, thank you very much."

Peter sat back in his chair, his muscles warm as they relaxed. Liv was going to be okay. No more cancer. How long had he been sitting near the edge of this chair, his shoulders hunched up by his ears? He wished she were here in person to witness how physical his concern was. "When are you showing her the cut?"

"At the last possible minute," Liv answered. "I want to make her squirm. I want her alone in the screening room while I watch from the projection booth."

"I think you should sit next to her, Liv."

"What?"

"If you make it seem like you take her seriously—even if you're faking it—she'll like you. If she thinks you like her, she'll want to please you in order to get more of your attention." Peter liked how insightful he sounded. He was talking about *stuff*. He told Liv that he did this with Joy, and it worked; they had a great working relationship. Joy and Beth were the kind of people who needed to be filled up.

"Since when have you become a student of human nature?"

"Liv, come on. I know about this stuff," Peter said.

"Have you seen Naim lately?" Liv asked.

Peter suddenly wanted the conversation over. Liv wasn't going to die, so could they just get on to figuring out what to do about Beth and the film?

"Cranky. Kind of jerky, as per usual," Peter said.

"He's not jerky."

"Liv, wake up. He's jerky. He talked into his camera, and he pretended to be a Muslim because he knew that's what you wanted. His mother was dead two years before you made your doc."

Liv watched Yasser drink frantically from an ashtray filled with sprinkler water. Naim's mother was dead. Who else knew this?

"Beth said you're with the craft service guy," Peter said.

Yasser pounced on a bug.

"Beth's an uptight freak." Liv picked at the skin under her nail to tear up a good flap. *Naim's mother was dead.*

"Do you think your father ever prays, or has prayed for me?" Peter asked.

"What?"

"Does he say my name in his prayers?"

"How the hell should I know?" Liv snapped.

"Can you send a tape of the film by overnight mail?" Peter asked.

"Why?"

"Because I want to be able to tell Beth that it's good, and she doesn't need anyone to save it."

"You don't need to see it. You take my word for it. You tell her that the film's good because I'm a fucking great director who should be trusted."

Liv pressed the "off" button. Her lips curled like she smelled rotting fish. *She* was the one on top. *She* was the one with the talent. *She* was the one who had beaten cancer. No one was going to take her movie away.

The first thing the next morning, Peter said into his cell phone as quickly as possible, "Beth, I talked with Liv, and she thinks you should see the film before we make plans." He was determined to put the problem back in Beth's court. His cell phone battery beeped, and he hoped the phone would die and cut Beth off before he had to say more.

"You're taking her word for it?" Beth asked.

"She's a very good filmmaker," Peter said, wincing at how he sounded like he was on a panel with people like Martin Scorcese, talking about master filmmakers.

"She's stoned."

"Jesus, Beth. You only have to wait four more days. Watch the film and then make a decision."

"Her film has a release date; yours doesn't. There are still a lot of territories to sell for *Bound Lover*. Which, given how the industry is going these days, might mean a very late release, maybe even a year from now, Peter. Liv has a firm date. We've got the poster."

Peter knew she was threatening to bury his film. "She's very good," Peter whimpered.

"You already said that," Beth said. "I'll talk to Joy. Maybe we can work something out with your schedule." She hung up.

"Fuck you," Peter said to his cell phone as he stood in the middle of the school playground where they had been shooting for the last two days. The streetlight switched off.

"Hey," Joy said, putting her hand on his neck.

"Hey," he said. She looked good today.

"Nick's gone."

His phone beeped. "My battery's dead," Peter said, pocketing the phone.

"I should say he's missing. There's a police file, and I hired a private detective." Joy reported the information as if it were a *TV Guide* log line.

"God," Peter said. "How long?" He noticed that she was in pants and a new sweater. No shapeless gray skirt. She did look good. Her husband was gone, but she looked relaxed. "You don't seem so freaked out. Most people would be freaked."

"It's redefinition time," she said, shrugging. "Opportunity, not tragedy."

"But what happened?" Peter asked.

"Nothing. He just picked up and left," Joy said.

Peter heard her voice waver, and he knew not to ask more.

A production assistant came over with checks for Joy to sign.

"Look, I have two appointments with real estate agents tomorrow, so I'll be late to the set. You're just doing that walk and talk. Do you think you'll be okay without me for the morning?" she asked Peter as she signed the checks. "I'm looking for a place in Battery Park."

Peter thought it would be okay. "You look nice today," he said.

"You do," the production assistant added.

"I do?" Joy's face lit up. "Thanks."

"Can someone tell Peter that a guy named Cyrus is at craft service looking for him?" It was Sally over the production assistant's walkie.

Peter nodded.

"Copy that. I'm with Peter now," the production assistant answered Sally as Peter headed to craft service.

"Cyrus," Peter said, shaking Cyrus's hand. "Why the hell do you want to be a personal assistant to someone like me?"

"I'm not sure I do. What's someone like you like?"

Peter liked the answer. The guy wasn't a wimp. He didn't want a wimp. He wanted a friend. "You won't mind picking up dry cleaning and shit?"

"Shit I might."

Peter smiled. Cyrus wrinkled his forehead. Like Thumper, Peter thought. He's a black Thumper.

"You don't look much like a dry cleaning man," Cyrus said.

"You're right, but that's always what people say when they talk about personal assistants."

"Is it?"

"Yeah." Peter went on to tell Cyrus that he had never had an assistant, so it would be a learning experience for the two of them.

"What are you going to do about school?" Peter asked.

"Drop out. I'll get my GED."

"And college?"

Cyrus shrugged.

"I didn't go either," Peter said.

Joy watched Peter talk to Cyrus. A personal assistant meant that he was taking himself seriously. A good sign. She and Peter were growing into their new roles. She was smart to have stuck with him.

17

$\mathscr{L}$iv and Beth were alone together in a small screening room to watch Liv's version of the movie. Liv was highly aware of every physical reaction Beth had to the film. Beth crossed her legs when Robert, the art thief, counted the money from a spectacular sale to the gullible New York gallery owner. When the gallery owner's wife—the observant Jew—longingly watched Robert count the bills, Beth flexed her hand. When Brigitte, the Europol investigator, and Robert had sex on a train, Beth ran her fingers through her hair. When Robert walked out on Brigitte, too addicted to art theft to commit to any woman, let alone a Europol officer, Beth recrossed her legs. All totaled, Liv counted thirty-two physical gestures during the one hour fifty-five minute running time. (Liv and Cody had decided to leave in an extra fifteen minutes so that Beth could feel useful when she suggested cutting fifteen minutes.) Beth waited until the last shot cut before she leaned into the mic to the projection booth and said, "I'd like to see the second reel again."

Midway through the second viewing of the second reel, Beth leaned into the mic and said, "Okay, that's fine."

The lights came up, and Liv waited. Beth put on her jacket. "You look good, Liv. Really. It's a miracle, isn't it?"

Liv knew Beth was talking about the film.

"I think you can lose a good fifteen minutes," Beth said.

"Can I lose them, or do you want to bring Peter out to do it?" Liv asked.

Beth turned her cell phone back on, and reapplied her lip gloss. She wasn't going to react to Liv's passive-aggressive reference to her plan to get Peter to "save" the movie. Why doesn't she see that I'm capable of anything? Beth wondered. Sometimes people get killed in business, Beth thought, and *someone* has to order it. Why doesn't Liv understand that I have no problem ordering *stuff* to happen? Why doesn't she get that I'm too scary to tangle with me? That I am a life-size totem for this nation's number one export sector? $60.18 billion. I *cover*, Beth thought. I *smooth*. I am the picture of unruffled.

"I think you can handle it," Beth said, flatly. "We're done," she called up to the booth, waving and smiling to the projectionist.

Beth called Germany from the car to say that the cut looked good, very good. She used the word "fantastic." She wanted to talk about the ad campaign. "I'm almost wondering if it would be better to sell it as a love story," she said. *Almost wondering*, she thought. I *published* as an undergraduate, and I just said, "I'm *almost wondering*." Beth shook her hands as if flinging off a sticky spider web.

Arno wanted to know how the sex was.

"It's affecting," Beth said. She winced again. I used the word *affecting?* Jesus.

"It won't get an NC-17, will it?"

"Oh, no. We'll get an R rating."

"But will the sex be as good with an Ahh?" Arno asked.

Beth hadn't had sex for almost two years. "It depends what you mean by 'good,' Arno," she said.

"I'm flying in on Wednesday."

"Great. I'll have Crystal get you a hotel."

She was going to have to start being nice to Liv. It was a great movie, and Arno had to think of them as a team, even if the thought of Liv Johansson made Beth's fingers curl up on themselves.

"Get me something in Santa Monica," Arno said.

Liv found Cody sleeping in his car when she came out of the screening room.

"Why didn't you come in?" Liv said, opening the door.

"Because it's weird. She doesn't know how to deal with the whole thing, and we needed her to be as comfortable as possible."

"You're a saint, and she's evil."

Cody shrugged.

"She wants us to cut fifteen minutes," Liv said.

"What an amazing and insightful note. She's a genius," Cody laughed, and then he got serious. "Us or Peter."

"Us." Liv smiled. "We're almost done, my sweet."

"You called me 'my sweet.'"

"Because you are."

"You remember what you said?"

Of course Liv remembered. She'd make sure that Arno and the German cabal would finance Cody's film. She would convince them that Cody was the secret to her film's success and that he deserved a break. She would do these things, but couldn't they spend a day—today—in a hazy romantic bubble without thinking about deals and promises? "Of course I remember. Don't worry."

Cody kissed her. "This is complicated, isn't it?"

"You help me. I help you. That's not complicated. It's classic," Liv said.

"Yeah, but then we add sex into the mix, and it gets complicated."

"I think that's pretty standard fare, too," she said. She imagined sex. Why not right here in the car? She was strong again. He was great. Everything was in its place. She unbuttoned her jacket.

Cody put on the glasses that he needed for staring at the editing monitor, and he opened his door. "If we jam on it, we'll make the deadline for Cannes," he said.

*T*he minute she drove around the corner, Joy saw him sitting on the front stoop. She stopped the car, letting it idle in the street as she stared at him. His hair seemed longer, but could that be? He had been gone only two weeks. Sixteen days, Joy corrected herself. He was wearing jeans. Had she ever before seen him in jeans? It was Saturday, and he wasn't wearing a yarmulke.

A car honked behind her, and Nick finally looked up to see Joy down the block. He held up his hand. He's waving? Sixteen days missing, and I get a wave? She found a parking space, turned off the engine and then continued staring at Nick who wasn't moving from the stoop.

My husband, she thought. My husband has come back.

Joy had spent the day looking at twelve apartments in Manhattan. What had seemed exciting two weeks ago had turned into drudgery. It was all different looking for a place that could accommodate a child and all her stuff. Many of the apartments she looked at had children. Strollers in the hallway, large plastic toys infringing on the sobriety of the living room, couples relegated to sleeping in the dining room. The smell of baby infected these apartments as surely as an unclean cat box. The word "squalid" had come to mind in a six-thousand-dollar-a-month apartment.

Nick got up and started walking down the block to Joy's Saab. He had walked out of their life without much of a plan. All he could say for certain was that it hadn't been working, *it* being the home life in Brooklyn, playing the Jewish *paterfamilias*, acting as if he were wise. He had thought that this package would set him right for life, but he found he couldn't keep it up. He had seen the Nigerian three times in the month before he left. He was coming into work later and later, preferring to spend his mornings reading magazines at a Barnes and Noble. In his mind, he tried blaming his dissatisfaction on Joy: she was vulgar; she took up too much space; she didn't understand him; she was selfish. While he could get up a good head of steam with this list, he knew it explained nothing. He bought a ticket to Dublin. His father had been born there, which meant Nick was eligible for Irish citizenship. He would take only a carry-on bag. He'd start over in Dublin. The loner, the expat.

Nick got to JFK yesterday seven hours before his flight. He ate and walked. He shopped. He leafed through magazines at newsstands. A security guard looked at him suspiciously when Nick passed him for the fourth time in an hour. At a Bally shop, he bought the expensive boxy leather jacket he was now wearing.

At the gate, Nick watched the mechanics service the 767. He wondered if the plane would make it. Would his last sixteen days end with an air disaster—a free-fall over Long Island? He imagined the airline investigator calling Joy with the news. She'd cry and maybe even tell the investigator that her husband had been missing. Nick wondered if Joy even knew who his dentist was. They'd need his records to identify his remains. He watched the food service carts be loaded into the plane, and Nick remembered that he hadn't ordered a kosher meal for the flight.

The plane was boarded by groups. Nick was in group three, but he never got up from his chair. He watched the stragglers rush for the door. He watched the airline's representative close the jet-way and turn off the LED sign behind the ticket counter that read, Flight 45, Dublin. Nick watched the plane push off.

Nick was alone in the waiting area. He needed someone to tell him what to do.

Eventually he headed for an exit where he had to talk his way out of the international departures area, passing through passport control without having gone anywhere. A security guard accompanied him to the taxi stand and waited until Nick got into a car.

Joy rolled down the window. "What's going on?" she asked. Her voice was firm and annoyed, as if Nick was a troublesome boy she was ready to thrash.

Nick was relieved. "I think I'm lost, Joy," he said.

"No shit," Joy said.

They talked at the car, Joy in the driver's seat, Nick leaning into the window. Nick told her about the day at JFK, about the days wandering around New York. About how everything, from his job, to the apartment, to his Judaism was all an act.

"But the problem is I don't know what or who I am, outside the act." Nick didn't mention the Nigerian.

Joy told Nick about how she had already figured this out about him. She told him about the private investigator who hadn't been able to find him.

"I want to come back. Please," Nick said.

They were quiet. A group of kids were hanging out at the corner; one of them couldn't stop laughing. Joy watched the two girls in the group. Were they fantasizing about which of the boys will be president someday? Joy wondered. Are they pegging their imagined futures to the status of these 16-year-old boys—*guys*—with tattoos on their necks?

"If you come back. If I let you come back, I'm in the driver's seat," Joy said.

Nick wasn't going to be president, she realized. Her husband wasn't going to make everything clear and easy for her. She was the one in charge. Joy understood that *she* was the presidential material in this relationship.

"Yes," Nick said. "That's what I want."

"No more Brooklyn," she said. "We're moving."

She got out of the car, and she saw him looking at her new pants. She knew she looked great. "I like your jacket," Joy said. "I've been looking for apartments in Manhattan. Expensive, but we'll find something."

Nick turned to cross the street, stepping into a pool of light cast by the park lamps. Joy was startled by how handsome he was. His black hair shone. His shoulders were broad and open. His cheekbones were defined. Joy imagined Nick in Los Angeles, stepping out of his car, handing his keys to the valet parker. Hollywood, she thought. We could get a big place in Hollywood for the same price we'd spend on something cramped in Manhattan.

19

$\mathcal{S}$ara sat in an empty classroom, making the final decision on Lucia. There was her F on the midterm, which counted for twenty-five percent of the grade. A C– on the final. No book report: ten percent. Class participation: nothing, unless twirling hair around a finger while staring open-mouthed out a window counted for something. Attendance: one hundred percent. Yes, Lucia did well at occupying a desk.

Sara gave Lucia a D and opened her lunch. Clam-shell boxes from the restaurant with foul madamas, pita bread, olives, rice pudding with a hint of rose water. She thought about calling Naim, but decided not to interrupt him when he was shooting two karaoke backup videos for Rai songs popular with a community in Queens. In two weeks there had been four weddings, two confirmation parties and a birthday. Ten more events already booked for next month. Last week, when Sara told Naim that the one bedroom next to them was coming onto the market and that they could break through their living room wall to double their space, he had smiled. He had even gone outside with her to see how their view of the promenade would be more direct. Sara suspected that his doctor had put him on Zoloft, but she decided to never ask.

Her cell phone rang. It was Jan, the Dutch yoga instructor. Nancy had had a heart attack.

Sara put her hand on her heart and pictured Jan standing in front of the list of important numbers taped to her mother's new refrigerator in her Florida condo. What was it called? Whirlpool? No, not that brand.

"She went so fast," Jan said. His voice sounded weak. "So fast." Jan was crying.

She died, Sara finally thought. She *died*. My mother didn't survive. Seven syllables. My mother didn't survive. The statement. My mother didn't survive? The question. My mother didn't *survive*. The incomprehension. How *dare* she not survive, Sara thought.

"Oh my God," Sara said.

Jan was sending the body to New York, because that's where Nancy wanted to be buried.

Sara remembered that her mother's refrigerator was a Sub Zero. She changed Lucia's grade to a C.

Peter asked if they should sit shivah. "She was Jewish, after all," he said. He and Sara were sitting in her kitchen drinking beer.

"No." Sara said. "She was an atheist. She never did anything Jewish."

Peter lit a dusty half-melted candle that had been shoved into the gap between the refrigerator and an upper cabinet. Its flame shot up.

"Okay. We'll do a Jewish funeral, but you have to find the rabbi." Sara said. "And no shivah."

Although she knew the *New York Times* didn't run every submission, Sara e-mailed them an obituary. Her mother had had a certain profile: a businesswoman; a lifelong New Yorker, if you didn't count the last few winters in Florida; a founder of Sara's alternative high school, which had, in recent years, become quite tony.

Joy found a rabbi for Peter. There were scheduling conflicts between the funeral home and the rabbi, and there had to be time for out-of-town people to get to New York. Everyone agreed that, given Jewish law, the funeral should be sooner, but there was no choice but to schedule it for Tuesday.

Nancy's body arrived in New York on Saturday, the same day her obit appeared in the paper.

Naim told Sara to take Monday off, but that wasn't what she needed.

"I can't," she said. "I'm diagramming sentences."

Great literature, which challenges the intellect, is sometimes difficult, but is also rewarding.

Sara walked up and down the blackboard, pacing off the subordinate clauses, making solid and dotted lines to form a neighborhood's through-streets and dead ends, jogs and blind alleys.

"See, it's fun," Sara said, drawing a dotted line from "is" to "challenges" and down to "but."

She wrote a new sentence that extended the full width of the board, twice:

Just when things are easy and you feel as if you can relax, the breath catches, because, even if the brain won't admit it, the body already knows that the other shoe is about to drop.

When she turned away from the sentence, she already knew that over half the class had walked out. But Lucia was still there, running her hands through her braids, brushing a cloud of dandruff onto her desk.

Sara insisted on going to work at the restaurant. The waiters and cooks kept telling her to sit down and relax, but she restocked the walk-in refrigerator and cleaned the meat slicer. During her shift, Peter called her five times from the editing room. He couldn't focus.

Sara said that it would pass. This was normal. She had lost Thumper, and she claimed to know "normal."

There was a ceremony at the funeral home where people could speak. Sara gave a eulogy that included details about her trip to Mexico. She saw Jan smile. She talked about discovering the power of the word "honey" during a phone call with her mother after she had met Naim, and she saw her husband touch the cross around his neck. She talked about her mother's physical strength and her emotional needs. She made some people cry, and she got a few laughs.

After speaking, Sara took Naim's arm. The yarmulke he had taken from the bin at the room's entrance had slipped to the back of his head. Someday his hair will be thin there, Sara thought.

Peter spoke about his "best friend," his mother. Then Jan spoke. Then a woman with whom Nancy had started Sara's school. The room was full, the crowd spilling out into the hall.

The cemetery was wet, the ground not yet thawed. Jan put a spray of tropical flowers from Florida on the casket—garish purple and yellow against the muddy ground.

The rabbi recited Kaddish, and Sara wondered about the inscription on the gravemarker. "You have a year to think about that," the funeral director had told her this morning. "You'll have an unveiling in a year; that's what Jews do," he had said as Sara fingered the sample pieces of gravemarker stone, each one smooth and cool, one of them glinting slightly under the fluorescent light in the funeral director's office. "Take it," he said, handing her the rock. "It's limestone. People like it."

Sara wondered if the gravemarker inscription had to be in Hebrew. She looked at Joy and Nick across the open grave and wondered if one of them knew enough Hebrew to translate the eventual inscription.

A hard woman.
A loyal one.
Brutally honest.
Supportive, with strings.
Loving, sometimes with conditions.
Not *easy for her daughter, ever. Easy for her son, always.*
Often just plain mean.

Sara put her hand in her pocket and found the sample piece of limestone, rolling it between her fingers. Maybe a line from Ginsberg's *Kaddish* would be better: *Like a poem in the dark trapped in its disappearance.* No, that's not it, Sara thought. I'm mashing lines together. She would have to look it up.

A backhoe beeped as it made its way down a narrow path between plots. A couple got out of a Volvo station wagon, carrying Mylar balloons to a grave. Sara saw a dog behind an evergreen. She looked again. Not a dog—a man bending over to tie his shoes. Cyrus? Sara smiled to herself. How nice that he came. The job with Peter had definitely worked out. Cyrus started walking toward the cemetery's front gate. He took off his cap. Not Cyrus. This guy was white.

Sara took off. Jumping over a low gravestone, her ankle turned, but she kept going. The guy was running now. The rabbi stopped talking.

"Oh my God," Peter said, his hand to his mouth.

It was Thumper.

"Stop, you fucker," Sara screamed, heaving the piece of sample limestone. A direct hit to the back of his head. Thumper was slowed up. Sara tackled him, and he was face down in the wet grass.

He refused to go to the hospital, even though everyone said you never know about head injuries. He hugged Peter, and he shook Naim's hand.

"Do you want to get a beer?" Thumper asked Sara.

Sara looked back to the grave. Was it over? Had she missed the part when they shoved dirt on the box?

Sara walked back to the grave. The rabbi was on his cell phone, unlocking his minivan. Exhaust billowed as the mourners warmed their cars. She noticed that the gravemarkers around her mother's plot didn't have inscriptions—just the names and some symbols. It was disappointing.

"No one has ripped their clothes," Naim said, coming back to the grave.

The yarmulke was still on his head—straighter now. His eyes looked swollen. Sara couldn't remember if she had seen him crying today.

"What?" Sara asked.

"You tear a piece of clothing. If you're mourning a mother or father, you tear it on your left side—closer to your heart. I don't like this cut ribbon thing," he said, flipping the torn black ribbon that the rabbi had given the mourners to pin to their clothes. "It's too, I don't know, too clean or manufactured or something. Tearing the clothes is better. It's more dramatic. It's called K'riah. The tearing of garments. Like you said, I know about Jews." He tugged at her down coat. "I won't tear this because the feathers will fall out."

She unzipped the coat and pulled out the collar of her cotton blouse. "Do you have a knife?"

Naim handed her a Swiss Army knife and she slit her collar. He gave her the car keys and then he ripped her collar away from the blouse's neck.

"I'll go back with Peter. Go have a beer with him," Naim said, looking at Thumper waiting near the front gate. "She'll be okay," Naim said, talking about Nancy.

Thumper had walked out of the Quito hotel with no plan other than to stay in Ecuador. He had wound up with a wife, Carmen, and a son, Edward. He had a small factory, which made a part used in nearly every Ford muffler sold in North America. He knew about the funeral because he always read the *New York Times* online.

He answered Sara's questions as if this were a publicity junket: Yes, he had no contact with anyone in the States, even his family. Yes, he thought about Sara and about Hampshire. Yes, he had been a little "nutty" when he left New York for the eco-tour. No, he didn't miss America. What he had missed were bookstores, but then there was Amazon.com, which was better. It was amazing how easy it had been to start a life in Ecuador. His Spanish was decent. His son spoke English perfectly, and he hoped to send him to an American university.

They were quiet, and Sara watched him peel off the beer-bottle label. The tip of his ring finger was gone. "You lost part of your finger," she said.

"I worked in a mine for a year," he said, folding his finger into his palm.

"What did you imagine would happen when you came here?" Sara asked.

"I thought I could get away without being seen."

"Really?"

"Yeah," he said. "You're thinner."

Sara heard a truck beeping outside, and she thought about the backhoe digging the hole for her mother. What was she doing in a bar with this man after her mother's funeral?

"Your husband or boyfriend . . . he's a good looking guy," Thumper said.

"Husband," she said.

Was this all there was going to be? she wondered. He had disappeared. She had been medicated and closed off. Why wasn't he begging her forgiveness? Why wasn't he at least making more of an effort to explain himself? She wanted to break a beer bottle and threaten his face.

"A lot of time has gone by," Sara said. She put on her gloves. Thumper shrugged.

There were no questions about her job or plans. Or the past decade. Nothing about Peter or Nancy. He was staying at a Sheraton in midtown. He only came back for Nancy's sake, Sara realized. Shit, she thought. Now I'm jealous of my dead mother.

He hugged her outside the bar, and Sara waited for it to end.

On the highway entrance ramp, her cell phone rang. It was Beth.

"I know we haven't talked for forever, but it has been crazy. If I had had any idea what this new deal meant, well, between you and me, I'm not sure I would've done it. You can't believe these Germans."

She doesn't know that my mother's dead, Sara realized.

"So if it weren't crazy enough, the Germans are getting in bed with one of the only new technology success stories around. This company went through a contraction, but they're a real powerhouse now, and they have capital to back it all up," Beth said.

Sara remembered that Beth used to say brilliant things, pithy and surprising expressions. But now she said things like: *new technology success stories*, *contraction*, and *powerhouse*. The sun flared through the windshield's smear. How long was it going to take to get to the point of this call? Sara wondered.

"Still, I can't really complain. Two pictures in the can isn't bad. FYI, your brother's brilliant, and Liv's going to Cannes."

It's the "Entertainment Tonight" pod people. They've eaten Beth Meisner, Sara realized.

"There's a new director that I have a real feel for. I found him doing craft service. Can you believe it? He's young, and a bit of a stoner, but who wasn't once, right?"

Sara kept herself from answering, You, for one, Beth Meisner.

"Anyway, I'm calling to see if I could lure you away from Brooklyn to come work for me out here. I really need a development person, someone who knows about story and structure. Shit, someone who can *read*. You can't imagine the pile of scripts I've got backing up. And these Germans keep breathing down my neck."

A car honked. Sara looked at her speedometer: thirty-five mph. She pulled onto the shoulder, turned off the ignition, and felt the car shake from the passing traffic.

"I've *got* to green-light three more projects in the next eight months. I know it sounds easy, but believe me, it's not."

Sara climbed over the gearshift and opened the passenger door, banging it on the guardrail. She was on an elevated stretch of highway over streets lined with squat two-flats. Directly below her, a tennis court had been flooded to make a skating rink, and a girl in a white parka was doing spins and shaky jumps.

"Where are you?" Beth asked.

"I'm on the highway. I pulled over."

Two boys in hockey skates dashed in wide circles around the spinning girl who was looking up past the highway and into the sun.

"So, what do you think?" Beth asked.

Sara knew that Beth was expecting a breathless acceptance. Everyone wanted to work in the *movie business*.

"I don't know anything about it. Development." Sara said.

"You know story and structure. The rest you learn."

"It's a big thing," Sara said, trailing off. If she talked, she might end up talking about her mother's death. Then she remembered that

Beth knew Thumper, and she didn't want to talk about that either. Boundaries had to be kept. I am not Beth Meisner, she told herself.

"Well, think about it. I'll give you a couple of days. I'll e-mail you all my numbers," Beth said. "I'm really serious about this."

Sara pushed "off" on the phone. The skating girl fell, and the boys skidded with long hockey stops to help her to her feet.

People from the funeral came to the apartment with food, and there was an unlikely buffet of lasagna, cheese and crackers, Swedish meatballs, honey cake, lemon cake, Turkish salad, falafel, and cold cuts. There weren't enough chairs, and people clotted in doorways. Jan collected dirty dishes and Joy and Nick washed them as they piled up. The mirrors in the apartment were covered with cloth. That's what Jews did, Sara had been told.

Sara made her way to the dining table where Peter sat with his new girlfriend, the actress whose name she couldn't remember. She knew that everyone wanted to hear what had happened with Thumper at the bar. The day was supposed to belong to her dead mother, but a good story is a good story. We're all narrative junkies, Sara thought.

"He's married. He has a son and a factory in Ecuador," Sara said to the table. There. Enough bullet points for people to pass around, she thought, noticing that someone had covered the Paul Klee print that Linus had given her when he had closed his practice.

Was it covered because the glass was too reflective? Sara wondered. Paul Klee: making the invisible visible, Sara remembered. She thought about Linus, about how he found her so difficult to read. I'm an open sore; why couldn't he see that? she wondered.

"Where's Naim?" she asked Peter.

"On the roof."

Sara found Naim eating a falafel sandwich at the edge of the roof terrace, a feature that had been emphasized by the realtor when Sara bought the apartment. "Everyone in the building shares it, and there are some terrific barbecues up here. There's a real *community* in the building," the realtor had said.

Sara had been to one potluck, which turned out to be a pretext for enlisting new members in a pyramid scheme called "Pilot."

A pigeon landed on the roof. He butted a piece of fallen falafel with his beak, and Sara started to cry.

Naim dropped his sandwich and wrapped his arms around her. An exhaust fan on the next-door building turned on, and Sara smelled chicken. There was a crash on the street: garbage collectors. She looked up at Naim. The muscles in his face were loose. She touched his cheek and it was wet, and she put her mouth there.

"Beth Meisner offered me a job in California," she said.

Naim let her go, and she sat on the roof's parapet.

"That's big news, Sara."

She still loved how "Sara" came out of his mouth. So much better than an American's nasal "a."

"Look," she said, pointing to the crowd of pigeons swooping onto the falafel. Naim swung his leg back and kicked the sandwich hard, the lettuce, bread, and falafel bursting into the air with the birds. His yarmulke finally fell off.

"What happened?" Naim asked.

Sara shrugged. "He lives in Ecuador."

"How do you say 'Thumper' in Spanish?" he asked.

"'Golper.' That's the verb, I think," she said, ninth-grade Spanish rushing back. *Golper*, to hit or thump.

Naim pulled a winter wool cap from his pocket, unrolled its face mask, and put it on. "*El Señor Golpe de la lucha libre*," he said, puffing up his muscles, playing a Mexican wrestler.

This is my mom's funeral, and I'm laughing, Sara thought.

"Tell me how you wanted to be with me the minute you saw me," she said.

"Oh, no, not the Fairy Tale," he said, still in his *Lucha Libre* announcer voice.

"Yes," she said, pulling him to sit on the parapet next to her. "But no funny voice." She pulled the mask up to see his face. "Okay, now. Now you can start."

"I start," he said, clearing his throat in a high-school-speech way. "You were standing at the flowers."

"No," she said. "Start at the beginning."

"You're a child," he said.

"Yes," she said.

He leaned over, cupped her chin, and whispered in her ear, "The minute the movie was over, everyone started talking very fast, but they weren't listening to each other."

Sara turned her head so that their foreheads touched. Joined at the head.

"I couldn't understand because they talked too fast, but I knew that they all wanted to show off how smart they were," Naim said, sitting up straighter. "They made me dizzy and confused. How do you say it?"

"Dazed and confused," she said.

"Yes. Then I saw you next to the flowers, and you were quiet and still, not like a statue, but like a wise person. Like someone who sees."

Sara teared up. He had picked her out of a crowd as someone special.

"I knew that you could stay or go. It didn't matter, because you were solid. Not frozen, but strong. That kind of solid."

Although she had given him all the proof to the contrary—the stories of her retreat to her mother's house, the years of medication, the reliance on Verizon's reminder call option—Naim's belief in her solidity had never been shaken. Maybe he had a better perspective on her because he was an outsider, Sara thought. Maybe he was able to see the benefits of being ill-equipped for a fancy career and a sexy personal life.

"I thought you could teach me something. You were someone who knew things that I needed to know," Naim said.

And that was the end of the story. This was the part where they lived together happily ever after, which of course had not exactly been the case.

"Rip some more," Sara said, holding out her collar.

She felt his breath as he ripped the collar back to the top of her spine. Then he got up to retrieve a notebook sitting at the edge of the roof.

It was a sketchbook filled with pencil drawings, every page devoted to water: the river she could see from this roof, ocean shorelines, a dripping spigot, a water park slide, a hotel pool. Even with pencil, he had finely rendered liquid. They were beautiful.

My husband is an artist, she thought, seeing these words as an electronic news ribbon in Times Square. Why hadn't she seen this? He had been able to see *her*, but she hadn't seen him. She took his hand. He is a superior being, she thought. The muscles around his mouth softened.

"You should paint," Sara said. "It's time to paint."

"I know," he said. "I'll need more room."

For the first time, Sara thought about the money that her mother had probably left behind.

"I want to go back to Palestine," he said.

But there is no Palestine, Sara thought. Not really. Not yet. There had been the Ottoman Turks and then a British Mandate and then partition and then Israel. Then a thing called the Palestinian Authority. Does that really count as a country? she wondered.

"What?" she asked.

"I want to go back, and I want you to go with me," he said.

"What?"

"Stop saying 'what,'" Naim said. "You have passion, Sara, and you don't know it."

La Pasionaria, Sara thought. Liv had called her that. Her mother had been there. It was dinner. There were oysters, and she had had things to say about America. She had made a point about how everyone just nodded at each other because thinking about big problems was too hard, and that people would rather maintain their "mellows."

"La Pasionaria," Sara said.

"What's that?"

"She was a Spanish revolutionary," Sara said. "She was full of passion. You're wrong. I know I have passion."

Sara tugged her ripped collar. "What's it called?" she asked.

"*K'riah*," he said.

"*K'riah*," she repeated.

A helicopter was making its way over them toward Manhattan.

"You'll like it over there," Naim said.

"Like?" Sara asked.

"Okay. Wrong word. It would be *interesting*," Naim said.

"I'm interested in Brooklyn. I could be interested in working for Beth," Sara said.

"It's soul death," Naim said.

"Why do you want me to go there?"

"Because you're going to sink in this," Naim said. He was talking about New York, California, maybe all of America.

Sara imagined herself alone in her apartment, eating out of the microwave. Working and coming home. Reading and staring out her window. She'd drink one bottle of wine every two days. She'd rent videos. Her mother had had her yoga teacher at the end. She had made sure that she wouldn't be alone when she had a heart attack. Her mother had made sure that someone was there to cry for her and to make the calls that needed to be made. Sara saw herself lying dead on her kitchen floor for days before anyone noticed.

"I'd have to learn Arabic, right?" Sara asked.

"Yes," Naim said. "Who else do you have, Sara? Your brother?"

Sara imagined dusty streets and crumbling buildings, the plaster chipping off the concrete blocks. She thought about army bulldozers and about kids throwing rocks. She imagined shopping at a market where she'd see women in veils. She imagined living with curfews.

"You want me to move to a war zone," she said.

Naim nodded.

Sara knew he would go, with or without her. She imagined going alone to Los Angeles and working for Beth. Reading scripts, learning how to talk like Beth talked. Box office. Story arc. Payoff. She imagined having drinks with her brother and his new girlfriends. She'd have to buy a car. She imagined a city filled with special people, shiny people. Sara wondered where Linus was. What would Linus say? Hollywood or Palestine?

Naim pushed the hair out of Sara's eyes.

"Why did Thumper disappear?" Naim asked.

Sara realized she had never asked him. "I guess he didn't want to come back to me."

"Really? That's the reason?"

"I don't know," Sara said. "No, of course that's not the reason."

Sara thought that she would have to live near the water. In a place as arid as Palestine, she'd need the sea.

"I want to live on the water," she said. "The Mediterranean."

"Okay," he said. "We can do that."

A streetlight came on. Sara smelled fireplace smoke. The wind picked up, and she felt rain, maybe snow. She could always come back to Brooklyn. The decision would be easier if she thought like that. In the scheme of things it's always important to have an out, Sara realized. Brooklyn would always be here if the Palestinian thing didn't work out. Of course it wasn't so sure for Palestine. It might be there in the future. Then again, it might not, she thought.

"I guess I should catch Palestine before it disappears again," Sara said. "Palestine: my future ex-country," she said to her husband.

"What are you talking about?"

She kissed Naim. "I was playing with words," Sara said.

The wind blew and Naim pulled his hat over his ears. "It's my last winter," he said.

20

$\mathcal{C}$ody's script was about four losers, loosely based on his two brothers and their next-door neighbors, who discover that one of their ATM cards can access money from any account in the bank system. Three get arrested. One gets away. A little *Lord of the Flies*, a little *Treasure of Sierra Madre*, some bonehead humor.

"For this to work, it has got to be funny," Liv said. "And it's not funny enough."

"Yeah, I know. Beth said the same thing," Cody said.

Liv looked down at her coffee and forced herself to count to ten. He had let *Beth* read the script before her? She sipped the coffee. What the hell was that woman still doing in her life? Was she condemned to be with Beth forever? Liv wondered, imagining shoving her producer out the door: *Here's your hat; what's your hurry?*

"She has a good eye for story," Cody said. "She's not totally lame."

"Well, then you don't really need my notes, do you?" Liv said, tossing the script across the kitchen floor. "I mean, you have Beth."

I'm going to lose Cody, she realized. He's going to leave me.

"Come on," Cody said. "Don't be psycho."

"No, *you* come on."

This felt good, this wind-up to an explosion. They hadn't had sex for a long time. A fight might be an adequate stand-in.

"What's your problem?" Cody asked.

"My problem is that you're thinking more about Beth than about me."

"Are you on crack? I edited your movie. We're joined at the hip. We might as well be the same person," Cody said, low and firm.

"She's a terrible producer."

He slammed his hand against the cabinet door next to her head. "Why are we talking about Beth?"

She kept herself still. No flinching. The dishes in the cabinet rattled, and Liv felt light, almost like giggling. I'm in it, she thought. The black, icky emotional stuff was flowing just like she wanted it.

"This isn't about me and Beth, you know," Cody said.

"Then what's it about?" Liv asked.

"Is there anything in your head at all?" he said. "This fight is about us, but I sure don't know why. Do you?"

"There is no *us*. We don't have sex," Liv said. She was whining.

He leaned very close to her. "Let me tell you our story. We *had* sex, and you rejected me because you wanted to be with the Director of Photography. And then we had sex *again*, but you got cancer, and we stopped. But we're going to start again."

Liv stared at his left eye where a faint gray ragged ring pulsed around the pupil.

He slid down the wall to sit on the floor.

Liv traced a circle on the Corian countertop, her finger sliding around an invisible bull's-eye. Don't make Cody the target when he's not, Liv thought. She wanted to take off her skin to fumigate it. She wanted to remove her eyes from their sockets and wash them. She wanted to shave her skull and give it a glycol peel. She had to change everything.

She heard John come in. "I'm back," he yelled.

Liv climbed onto Cody's lap and wrapped her legs around his waist.

"The chemo made you twisted," Cody whispered to her.

"Yes, and other things," she said, brushing his earlobe with her teeth.

Out of the corner of her eye, she saw her father step into the kitchen and then step quickly back out.

Tonight would be the first time they had ever eaten in the dining room with its view of the L.A. basin. Gnocchi, pesto, greens, salad, a black cherry soufflé for dessert. Cody cooked.

"Where did you learn to cook?" Linus asked as he finished his salad.

"The normal way. My mom," Cody said.

"Our mother never taught us." Linus said. "Of course it was all boiled potatoes with goat grease—the national dish of Armenia. Who would want to learn how to cook that?"

"That's not true. We ate very well," John said.

"You're delusional," Linus said. "Name one good Armenian food."

"The bulgur dishes," Cody said. "They're Armenian, right?"

Liv's stomach heaved with the word *bulgur*. *Bulgur*. Blank it out, she told herself. Push it away. *Bulgur with chopped dog meat*. Don't think about it, she thought. *Bulgur*.

"Okay, I'll grant you that. Yeah, that's pretty good," Linus admitted.

"What are some of them? Like some recipes," Cody asked.

"There's *havgitov kufta* which is bulgur with egg and tomatoes," Liv said. Keep saying the word, she told herself. "And there are *dolmas*, which are vegetables stuffed with bulgur." Strip the word of all its associations, she thought. "And there's *Madzoon Abour*, which is yogurt soup with Swiss chard, garlic, and mint," she said. "But wait, there's no bulgur in that one." *Bulgur with chopped dog meat*. She couldn't help it; it was all she could imagine. "I'll get the cheese," she said, jerking herself to standing to get the cheese platter. Maybe if she moved, she could tamp down the picture of the dog in her head.

It worked, the dog was gone. She was back in Hollywood, holding a cheese plate for her father as he cut a piece of Camembert. From this angle she could see that even though his hair was finally gone at the crown, his arm muscles were defined. He could be 50, not 65, she thought. Sixty-six, she corrected herself. How much older would he have looked had he stayed in Armenia? Maybe he'd be dead by now.

"Thanks," John said, and Liv held the plate out to Linus.

The Christmas card photo, she thought: her father savoring his Camembert, her uncle, Mr. Dirty Old Man, with his greedy slice of Manchego. If I hadn't gotten sick, they would have been stuck in another New York winter, and Cody would be serving buckets of trail mix to another film crew. My cancer has given their lives shape—a good shape.

"Do any of you realize that all of this has a very good chance of coming back?" Liv asked, pointing at her body. "The cancer. Statistically there's a good chance that it'll come back. It comes back, you know."

They were quiet.

"I do," Linus said. "I know that."

His face was pale, and his nose seemed larger. He's gotten skinnier, Liv thought, opening the doors to the deck. A breeze blew, and she shivered. She looked at Cody, who was concentrating on carving the wax from a piece of Brie. I'm embarrassing him, she thought. I'm too confrontational for the Cody Man.

"The movie's done and I'm doing okay for the moment, so I wanted to know what you're thinking," she said. She looked at John, then at Linus. "About the future, I mean."

"I didn't think I'd stay once you got better, but I've been enjoying myself," her father said.

Yeah, Liv thought. *Enjoying* yourself.

"I guess I, we, will be going back to New York," John said. "But it feels aggressive to ask us here at dinner like this."

Linus shook his head slightly at his brother to make him tone it down.

"No, no. I have to say this," John said to Linus. He turned to Liv and said, "Why are you asking me when I'm leaving your house? I never asked you when you were moving out of the apartment."

The small muscles in her arms spasmed. "It's so fucking cold in here," she said, wrapping the afghan from the couch around her.

Cody got up and closed the deck doors.

"No, you didn't. But I want to have the house—this house—to myself," she said.

Please don't be mad at me, Daddy, Liv thought.

"Production stops paying rent in a week," Linus said.

"I was thinking about picking up the lease after that," Liv said.

"It's a fortune," John said.

"But we're loaded," Liv snapped. "Remember?"

"There's a place on Crescent Heights that I'm going to rent until I find a place to buy in the hills," Linus said.

"You're staying here. In L.A.?" John asked.

Linus nodded.

John felt his shoulders round. His throat narrowed. He had never been alone in New York.

"You're ungrateful, you know that," he said to his brother. "You're cynical and narcissistic."

Linus laughed. "Whoa there, big boy."

"I won't whoa," John said. "You laugh at people, and you're lazy. You wrote a script about a James Bond wanna-be because you're emotionally retarded. You're stuck in a fantasy. What have you ever done to help this family?"

His voice embarrassed him. He was a father, a businessman. A homeowner. A man of deep faith. But he sounded whiny. Why didn't his brother know how lonely he'd be?

"I schlepped my share of crosses," Linus said. "I got the truck to port. I'm part of this family. I've done my part. You would've been nailed at the first checkpoint if I hadn't been there." His eyes never wavered from the candle's glare off a spoon. I've been moving into the light, but John hasn't noticed a thing, Linus thought. It's so discouraging. "You'd still be in Spitak if it weren't for me. If I hadn't figured it all out, you'd still be stuck there eating gray meat. I made things happen."

"Mr. Joker, driving a truck wearing the priest's crown," John said, picking up his soufflé cup.

"That old saw. You want to argue about that?" Linus asked. It was a taunt.

"Yeah. Why not?" John said, turning to Cody. "He stole this beautiful hat from the priest's vestry, because he just *had* to have a driving cap and a regular cap wasn't good enough. He had to wear the priest's hat."

"Oh, I see. Now we tell everyone everything," Linus said, motioning to Cody.

"Why not tell Cody?" John asked. "He's a lot more respectful than you."

Cody turned to Liv, hoping for clarification.

"Hello, we don't talk about this stuff in front of outsiders, remember?" Liv said to her father.

"I said I don't care," John said.

"Hello, the outsider needs cluing in," Cody finally interjected.

"It's our family's migration story," Liv said. "It's our Donner Party, but we ate sausages, not people," Liv said.

"Don't you dare make this into a joke," John said.

Liv held up her hands and then folded them in her lap like a naughty student relegated to the corner of the classroom for having talked out of turn.

Linus mimed zipping shut his mouth.

John turned his back on his brother and daughter to face Cody. "I'll tell you," John said to Cody.

A candle hissed. The heater blower kicked on. He ran his finger around the rim of his wine glass, and then he started the story.

He spoke casually as if he had often recounted the narrative on talk shows. He shaped the events into a plot of international intrigue, roguish heroes, and large sums of cash. He described Crete, the sleazy art dealers, and the way he stored the cash—always cash—in an empty septic tank in the back garden.

We're Americans, Liv marveled. Thirty years later, and we're finally like them. Our history is now officially consumable anecdote.

But Liv didn't find it so bad, this letting the boundaries go fuzzy.

It's a good story. What the hell. Let the Cody Man hear it, Liv thought.

There was pushing the truck out of the mud when they left Spitak. And eating cheese sandwiches by the side of a road next to a donkey tied to a pole. She remembered the man who had walked up to the donkey, and without a word started beating it with a stick, and she remembered crying and yelling at the man and then throwing up. There was Linus rushing at the man. There was money—Linus paid something—and then a woman came to unhitch the donkey. Liv remembered petting the donkey's suede nose.

They slept and ate in the truck for 21 days. Liv remembered shitting behind a tree and how every place was gray and wet, until one day, when she woke up after sleeping for hours, spit dried on her cheek, it wasn't. Gray or wet. "We're close," her father told her.

There was the ferry to Crete where Linus insisted on staying in the truck while John and Liv stood at the edge of the boat so she would watch the waves, and he could be seasick.

Then in Iraklion, they gave the truck to a man who wanted the parts. He lived at the end of their street, and Liv remembered how he set the truck's seats under an olive tree in his garden. Liv, John, and Linus had a white house with thick walls and a blue door. There was a yellow Renault. A woman came every day to sweep the packed dirt yard and make lunch and dinner. There was an English school with a long white stone loggia, a big classroom with high ceilings and fans. There was her teacher, Mrs. Pavlos, who closed the shutters to keep out the afternoon sun and who demanded correct prepositions even from 6-year-olds.

Her father walked her to and from school three times a day. Morning, lunch, and afternoon. The other fathers came to school only for the Christmas pageant, because they had jobs with Ford Motors or with tanker companies. Her father was a thief, which meant he had more time for his daughter.

When John finished the story, Cody said, "The movie's about you guys. Why didn't you tell me?" He was asking Liv. "All those hours, and no one said a thing." This was directed at John and Linus.

"That's how we are," Liv said, proud to flaunt her membership in the club of three. "Do you remember the donkey?" she asked her father.

"Yeah," John said, turning to Liv. "You tried to convince me to take him with us in the truck. You said he could sleep in the crèche. It was solid gold. Fourteen carat, that crèche."

John took Liv's hand. She didn't remember this. She couldn't picture the crèche.

"Liv, I moved Sparkle Life to Spitak," John said.

"What?" she said. This was a new story. She didn't know this one. "You left New York?"

"Yes," he said.

"For cheaper labor?"

"Not entirely," he said.

"Not entirely," she repeated. "Why else do factories move offshore?"

The tension was back. She watched her father swallow and look over her shoulder toward the Strip.

"So, I'm listening," Liv said. "Cheaper workers to make leotards because . . . Because why exactly?"

"We make a lot more than leotards, now," John said. He got up and straightened the shelf of videotapes and DVDs behind Liv. "We make clothes like what Cody wears."

Liv looked at Cody's pants. Baggy with lots of pockets, a miracle fiber that wicked his sweat. "So what?" Liv said. The idea was still the same: her father had kept something very big from her. He had sprung his secret on her in front of Cody, a stranger. For the first time ever Liv felt what it might be like to be someone other than her father's daughter.

"It's true I'm making more money there, but I'm not keeping all of it. I'm building a church in Spitak," John said. "Linus and I are going back to ask for forgiveness for what we did. I have a guy looking into buying television time."

"You're going on Armenian television?" She could laugh.

"Yes. We need to apologize to the whole country."

He's crazy, Liv thought. Of course that's it. The way he prays before every meal, even the popcorn at the movies. The manic running. No women for years and years. My father's psychotic.

"I want you to go with us, Liv," he said.

"My zipper broke," Linus yelled, miming unzipping his mouth. "I'm talking now. Professional opinion: you're crazy."

"No, I'm not," John yelled back.

"Delusions of grandeur. Nuts," Linus said, no longer yelling.

"I'm—*we're*—going to go on television and *we're* apologizing. It'll be very pure and simple. Just 'we're sorry,'" John said.

"Bullshit," Linus said, shoving his plate away. His wine glass tipped, and no one reached for it. The red liquid pooled around the wooden salad bowl.

"And how much have you spent on this church thing?" Linus asked John.

John looked at his lap.

"Come on," Linus said. "Say it."

"Two and a half," John whispered.

"That's *million dollars*, ladies and gentlemen," Linus said.

"Wow," Cody said, getting up from the table.

"Where are you going?" Liv asked.

"You could make a movie with that," he said, collecting the plates and putting a napkin on the wine spill. "That's all the investment my movie would need, but you build a church instead."

For the first time in Liv's memory, the Cody Man sounded judgmental.

He left the room, and Liv heard water running in the kitchen. Linus left the table, his shadow thrown large on the far wall by the courtyard's garden lighting. John pulled the fruit plate toward him and began denuding a date branch.

"Well, we've cleared the room," John said.

Liv picked up the napkin and wrung the wine into her glass.

"What do you think of the plan, really?" John asked Liv.

Liv shrugged, and drank the last bit of wine.

"A shrug? What does that mean?"

You should've told me, but not like this. If you want to be famous by giving all this shit back . . ."

"It's not about fame," John interrupted.

"Whatever," Liv said.

"It's not 'whatever' either."

"Okay, what do you want me to say?"

John wanted corniness; he prayed for it. "Why can't you say you're happy for me?"

Liv heard the lump in John's throat. "Dad, this religious thing . . . I can't really go there."

"I'm not asking you *go* there. I'm asking you to be happy that I'm doing what I want," John said, cutting a piece of olive bread, separating the crust from the spongy middle. "If you come back to New York, I think you should get your own apartment."

And here it is, Liv thought. Finally. Her head felt light, and she thought about heart arrhythmias, blood clots, and blood pressure. She was sure her vision had degraded and that if she were tested right now, she'd need glasses. All landmarks are socked in by fog, Liv thought. Anchor cut. Buoy sinking. She wanted Cody back at the table. She could use someone next to her right now.

"It'll probably be better if I stay out here," Liv said.

John shrugged. Whatever.

"I brought you this, you moron," Linus yelled, stomping into the room, slamming Thaddeus's stone hand onto the table. "How dare you say that I've never done anything." He was whispering now, bug eyed. "This cured her, and you know it."

He's crazy, too, Liv thought.

John got up and took Linus's head in his hands. Covering his brother's ears, he put his lips to Linus's forehead and kissed him. "Yes. Thank you for bringing the hand into this home," John said.

The motion detector light flicked on at the front gate. The door buzzed. It was Beth.

She had a magnum of champagne and breathlessly apologized for interrupting dinner. "I just had to come *pour fêter le film*. It's sticking with me. It really sticks," she said, smiling.

Liv glanced at her father and uncle: they were all back in line, lips zipped. Beth wouldn't be privy to what had been going on at dinner. Maybe they were all coming closer to being like other Americans, but they hadn't yet totally crossed the line. There were still limits.

"No reason we can't switch to champagne," Cody said, coming into the room with flutes. "Let me get that," he said, taking the bottle.

Liv glanced at Cody. It was clear that he'd keep his mouth shut, too. The family's secrets would be safe with him.

The cork bounced off the deck doors.

"To the film," Beth said.

"To the film," John said.

"To Cody," Liv said. He had saved her ass, so from now on any time she had the opportunity to direct attention to Cody and his projects, that's what she had to do. All Cody, all the time. It was their deal.

Liv watched her father sip champagne. I'm breaking up with my father, she thought. This is the champagne toast to our separation.

21

"Can we cut to the chase?" Liv asked Linus. "I've got to give him something."

She looked at her watch. She was meeting Arno at his hotel at the beach, and traffic could be awful this time of day.

"It's a total departure," Linus said.

"Just tell me."

Liv wanted to go to this meeting armed with ideas for her next movie. She had some vague notions of her own, but Linus had told her that he had the beginning of a real script. What Liv needed for the meeting was a log line. Something simple: one sentence, maybe three describing the story. Was it a love story? Science fiction? Romantic comedy? Action? Thriller?

"It's a love story, which means of course it's a tragedy, because that's what all love stories are," Linus said. "It's about a failed shrink who finds his salvation in his love for a cello player, but the cellist is sick, and their love story becomes a battle for time."

"It sounds pretty down. Is it?" Liv asked.

"Not totally. The shrink's funny. Ironic and wry. And the cellist can be pretty wacky," he said.

"So they live life to the fullest," Liv said.

"Yes, each of them takes whatever two sticks are available, and they rub the hell out of them," Linus said.

Liv had put on a dress for the first time in years. It was sleeveless and tight and it didn't feel right: this dress, this close to her uncle.

"Don't be uncomfortable," Linus said.

"I'm not. It's just this dress," Liv said, squirming.

He took off his sunglasses. "Look, I know."

"Know what?" Liv asked.

"I'm 60 years old, and I'm still a smart aleck with a superiority complex," he said. "I need something to reign me in. I need a tether, Liv."

Liv pictured the knot of traffic that would be building up in downtown Beverly Hills. She'd have to cut all the way down to Olympic Boulevard to avoid that. She picked up her bag. She'd call Linus from the car to get more details on the script.

"Wouldn't you agree?" Linus asked.

"What? That you're a smart aleck? Maybe. I don't know. Yeah, you are," she said. "I should get going." She didn't want to hear more of her uncle's confessions. Not now. Maybe not ever. Wasn't this a violation of boundaries, and hadn't he already done that on the hillside with his hands?

"You've got time," Linus said. "I need you to listen to me, Liv."

This was new, this sounding needy thing, Liv thought. His eyes were clear. Everything about his face looked different. Less hungry. When was the last time she had looked at his face? Liv wondered.

"I meditate six days a week, between two and four hours a day, at the Vedanta Center, so that I can lose my maya, which means illusion. It's the veil that covers our real nature," he said

"I thought you went to the movies," Liv said.

"Nope," Linus said. "I don't want to say that I'm becoming a Hindu because it sounds trendy, but I am sort of becoming one."

Her uncle spent his days finding God? The Vedanta Center?

"Didn't Christopher Isherwood hang out there?" she asked.

"Yes," Linus said. "Some people say that meditation is like being a boomerang. By looking for and finding your divine nature, you're coming home. But that's not how it is for me. I lost my divine nature lifetimes ago. There's nothing boomerang about any of this.

It's all new," he said. "I never apologized for the thing on the hill when you found the dead cat."

"No, you didn't," Liv said.

"I'm sorry."

"I really have to go," Liv said. "Traffic."

Linus watched his niece cross the courtyard to the front gate. He wanted her to turn back and smile at him, but then he told himself not to desire that smile. Whatever she gave him was enough. She was part of him. She was part of the world, and it was all part of him, of all of them.

"Do you want to come with me?" Liv said from the door. "You can finally meet Arno, the German."

"Yeah," he said, grabbing his jacket.

Liv knew she could provide a place for her uncle's stories. The love-story script would probably be good. She and Linus could share it and maybe others in the future. The project would be their neutral field, swept of landmines.

22

$\mathcal{L}$iv's film was screened in the International Critics Week section of the Cannes Film Festival. Liv gave twenty-five interviews after the screening, and there was a party thrown by the Germans at which Liv split a bottle of champagne with Kim on a dark terrace that waiters were using as a staging area for trays, wine, glasses, and ashtrays. The response to the movie had seemed pretty good, but who could tell at Cannes where people answered their cell phones during screenings?

"I want you to know that I think the film's great. My tantrums during production, well none of that was about you," Kim said. "I would work with you again in a second."

"Ditto," Liv lied, pretty sure that Kim was doing the same.

During an interview that afternoon, Kim had announced that she was pregnant. "I can't have journalists see me drink, so let's load up now," Kim said, refilling their glasses.

Liv stayed out on the terrace after Kim went back into the party. She asked a waiter for a glass of wine, and he gave her a full bottle of a St. Emilion.

"*C'est plus pratique*," he said, kicking open the door to reenter the party. A wave of chatter and French house music broke onto the terrace.

The doors swung shut, and Liv settled down onto the cool slate with her bottle and a glass. She wished things were back to the way they used to be with Cody, so she could ask him to go to her room to get the small gummy wad of opium she had tucked into the nightstand. But they were no longer the way they used to be; since the final mix, she and Cody were "exes." He was at the party as Beth's new director and Arno's new best friend. "A director *and* a surfer. We should all be like the Cody Man," Arno said as often as he could.

She could hear lanyards hitting sailboat masts in the harbor across the street, and she relaxed against the building's limestone walls. Church bells struck the time somewhere in town. It was three a.m. in Armenia, Liv calculated. Linus and John had landed in Yerevan yesterday.

If Arno's inflated worth on the European market didn't deflate to conform to reality, and if her movie did any business at all, Arno with the German cabal would finance her second movie, with Beth producing. Liv would help Linus finish his script, because, as depressing as it was, Arno liked the idea. "Very *Love Story*," he had declared at their lunch. "I loved *Love Story*. My first date was to see *Love Story*."

Her cell phone rang.

"You're in our country." It was Peter.

"Paris is ours. Not France."

The moving billboard at the bus stop below whirred, changing from Kinder Surprise Chocolat to a Volvic ad with Zinadine Zidane in a locker room with his soccer ball.

"Whatever. I hope you're in better shape this time."

"It's not hard. Where are you?"

"L.A."

He sounded stuffed up with a cold.

"Julie dumped me for my assistant, Cyrus. Is that the most fucked-up clichéd thing? He's eighteen."

"Was it serious between you two?"

Peter laughed, a loose laugh, something that could go very manic very quickly. "No. Still it was romance, Liv, you know?" His voice caught. "Oh God," he said. He was crying. "Romance is never funny."

A kid drove a skateboard at the concrete posts separating the sidewalk from the street below Liv. The board flew up; the skateboarder tucked and came down, only barely avoiding landing on his knees.

"Where are you living now?" Peter asked, his voice stronger. Liv heard him drinking.

"I don't know. I haven't decided," she said. She reached for a long cigarette butt wedged between two slate tiles.

"Are you going to keep your house in the hills?"

She pictured her house: Yasser in the olive tree, watching the hawk circle above, the cleaning lady making sure that the cat bowl was filled with food. She dug a lighter from her pocket and lit the cigarette butt. It was her cat's house now. She waited for Peter to say what she knew he would say next:

"I was thinking that if it's empty I could take on the lease. Joy's got this big place in the hills. Her husband's working for a California senator, now. Anyway, they have a lap pool," Peter said. "My apartment has this great deco bathroom—original tile and everything—but it's not that great, you know?"

Her phone clicked. Another call. "That's my other line," she said. "If I decide to give it up, I'll let you know."

Neither of them was unhappy to get off the phone.

It was Linus. "Just checking in from the shithole," he said. "How's the party?"

"Not to sound too been-there done-that, but it's boring. The weather's nice, though," Liv said.

"It's raining here, and we had dinner with five priests," he said. "It was incredible. We're eating at the only decent restaurant around, and while everyone's acting like we're in the light of the Lord, I'm watching three girls shoot up outside the front window," Linus said.

"Lovely," Liv said.

"Isn't it? The priests are trying to talk him into restoring a bunch of churches that have been falling apart for two hundred years. These guys can be pretty convincing, and your father's there with his calculator making projections on how to rebuild. They're on a fault line," Linus said.

"Oy," Liv said.

"Oy is about it. Sometimes I think I wouldn't know how to talk without Yiddish. *Oy vey*," Linus said. "There were a bunch of reporters when we landed, and you won't believe what your father said first off. The first thing."

"What?" Liv asked.

"He tells how much everything cost—the construction, the statues, the windows, even the pews. Now after the fucking Armenian gangsters steal everything in the place, they'll know the market price for the resale."

"You're supposed to be seeing everyone's divinity," Liv reminded him.

"I can see an Armenian gangster's divinity and still know what his job is."

There was a crackle in the connection and then the sound of a truck engine.

"What's that? Where are you?" Liv asked.

"I'm in a parking lot. That was the last truck from Germany with this huge gold cross. Our so-called security guard's been throwing up vodka for the last hour, and I thought someone should be here to make sure the cross actually made it into the church."

There were more crackles in the line and then an echo.

"Are you still there?" he asked.

"Yeah, but the connection's getting funky."

"You know what the security guard told me?" he asked.

"The one throwing up?" Liv asked.

"Before he started puking."

"What?" Liv asked.

"He said he read on the Internet that the universe is shaped like a soccer ball, and that if you go off into space, after billions and billions of light years, you'll wind up back on earth."

The moving billboard on the street below Liv whirred to show the ad with Zidane and his soccer ball. Liv felt comforted knowing that everything comes back. "Are you there?" Linus asked.

"Yeah, you sound better now," Liv said.

"So you see? We come back. We'll always come back," Linus said. "Liv, he's really happy. He is a righteous man, and we shouldn't make fun of how corny he is. If you were here, he'd be so happy. Beyond happy."

A waiter rushed onto the terrace to grab a crate of bottles, and Liv caught a glimpse of Arno dancing a sort of stiff pogo with Kim before the door swung shut.

He came and got me and then strapped into the airplane seat with him, Liv thought, imaging a baby—herself—wrapped tightly in flannel, pressed against her father for her first flight, Stockholm to Yerevan.

"Liv?"

"I'm still here," she said. "Okay. I'll come. Of course I'll come."

Back in her hotel room, after the first bit of opium, Liv felt tall, substantial, and weighty. "I am a giant among men," she announced to the empty room, opening the balcony doors. There was a high-pitched hum below. Was it the DJ at the party? No, he was too many floors below her. How many? She remembered seeing "5" in the elevator, but that was a long time ago. How long? Her cell phone rang.

"Hello," she said, the two syllables long and languid like a muscle softening.

The opium was everywhere in the body.

"I slept with Joy," Peter said. He was drunk.

"Oh," Liv said.

"I slept with her when you and I were together," Peter said.

The flashing green cross on the *pharmacie* next to the hotel bloomed through her room's voile curtains in a diffuse green cloud. A breeze blew, and the green voile cloud floated in and out of the room. She laid down, half on the balcony, half in the room, the curtains billowing across her body. We're breathing, she thought, imagining the earth had lungs as she listened to herself and to Peter breathing.

"Liv?"

"Why are you telling me this?" she asked.

"Because you're always so separate and in your bubble, and I never can get to you. Maybe this'll get to you."

Something dug into her back. It was the metal threshold between the floor and the balcony. She rolled away from the threshold and back into the room.

"I'm a person, Liv, and I can affect and be affected. I'm in a context. I'm as complicated as you are, Liv."

"Go live with her in her big house, then," Liv said.

"We're not together *now*. She's my *producer*." He was whining. "I don't want to live with Joy. I want your place. I'm serious."

"It'll be too hard for Yasser to accept a new person. Cats are creatures of habit," Liv said. And she hung up. "He's gone now," Liv said to the room, turning off the cell phone.

Liv watched the green neon cross blink and thought about the opium in her brain folds. She imagined farmers scoring the poppies' seed-pods in the late afternoon, the opium oozing and coagulating on the pod's surface, the farmers scraping the resinous gunk from the pod, working quickly to avoid too much sticky build-up on their knives. It was the stuff that stuck that counted. Peter had never stuck.

Liv smoked the last bit of opium on the empty observation deck at Charles de Gaulle. A Lufthansa airbus turned its nose to face the deck, its engines racing. Liv leaned backward over the railing to look up at the gray metal netting strung over the deck. The engines shut down. She could hear her heart.

She went to an airport store and bought a few of the store's top ten CD recommendations, which strangely included Carole King's *Tapestry*. She held her wallet open to the clerk, for she was too high to count out the money.

Liv drank a Bloody Mary and listened to her voicemail in the Air France lounge. A message from Beth reading her the *Daily Variety* review. Mixed. More nice than mean. A good word for Kim and the camera work. Linus's script was a tad too dark. Liv booted up her laptop and inserted a CD. *Tapestry*.

The woman who kept the bowls of crackers and peanuts full tapped Liv on her shoulder. She lifted one earphone. *I feel hot and cold all over*.

"Your flight is ready for boarding," the woman said.

The gate was crowded with thick men and women in cheap shoes. Their Armenian chatter bled through Liv's headphones. Her eyes hurt from the Bloody Mary, and she fished sunglasses from her carry-on.

I feel the sky tumbling down.

Liv's arms were cold. Why had she put her sweater in her checked bag? The teenager across from her was wearing a zip-up sweatshirt—a much smarter traveler than I, Liv thought. He wore surfer pants (made in Armenia by Sparkle Life?), a T-shirt from the Amsterdam Hard Rock Café, and a Maori-style tattoo around his wrist. His thumbnail was black as if he had smashed it in a car door. He's going to lose that nail, Liv thought before starting to cry.

Liv went to the desk and told the ticket agent that she wasn't feeling very well. Would it be possible to get something out of her checked bag? The answer was no—security reasons. The tears were drying, leaving her eyes crusty. The ticket agent examined Liv's ticket and opened the door to the jetway.

"You can board," the agent said.

In the gap of the galley curtain, Liv could see the flight attendants arranging trays of orange juice and champagne. One was giggling about a movie she had seen the night before. Liv wrapped two blankets around her. Her teeth were chattering.

A flight attendant came out of the galley with a full tray. "Can I get you something?" she asked Liv.

"Another blanket," Liv said.

The flight attendant wrapped the third blanket around Liv like a mummy. Liv was asleep when the other one hundred and fifty-seven passengers boarded. Carole King was still playing. Liv's sunglasses were still on.

23

$\mathcal{T}$he church in Spitak was filled to capacity—175 people—for its inaugural service. The old icons and statuary that John had bought from religious art auctions around the world were covered in white gauze cloths poised to be pulled away by young boys in a choreographed sequence.

It was bright where the light from the stained glass windows hit the statues on high pedestals, but it was dim down where Liv and the people sat. There was a TV camera crew from the most important national station, but they had nothing more than a single floodlight to illuminate the whole nave. It wasn't enough light, and Liv knew the TV images would end up off-color and unstable. The camera moved in on Liv for her close up: the daughter of the Armenian success story who was now the Armenian Church's most important benefactor. The cameraman was too close, and Liv knew she'd wind up an unrecognizable lump on the evening news. The cameraman moved on to the next pew. A cloth was pulled off to reveal icons of Saints Gregory and Thaddeus, the same worried eyes and thick eyebrows as her father and uncle, as all the other Armenians in the room. Another cloth pulled: St. Kevork in a brilliant red cape.

Liv remembered Artur's red T-shirt. She had said, "Run," to Artur and pushed him toward the coppice at the edge of the pasture. She watched his red T-shirt move across the grass until she couldn't see him anymore. Then she held up her blue U.S. passport and screamed "American." She puked and dry heaved into bright green grass. The cows watched it all, continuing to make white milk as Marina's family was killed and Artur disappeared forever.

In the church pew, Liv brought the pasture back. What clues about Artur had she missed? Had he ducked into the woods to the north? Was that why she never saw him again? Had he slammed himself to the ground, hiding his small body behind a rock, or a sleeping cow? Had he waited for the killers to leave, before he stole away to the safety of a nearby village? Maybe he just went up, Liv thought. Snatched up to heaven by a patron saint on the lookout for trouble.

"That's the one that came last night," Linus whispered to her, his breath smelling of the licorice drops he kept popping ever since giving up alcohol. Liv looked up; a large gold cross had just been revealed. Gold filigree. Red jewels. Rubies or paste, she wondered.

She smelled incense, and three altar boys came up the aisle, their burners swinging, athletic shoes beneath their robes. Liv looked around and saw that every man around her was also wearing athletic shoes. Counterfeit Nikes, mainly black. Some Adidas. The women, in their bright-colored silk dresses, wore pumps with rubber soles. In the twenty-first century we walk as quietly as cats, Liv thought. She wondered what churches must have sounded like in the fifteenth century, wooden shoes making a raging racket on stone floors.

Artur had worn canvas slip-on shoes. Blue, Liv remembered, worn at the back edge. She worked her way around his body, trying to bring back every detail. A scraped calf. Thin blue pants, its waistband taken in by Marina with yellow thread. The red T-shirt. A heat rash on the inside of his elbows. A mole on his neck. Green eyes. Hair shaved to ward off lice. Long ear lobes. How could such a solid body disappear? she wondered. Where are you? She mouthed to herself. I was watching you and the cows and then you were gone, she thought.

The priest emerged from the back wearing a tall red crown that looked like a chef's toque. A cap to symbolize the salvation of the soul and the royal attributes of Christ the King.

The sun shone through the stained glass window, and Liv tipped her face to catch the light. She closed her eyes and watched the colors swirl under the lids. Brown, gold, mainly red. The priest was talking, the Armenian echoing off the stone walls. She heard hard-soled shoes. Who was this? No one wears hard soles, she thought. Liv heard more hard soles now, and she imagined dozens of men in fancy Italian dress shoes. Had a tour bus from Milan just arrived?

"Look at the cows," Linus said.

She opened her eyes. It was a troop of cows, their hooves echoing off the walls, each of them dressed in floral wreaths. Some wearing crocheted harnesses. Each led by a young girl in a red folk dress.

Look at the cows, Liv mouthed.

"They're here to be blessed," Linus said.

A giant cow filled the open door, and the news crew approached her for her close up. She wore a headdress and a red embroidered blanket across her back. She took a step up the aisle, and the camera crew let her pass.

The big cow arrived at Liv's pew and stopped. Liv heard it breathing. She touched the cow's soft ear, and she mouthed "Hello." The cow's nostrils flared. What do I smell like? Liv wondered.

The girl minding the cow curtsied to Liv and then gently turned the cow's head to face back up the aisle. The cow moved on, her hooves clicking on the stone floor.

The cows that had been there the day Artur disappeared: they'd be dead by now, Liv thought. They've been long turned into shoes, steaks, and hamburger, their hooves ground up to make gelatin. Liv pictured red Jell-O cubes. Had a farmer found Artur, scared, but alive? Had local people come to dispose of Marina's family's bodies? Had they taken their clothes? There were button down shirts and T-shirts. Liv remembered one from a Baja cantina. She remembered Marina's blue knit top, soaked in sweat. Had they found Artur's corpse? Was there a bullet hole in his red T-shirt?

The boys carried the gold filigree cross behind the priest who stopped to bless each cow. A team of younger boys scurried with shovels and buckets to clean a cow's shit off the stone floor. The shit and the incense combined to make the church smell smokier and feel warmer. The priest traced the cross on each cow's wide forehead.

They're all going to rise up to heaven, Liv thought, knowing full well that there was no heaven. There was only a final place where the body is either left to decompose or an abattoir where each bit of flesh and bone is separated out for utilitarian purposes.

Had the killer hit his target? Had Artur's body become fertilizer for a cow pasture? Was it still decomposing, still fertilizing the pasture, but now for cows that hadn't even been born when Artur died in the grass? Was Artur dirt, now? Liv wondered. The cross and the cows were coming back down the aisle, and Liv stood up, her hand over her heart, her head lowered. "Artur," she said out loud.

Linus was pulling her hand. The people in the church were staring at her. Standing up to salute cows was not customary.

Liv sat down and the pews creaked as the people turned away from her to face forward again.

Liv slid down onto the prayer rail and held her face in her hands. She would find that field. With a map, she was sure she could find it. She'd take John and Linus. They'd rent a car and ruin the shocks, tracing cow and goat paths to find the field where she would place a stone. She'd have marble carved with the names of everyone in Marina's family. Maybe Artur was dirt. Maybe he was alive—a teenager in a local village playing video games and going to church. She'd have Artur's name carved into the bottom of a marble bowl, which she'd place in the pasture. The bowl would collect rainwater, and the cows would lick Artur's name. Dead or alive, Artur would like that.

Now, at 38 years old, this is what Liv Johansson knew: it's the quotidian that saves. Buying the refills for the tape rolls you use to lift cat hair from your pants. Making sure there's enough Tampax in the bathroom drawer. Getting enough exercise to burn off lunch's dessert. Living is remembering your credit card personal ID numbers, returning movies to the video store, understanding that the fabric softener is added during the second wash cycle. You get over seeing people shot or going through chemotherapy or anything at all by wrapping yourself in the details. Maybe it's constricting, but constriction's better than bleeding all over the floor.

"Come on, Liv. It's okay. *Mee mdadzir, Liv jan, amen ban lav glinee*," she heard her father say.

Liv kept her face in her hands and smiled; she knew those words. He had lifted her out of the crib in the back room of a Stockholm apartment. She had been cold, and he wrapped a blanket around her. He took Liv from the Stockholm apartment, promising his new baby that he'd take care of her. And he had made good on that promise.

"Come on Liv. It's okay. *Mee mdadzir, Liv jan, amen ban lav glinee*."

She looked up at her father standing in the aisle, backlit by the television crew's light, and she got up to join him.